Seed Seeker

Also by Pamela Sargent from Tor Books

Earthseed
Farseed

Seed Seeker

Pamela Sargent

A Tom Doherty Associates Book
New York

This is a work of fiction. All of the characters, organizations, and events portrayed in this novel are either products of the author's imagination or are used fictitiously.

SEED SEEKER

A Tor Book
Published by Tom Doherty Associates, LLC
175 Fifth Avenue
New York, NY 10010

www.tor-forge.com

Tor® is a registered trademark of Tom Doherty Associates, LLC.

ISBN 978-0-7653-1428-4

First Edition: November 2010

Printed in the United States of America

0 9 8 7 6 5 4 3 2 1

To
Chelsea Quinn Yarbro,
Renaissance woman

Part One

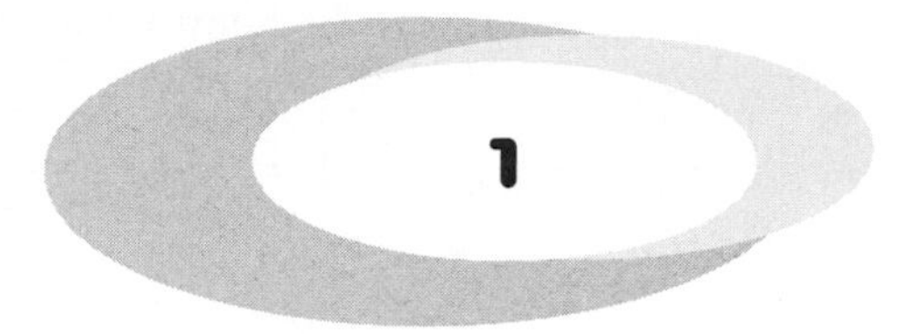

1

Bian's great-grandmother Nuy was the first to see the new pinprick of light in the sky.

Bian had followed Nuy downriver to the seashore only because her mother had insisted that she look after the old woman. "Don't let her out of your sight," Tasu told her. Bian did not argue with her mother, although Tasu knew as well as she did that Nuy often wandered down to the shore in search of solitude and was able, in spite of her advanced age, to look out for herself.

Bian found Nuy sitting on a hill overlooking the ocean, her basket empty of fish. The sun was nearly below the horizon in the west. Bian strolled along the shore, clutching her own small basket, kicking up sand while pretending to look for any fish that had washed up onto the beach.

"Go back to your mother," Nuy said at last. Bian halted and shifted her basket from one hand to the other. "Go on home, child. I don't need you here watching me."

It was no use telling Nuy that Tasu had only sent her here to fetch any fish that might have been washed ashore; Nuy could see through a lie as well as anyone. "I know you don't need me," Bian admitted, "but Tasu insisted."

"Tasu worries far too much about me."

"Not any more than the rest of us do."

"And then everybody wonders why I like to wander off by myself." Nuy waved a hand. "Lately it's because I can't bear to see all of your worried looks and sense everybody's concern for me. It's enough to make me feel I'm being smothered by your worries."

Bian dropped her empty basket and sat down next to Nuy. The old woman's long white braid hung over her left shoulder and down the front of her sleeveless tunic; her slim bare legs and arms were almost as muscular as those of a young person. She was much older than other great-grandparents in their village, because the first of her seven children had not been born until she was in her forties, and her children had followed her example of living for a long time with their mates before having children of their own. Her age was most visible on her lined neck and around her eyes, where deep wrinkles were etched around drooping lids.

"You're one of the First," Bian murmured. "It's natural for us to be concerned about you."

"I'm the only one of the First who's still alive," Nuy said. "That's what you meant to say."

Nuy was right, of course. She always knew what was lurking in the recesses of Bian's mind, sometimes even before Bian herself became aware of her own hidden thoughts.

Nuy had outlived all the first generation of Home's children, that first generation born of the people who had come down from the sky to settle this world. She had told the story of those sky people often. "All of us grew from the seeds sown here by Ship, that great vessel launched by our ancestors," Nuy would begin. "Some of those seeds were the people who came down from the sky, who flew down from Ship to live here on Home. Ship was the child of the people of Earth, and its purpose was to find other worlds like Earth, worlds where its seeds could be sown and where they would grow and flower and preserve true humankind."

At that point, Nuy was often interrupted by two or three of the youngest children, who wanted to know what and where Earth was, what "true humankind" meant, and whether the heavens were anything like the vast sea that stretched to the southern horizon. When she was much younger, Bian had imagined Ship as a very large boat sailing in from the sea and then up the river to disgorge its living cargo along the river's banks, but she had soon learned that Ship could not have been anything like their boats. Ship, Nuy had explained, was more like one of Home's two moons, an orb of rock, but with a hollowed out core and crannies where people could live, and with powerful engines that could carry it across the vast distances of space, and with a mind far more complex and all-encompassing than a human being's.

"Other seeds from Earth were scattered over Home," Nuy would continue, "and those seeds sprouted into the rabbits and horses and birds and cattle and sheep, the small and large cats, the dogs that befriend us and the wolves and bears that avoid us. None of those creatures existed on Home before our kind came here, and the greener grasses of the plain and many of the plants that feed us also sprang from the Earthseed sown here. If human beings were to survive, we could not live on Home as it was, or so Ship and its designers believed. Some of the life-forms of Earth would fill the niches that Home had left empty, and Home would in time become another Earth. That was their hope. But Home isn't just another Earth. And we may all be a part of humankind, but strands of Home also took root in us and live within each of us."

That was usually where Nuy ended her story whenever she told it to the youngest children. The rest of the story, a tale of the distrust, resentments, hatreds, and battles that had also made them what they were, could wait until they were older. Those battles had finally ended, and after that most of their people had left their original settlement to live along the banks of the river and near the sea. But a few had remained in the north, inside their domed dwellings, because they feared growing too close to Home and losing their true humanity. The battles among them might lie in the past, but distrust had remained.

"Will Ship ever come back?" Bian and some of the others had asked Nuy when they were older.

"I don't know," Nuy always replied. "Perhaps."

The sky had grown dark green. Bian sat with Nuy, not speaking, until the sun set. Nuy intended to stay here at least until the first moon rose; Bian sensed that as soon as the old woman lifted her head to gaze at the sky.

"I saw a strange light in the sky last night," Nuy said then. "Just before dawn, a light I've never seen before. It was only a tiny pinpoint of light, yet it didn't flicker in the way that the stars do. I wonder if I'll see it again tonight."

Nuy was silent after that. Bian sat with her until the sun had set and the first of the stars appeared. Nuy glanced from right to left, grew still as she gazed east, then suddenly clutched Bian's shoulder. "There it is."

Bian saw it now, a tiny beacon on the horizon. The unfamiliar speck of light shone steadily as it moved slowly across the sky. Nuy let out a sigh and Bian sensed a disturbance inside her great-grandmother. Nuy was afraid.

"You fear it," Bian said before she could stop herself from speaking.

"I'm afraid of what it might mean." Nuy's grip on her shoulder tightened. "You remember the story of how we came to be and how we were brought to Home. Not the story that I told you when you were very small, but the rest of it, the part of the story you heard when you were older."

"Of course." Bian gently removed Nuy's small bony hand from her shoulder.

"Most of the ones your age never did hear the end of that story," Nuy continued. "Your grandmother heard it, and I think your father might have heard it all, but I may be the only one left in our village who remembers that Ship made a promise to our ancestors."

Bian frowned. "What promise?"

"Ship's promise to return."

Bian turned toward Nuy, surprised. "But you never told us—"

"Ship promised to come back here," Nuy said, "to see what we had made of ourselves. That was the true end of the story. But as the years passed, most of us came to believe that Ship would never return, that in carrying out its mission to seed other worlds, it might have forgotten about this one. Others worried instead that some misfortune had come to Ship, that it was unable to return, or even that it might have traveled so far across space that it could no longer find its way back to

Home. What's the point in telling young ones about Ship's promise when it seemed likely that the promise would never be kept? I began to ask myself that after I'd been repeating the story for a while, so I started leaving that part out. When no one ever complained, I decided it was best to leave it that way. Maybe Ship would return, and maybe it wouldn't, but it was better to get on with our lives and not think about that."

"No one else ever told us the story except you."

"Yes," Nuy murmured, "I seem to have become the guardian of that tale in our village. I have grown to prefer the more uncertain ending I gave it." She looked up at the sky. "Maybe that new light is only a small planetary body that was roaming the heavens. Maybe Home has just captured it and made another satellite of it. That's what I'm telling myself now. It can't be Ship."

"There's no reason to think—"

"I don't want it to be Ship."

Bian waited for Nuy to explain what she meant by that, but her great-grandmother said nothing more.

2

Bian and Nuy watched the point of light cross the sky three times before they walked back to the village. In the morning, Bian woke to the sound of voices outside the entrance to her cabin, all of them chattering about the new light that had appeared in the night sky and speculating about what it might mean.

Tasu was already up. She sat just outside the entrance to their hut, cooking thin cakes of grain for their morning meal on one of the flat rocks around their fireplace. She did not ask Bian if Nuy had said anything about the light, although Tasu had to be wondering if she had. Not long after they finished their breakfast, nearly all the seventy people in the village of Seaside had left their huts to gather under the boltrees that bordered their orchards and fields. That was when Nuy told them the rest of the story, the part that most of the older people had forgotten and the younger ones had never heard at all.

In the northern settlement of the dome dwellers, Nuy explained, there was one dome where a library was housed, where the records that had been carried down from Ship were kept. The people who lived along the river had brought some of those records with them, which they could read and view on the carefully maintained screens in which the records were embedded. But there was a mysterious room inside the library that was also part of the tale of the sky people, a room barely mentioned in the records the river people possessed.

That room was called Ship's Room, and Nuy had visited it only a couple of times while living among the dome dwellers, since the door to Ship's Room was usually kept closed. The people who had come down from the sky used to speak to Ship from that room, sending their voices into the air and out to the great vessel through a device they called a radio. Although Ship had finally left its orbit around Home and was now too far away for any of their voices to have the power to reach it, Ship had promised to return. The settlers had pledged to keep Ship's Room as it was and to preserve their radio, in the hope of one day hearing Ship's voice again.

"Do you understand now?" Nuy asked. "That new light in the sky may be Ship, returning to see what's happened to the seeds it planted here. If so, the dome dwellers will be the first to find out, because Ship will have to contact them to learn anything, and speaking through their radio is the only way to do so. They could be talking to Ship right now."

Bian looked around at the others seated near her. The

oldest of the villagers looked worried, while the younger ones seemed puzzled, but all of them had clearly sensed the fear in Nuy's voice. If they possessed a radio of their own, they might also have been able to send a message to Ship, but they had never thought of making such a seemingly useless device.

"Does it matter?" Arnagh, Bian's closest friend, asked. "If they're talking to Ship, I mean." He stood up and took a step forward. At seventeen years of age, a year older than Bian, Arnagh was already the tallest of their people. "What difference would it make if they talked to Ship first?"

"They think of themselves as the true people, as true humanity," Cemal answered in his resonant voice. "That's what difference it makes."

Nuy nodded.

"It's why they stay in their settlement, why they avoid us." Cemal slowly got to his feet. "That's what they'll be saying to Ship, that they're its true children and the rest of us aren't." The old man stroked his white beard as he looked around at the crowd. "How do we know they aren't already turning Ship against us?"

Tasu looked up at Cemal. "We're Ship's descendants, too," she murmured.

"But with pieces of Home inside us," Cemal said. "How I wish that at least one of those sky people who once lived inside Ship were still alive to advise us. Then maybe we could figure out what to do now. We don't know how Ship might act, how it might regard us, or how much power it may have to harm us, if it comes to that." He sat down again and held up one hand, indicating that he had finished speaking.

Mari rose and glanced toward Nuy. "We're not even sure what that light means yet," the red-haired woman began, "but let's assume that it means Ship has returned and is in contact with the others. There's a chance that whatever they tell Ship about us will only rouse Ship's curiosity. It may want to speak to us itself, to find out for itself what we are, which means that sooner or later the dome dwellers will try to contact us."

Mari was always so reassuring, Bian thought. She had a placid temperament and seemed incapable of anger or anxiety, which was probably why most of them increasingly looked to the young woman for guidance and advice. Mari clearly believed what she was saying, and everyone sensed both her conviction and her calmness. Bian might have felt easier and less apprehensive herself, soothed by Mari's words and reassuring expression, if she hadn't noticed the doubtful look on Nuy's face.

Nuy said, "So all we have to do now is wait until someone from upriver lets us know what's going on, which will take a string or two of days if not longer." Bian could hear the skepticism in her great-grandmother's voice.

"Yes," Mari replied.

"And what if we hear nothing?" Clutching the spear she often used as a walking stick, Nuy slowly stood up. "Here are some questions for all of you. What if the dome dwellers decide not to let us know they've contacted Ship? What if they think it's to their benefit to keep whatever they can learn or get from Ship for themselves, without sharing anything with us? For that matter, what if they find out that this new light in the sky isn't Ship at all, but only a small worldlet captured by Home? They might still see some advantage in keeping that knowledge to themselves and leaving us in doubt."

"But we've no reason to think—," Mari began.

"—that they might consider only what's best for them,

even if it's not to our benefit?" Nuy finished. "The dome dwellers have had nothing to gain by acting against us in the past," she continued, "but now they do, or may believe that they do, and that could be enough to turn them against us. They seem to be grateful for what we can bring them in trade, but Ship could give them much more, maybe enough so that they wouldn't want or need anything from us."

Mari's smile faded; her mouth twitched as she tugged at the long braid that hung down over her chest. She sat down and folded her arms.

Bian stood up. "There's no reason to wait here and wonder about all this," she said. "We could send someone upriver, maybe with goods to trade to the dome dwellers, and see if we can find out something that way. At the very least, we'd learn something sooner than if we just wait here for information to travel downriver to us."

"Are you volunteering to go and investigate?" Arnagh asked.

Bian realized that she was, and prickled with apprehension. Nuy leaned forward, obviously pleased, while Tasu frowned with worry.

"But you've never gone anywhere, Bian," Arnagh said more gently. "You've barely gone more than a few paces beyond our fields."

It was true. She had been like a rit, hiding in its hole, afraid to come out. She had never left the village, not even to head upriver to Overlook, the nearest village to the north, or to hunt and roam the plains with a group of other young people or by herself; instead contenting herself with the stories Arnagh brought back to her of his adventures. She had often told herself that she could not leave Tasu, who had lost her mate, Kwam, while Bian was still a baby, and who still mourned for the father Bian had never known. It was also easier to stay at her mother's side, since they shared the same timid temperament. The other villagers had often wondered how there could be so little of the fearless Kwam and his grandmother Nuy in Kwam's daughter Bian.

But lately, Bian had grown discontented with her timidity. Once, it had protected her; now it imprisoned her.

"I'm willing to go," Bian said, knowing that she would have to follow through on her proposal now. "Everything upriver will be new to me, so maybe I'll see something that would go unnoticed by others."

"And maybe you won't know what to look for," Arnagh muttered. He was cutting off his words at the ends to make them sound harder, but underneath the hardness, she sensed his protectiveness of her. "You might not be able to tell if the dome dwellers are deceiving you, if you can even make it that far without turning back."

"Then come with me," Bian said quickly. "You've traveled north three times to trade. You've seen the dome dwellers, so you should be able to spot any lies they might tell us." The words escaped her before she could call them back.

Arnagh tensed, then looked away. Something had happened to him during his last journey upriver a little over a year ago; he had come back with a wounded, mournful look in his eyes and hardly spoke for days. He and his aunt and uncle had accomplished their trade with the dome dwellers and had gone through the usual exchange of information about births and deaths and other important events with people in all the villages along the river's banks. But Arnagh's bearing insisted that he would reveal no more about the trip. Even Bian had not wanted to press him with too many questions.

"We can't spare more than two or three people," Cemal

said, "not when the fruit will soon be ready for picking. And we can't afford to send a lot of provisions with them."

"They wouldn't have to take much," Mari said, "because they probably won't need that much. I doubt they'll get more than ten or twelve days upriver before they find out anything we should know. Any truly important news should have traveled downriver that far by then."

Tasu stood up and put an arm around her daughter. "If Bian wants to go," she said, "I won't stand in her way." Bian realized then that she had been hoping her mother might object and give her a way to back out. "As long as Arnagh is willing to go with her—"

"Oh, I'll go," Arnagh interrupted, but Bian heard the reluctance in his voice.

"Then it's settled," Nuy said.

3

The librarian said nothing. Safrah waited, still hoping to hear its voice, wanting to believe that it might somehow repair itself after not speaking for so many days, but the only sound emitted by the console was a low, almost indiscernible whine.

"Speak to me," Safrah whispered. The librarian continued to whine. Safrah could still call up any records that the library held, but now she had to write what she was looking for on a screen with a stylus, then wait until lines of writing and images appeared. Occasionally, the images and writings were only marginally related to what she was seeking. She had been here for much of the morning, searching for records on the subject of artificial intelligences, hoping that she might find something that would tell her how to restore the librarian's voice, but knowing that that kind of repair was probably beyond her and her companions' capacity.

The whining suddenly broke off.

Safrah rested her elbows on the table and frowned at the screen in front of her. The screen showed an image of a rocky worldlet against a black space dotted with pinpricks of light. The rock suddenly swelled in size, until she could see what looked like large metallic bowls on its surface and a flicker of light at one end. The library had responded to her search by offering her an image of Ship, the artificial intelligence that had seeded Home.

The door to her left slid open and Mikhail slipped inside. "Any change?" he asked as the door closed behind him. "Never mind," he continued as Safrah shook her head. "I can tell. It's still not speaking, is it?"

She nodded.

"We'll have to tell the young ones sometime."

"We don't have to say anything now."

"Sooner or later they're going to find out. Better that they hear it from us."

"They won't find out for a while," she said. "They don't care about anything in here." Once, they had been curious, pestering her with questions she could not answer and that they did not know how to ask of the librarian. Now they avoided this place. She, Mikhail, Awan, and Jina were the only ones who came to the library nearly every day. Perhaps by the time any of the others came here, the librarian might have repaired itself.

That, she told herself, was a ridiculously hopeful thought. For over a year, she had seen signs that the librarian might be failing, had noticed the hesitation in its voice and the ever longer silences before it responded to her queries.

She had said nothing, not even to Mikhail, even though he was clearly aware of the problem; she had noticed the worried look on his face, and on Jina's and Awan's, whenever they were speaking to the librarian. And then the librarian had fallen silent, responding to their queries with only a whine.

"We'd better keep this to ourselves," Jina had said, and Safrah convinced Awan and Mikhail to go along with her advice. Lately the younger ones seemed to value the four of them largely for their labor and their ability to tend and repair the technology that supported the settlement. If they failed at that, they would be of little use to anyone else here and would eventually have almost nothing to offer the outsiders in trade.

Mikhail sat down on the floor next to her and folded his legs. "We shouldn't just let it go," he said.

"We can get along without it." That was the truth, but she missed the librarian's voice; she had grown up with that voice.

"If we gave Awan more time here alone," Mikhail continued, "with nothing to distract him, he might be able to—"

"I don't think even Awan could fix this."

"We have to try. We have to hold things together, do what we can. If we don't do anything, things might get worse." Mikhail leaned toward her. "Right now it's just the librarian's voice. What if it loses its search functions?"

She looked up at the shelves of records on the level above this one, wondering how she would ever be able to find anything in them without the librarian's help. Then she looked down at the screen again. Too much had been going wrong lately. Lanterns and light wands flickered and then failed, weapons had to be recharged more often, fuel cells failed for the last time and could not be replaced. It seemed to her that such failures happened more often than they had when she was younger, but maybe she was only imagining that.

"It'll repair itself," she insisted.

"What if it doesn't?"

"It has to," Safrah said. "It always did before."

"Don't be so stubborn, Safrah. Even if it does, it might fail again."

They would have to embed more records in some of the remaining empty screens and keep those records where they would be safe. They would have to think about which of the records were most essential and which might be expendable. They might lose parts of humankind's past forever and never know what it was they had lost.

She looked toward the back of the library, where the closed door to Ship's Room was concealed by two shelves of old records, and thought of the radio on the other side of that door. She had not gone inside Ship's Room in some time, thinking it was better to keep away, to leave the door closed and the radio protected. Not that it mattered. The mind of the space vessel that had carried her people to Home had most likely forgotten them long ago.

As a child, whenever she had come to the library with Moise, Safrah had almost always visited Ship's Room with him. He had shown her how to press buttons and move dials so that they could listen to the snaps, crackles, and hums emitted by the radio. Moise had explained that many of the sounds were produced by lightning, even if the storms that produced that lightning were far away, and that other sounds came from space. The radio could also pick up Ship's voice, which Ship was able to transmit over a wide range of frequencies, so the radio would be able to hear Ship when it entered this planetary system, long before it was orbiting Home.

"We'll be able to talk to Ship then," Moise had told her, "and maybe when it finds out what's happened here, it will help us restore this settlement to what it might have become. Maybe it will even remain near Home and never leave us again."

"How do you know Ship will come back?" Safrah had asked him.

"That was Ship's promise to us," Moise had replied, "that it would return to see what we'd made of ourselves."

"Maybe Ship's forgotten that promise."

"Oh, no." Moise had shaken his head. "I have to believe that Ship would remember and keep any promise it made to our ancestors."

After that, Safrah had occasionally gone to Ship's room alone and whispered to the radio, hoping for an answer. Later, her hope had grown into fear. Ship might not be all that pleased to see what had happened to its people. Maybe it would be better if their radio did fail.

"We'd better go," Mikhail said. "We'll talk to Awan and Jina, see what they want to do now. Awan might want to try repairing the librarian again, or he might think it's better to leave it alone, but he's better at repairs than we are, so he's probably the one who should decide. As long as we can still search the records, we can get by."

Safrah stood up, reluctant to leave the library. The refuge of the library and her bond with Mikhail, Awan, and Jina were all that kept her here now, that and her lingering fear of the people outside the settlement.

Tina and Awan were keeping watch outside the entrance to the library, even though it was unlikely that anyone else would come that way. "The librarian's still not talking," Mikhail said to them.

Awan let out his breath. "Should we say anything about it to the others?" he asked.

"No," Safrah replied, "not yet."

"I'll take a look at it tomorrow," Awan said, "see what I can do."

Mikhail slipped a light wand from his belt and turned it on. To their right, the tunnel led up to the dining hall; to their left, downhill to the greenhouse. They turned right and walked through the tunnel in silence. Even with the dim light of the wand, Safrah could not help noticing that there were new cracks in the walls and that some of the patches on the ceiling above them were flaking.

Mikhail stopped in front of the door that led to their dome and pushed it open. A glance around the common room revealed that no one had entered their dome while they were at the library, although any of the young ones could easily have done so. Packets of food, folded-up clothing, pottery, and a couple of reading screens sat undisturbed on the shelves, and there were no marks on the walls or the table in the center of the room. Anyone coming there would at least have taken some of their belongings, perhaps broken some of the pottery, or carved an insult or a threat on the table or walls.

When they were all inside, Mikhail closed the door, then

set the pole they used as a brace against it. Anything stolen could be replaced, and damage could be repaired, but they needed to feel secure while inside their own dwelling.

Awan opened the small cooler in the corner and took out a bottle of juice and some bread and cheese, while Jina opened a packet of meat. They were running low on food and would have to get more from the dispenser in the dining hall soon. Safrah dreaded the prospect of going there, where the others spent so much of their time lately. At least the dispenser showed no signs of failing. She did not carry that thought any further than that.

Safrah went to a shelf for some pottery. They did not really need any plates for the food and could have passed the bottle of juice around; rinsing the cups and plates would only use up more water from their cistern. But Safrah preferred eating this way instead of grabbing at the food the way the children did. It was how they used to dine with Moise and the other elders long ago.

Awan poured out juice. "We have to start checking on the outpost signal again," he said. "Somebody might come there to trade soon." None of them had gone outside since the onset of the season of cold and ice, but by now the weather would be growing warmer; they had not needed to use their dome's heater for almost a month. One of the few traders willing to trade with them might come north.

"I'll take a look outside after dinner," Jina said.

"I'll go with you," Mikhail added. Safrah looked down. He and Jina were finding more and more excuses to go off by themselves, and she expected that the two would soon announce that they were making a pledge. It would be easier to wish them well if she knew that there would someday be a mate for her, but Awan shied away from her whenever she made any gesture toward him, even if it was only to clasp his hand a little too warmly.

Awan had even more reason to keep his distance from her lately. It had been only three months since she went to the dining hall to trade with Morwen for a bottle of his alcohol. Even though the liquid burned her throat, it had been surprisingly easy to drink enough of it to feel delirious and wild and ready to corner Awan in the tunnel near their dome. "We can do it here," she had whispered, and she had wrapped her arms around him and murmured about how much she wanted him and loved him, until he had finally torn himself away and knocked her against the wall. The shock of that, even though he hadn't meant to hurt her, had brought her to her senses; she spent the next day feeling ashamed and apologizing and blaming her behavior on the drink. It wouldn't have happened except for that, she had insisted; and it would never happen again. Awan had replied that he would never mention the incident to her or to anyone else.

Now, when she recalled what had happened before shame made her push the memory from her mind, she realized Awan had been struggling with her for a while, perhaps in an effort not to harm her, before at last freeing himself. Maybe that meant he did feel drawn to her, that he had been fighting against his own feelings for her. She had imagined that, after a while, he would come to her and tell her that he wanted her, too. It was only that she had taken him by surprise; that had to be why he had pushed her away. But lately it seemed that he was looking for reasons not to be alone with her. She had thrown out what was left of the alcohol, which had also made her sick and dizzy, and promised Awan she would never touch it again. She wanted to ask him what was wrong with her, what he wanted from her that she lacked, but had never summoned up the courage to do so.

There was no one else for her, and certainly no chance that she would come to care for anyone among the others in the settlement. But she would have to find someone to be her mate and give her children. Moise, who had taught them all about their duties and obligations, would have expected her to fulfill them.

She ate what was left of her food and pushed her plate away, missing Moise yet again.

Safrah lay on her mat, unable to sleep. Jina's mat, on the other side of their small room, was still empty. Jina and Mikhail, along with welcoming some time alone, would also be enjoying the spicy clean scent of the outdoor air after being inside for so long, and maybe they had spotted a lighted beacon in the tower south of the settlement.

Maybe all four of them could go to trade with the lake and river people this time, even if that meant leaving their dome completely unguarded. If they braced the door that opened onto the tunnel before they slipped outside, that might be enough to keep anyone else from breaking in while they were gone.

She thought of the first time Moise had taken her and Jina to the outpost, when she was still a child and Jina not much older. She had been apprehensive about meeting the people who lived outside the settlement, but the small man and woman, barely taller than she was at the time, had seemed friendly, and she had felt both generous and superior at being able to give them new light wands in place of the ones they had brought for recharging.

Traders had not come to the outpost for some time now.

That was perhaps just as well, since it meant less chance of any outsider learning the truth about their settlement. She almost hoped that Mikhail and Jina would glimpse no signal that night.

She longed for sleep. Lying there in the dark, too tired to sit up and find something else to do, yet unable to lose herself in sleep, she worried again over what had gone wrong and what she might have done differently.

Her earliest memory was of sitting with Mikhail and Jina and Awan in the library as the older ones told them how much they could learn there and how much more they would have to master. She could not recall exactly what the old people had said in that memory, but she knew that they had often spoken of restoring the settlement and preserving their kind. There were few of their kind left, the older ones had said, but as long as they had a new generation of true humankind to bring up, their species would survive. Perhaps their numbers would even increase to the point where some of them could go live in the eastern part of the settlement, which had been abandoned two generations ago and was now useful only for scavenging. The young ones would have to persevere after the old ones were gone, and care for the next generation.

The young ones had wept for days after Moise died, and Morwen mourned even more deeply than the others. Safrah and her comrades had tried to spare them the worst, burying Moise by themselves before telling the younger ones of his death. When they did, Morwen had thrown himself at her, hitting her with his small fists and refusing to believe her. Moise had gone away, he had screamed, and Ship had gone away, and someday Safrah would go away, too. She had held the little boy while he cried, promising him and the others that she would never abandon them.

"We'll all stay," Jina had said, reciting the same words the old ones once recited to her.

"You're our responsibility now," Mikhail had murmured, repeating more of those remembered words, "and we won't abandon you."

"This is our home," Awan had told them, "and you're as much our children as if we had sired and borne you ourselves."

The younger ones had eventually stopped mourning, but they had also started to keep more to themselves. They did not need Safrah and her companions anymore; or so they seemed to be saying. They did not want to depend on them. They would learn how to look out for themselves before they were abandoned again.

We failed you, she thought, imagining that Moise might somehow sense her regrets from his grave. She and her companions had done their best to look out for the younger ones, even after all the old ones except Moise were dead, felled by accidents, weakened bodies, chronic ailments that could be diagnosed by scanners but not treated easily or cured, or by the infectious respiratory disease that killed most elders who had not already died of other causes. They had stayed in the settlement even after being tempted to leave the outpost with the outsider called Tarki, who had traded with them more often than anyone else. "Most of your people chose to leave, you know," Tarki had said to her the last time she saw him, almost two years ago. "Almost every one of the First in your settlement, or their children, eventually realized that their future lay with Home, not holed up inside your domes."

She had thought then of never going back, of asking Tarki to take her with him. Just thinking about that, even though she had resisted such urges, nearly overwhelmed her with guilt. They would be abandoning those who needed them, betraying their people in the same way as had all those who had left the settlement generations ago to live south of the lake and along the river. However human-like those who lived outside the settlement might seem, they were not truly human. Receptacles of nonhuman genes and alien bacteria; that was what Moise had called them. Trading with those people was useful, because it brought in a few goods, and it kept the lake and river people from growing too suspicious of or curious about the settlement, but it was better to keep them at a distance. When Ship returned, it would see that those in the settlement were the ones who had kept to its mission of preserving true humankind. Ship would reward them for keeping to that purpose, then decide the fate of those who lived along the river.

Safrah turned over onto her back. The outsiders rarely troubled her thoughts these days. Lately, she was growing more fearful of the rest of true humankind, of all those young ones in the settlement who seemed increasingly belligerent and resentful.

"Safrah."

Surprised, she opened her eyes, realizing that she must have fallen asleep after all. "What is it?"

"Outside," Jina began, "up in the sky, we saw—I think . . ." She knelt at Safrah's side. "Come with me and see for yourself."

Safrah shook herself awake and got up. Jina had already slid open the panel that led to the room Mikhail and Awan shared. The two girls hurried through that room, past the closed compartment of their lavatory and its cistern, and then through another opening into the passageway that led outside. Awan was ahead of them, holding a light wand. He halted under a ledge, the one where he and Safrah had recently stashed two screens with some of their essential records, until they caught up with him.

Mikhail was waiting for them at the open entrance. Safrah followed the others outside, then turned to slide the doorway shut. The night air was cool, but not cold enough to make her shiver. The only sounds were the sigh of the wind and the gentle, distant swish of the windmills near the top of the hill.

Awan's wand went out. "Look there." Mikhail pointed east. Safrah looked up at the cloudless night sky. The second of Home's moons was well above the horizon, chasing the first moon. She continued to gaze at the vast black bowl studded with its familiar constellations and then noticed that one speck of light in the east was shining steadily instead of twinkling like the others.

Something new was in the sky.

"What is it?" she heard Awan ask.

"Jina noticed it first," Mikhail said. "It was just above us, and then we saw that it was moving across the sky, to the west. We watched it until it disappeared, and after that, we thought we'd better wait for a while to see if we saw it again or if anything else happened." He let out his breath. "So we waited for a long time, and just as I was thinking we might as well go inside, we saw it rising in the east. That's when Jina went to get you."

"What can it be?" Safrah asked.

"How can you ask that?" Jina responded. "You know what it has to be, either a planetoid or some other piece of space debris captured by Home, or else—"

"—it's Ship," Awan finished.

Safrah was shaking now, filled with anticipation and fear. "I can't believe it," she whispered.

"There's one way to find out for sure," Jina said. "If it's Ship, it must be trying to contact us." She darted toward the entrance and slid the door open. "Come on."

4

Safrah stood at the entrance to Ship's Room, stiff with shock, her mouth dry. The radio console still sat on its table, but the front panel had been removed and wires and small metal pieces scattered over the floor.

Jina let out a cry. Awan knelt in front of the radio, then began to move its dials and press buttons, going through every procedure Moise had taught them. But the radio remained silent, deaf to all frequencies. There was not even the crackling sound of distant lightning, or any of the other strange sounds the radio had once emitted. Had the radio been working as it should be, they would have picked up something, even if there was no message from Ship.

They should have come to this room more often. They should have guarded everything in this building more carefully, instead of assuming that the others would always continue to avoid the library. Maybe they should have left their dome and moved in here. She wondered how long Ship might have been trying to contact them, if the light that had appeared in the sky was, in fact, Ship.

"What do we do now?" Awan asked.

"Is there any way to repair it?" Mikhail said.

Awan scowled. "I don't know. I'll have to review some records, find out what parts we have and which ones are missing, see if—"

"Where are you? We know you're here."

Safrah froze. That was Morwen's voice; he was in the library. Jina looked around, then put a finger to her lips. "Don't say anything about Ship," she whispered, "or the radio." Awan and Mikhail nodded in agreement.

Jina rose. Safrah tried to stand up, but her knees shook. She had to grab Awan's hand to get to her feet. They left Ship's Room, slid the door shut as quietly as possible, and crept around the shelves to find Morwen and Terris in the large main room of the library. There's only two of them, Safrah thought, which partly made up for the fact that Morwen and Terris were the younger ones whom she now feared the most.

"Thought we might find you here," Morwen said, shaking back his long brown hair. "Went to your dome and banged on the door hard, but nobody answered. Pushed it open and saw you weren't there, so I figured you must be here." Even though he was a few years younger than Awan and Mikhail, Morwen was already taller than they were, while his broad shoulders and massive bulk dwarfed them. Terris was only slightly smaller, but his arms were even more muscular than Morwen's. It was impossible to ignore their muscles; neither boy was wearing a shirt, and their pants were hardly more than rags.

Safrah tried to recall the last time she had seen either of them in the library. All she could remember was the last time she had brought all the younger ones here as a group, still hoping they would show at least a little interest in learning how to read more than the simplest of sentences and how to search for more than visuals and games. Terris and Morwen were children then; it was hard to believe they had ever been so small and so young, so curious about the world they had not yet learned to fear.

"What were you doing back there?" Terris asked. "There's nothing back there except Ship's Room."

"Just looking for some old records on the shelves," Mikhail replied, somehow managing to sound calm.

"What?" Morwen chuckled, fingering the stun gun at his waist. "Sure you weren't in Ship's Room?"

Mikhail shook his head.

"Don't even think about going there." Morwen showed his teeth. "Think you're going to hear anything?" he continued. "Think Ship is ever going to talk to us? Maybe the old ones believed that, but I don't, not anymore."

"You never know," Mikhail said.

"I know," Morwen continued, "even if you don't. It dumped us here, and then off it went. If it ever comes back, I hope it loses control of itself and falls through the sky and crashes into the ground."

"If anything like that ever happened," Awan said in a subdued voice, "it could cause a lot of damage. You have no idea how destructive that would be."

Morwen laughed. "You're stupid to worry about that.

It'll never happen anyway. Ship forgot all about us a long time ago."

Safrah could not tell if they knew anything about the destroyed radio or not. Maybe someone else had done the damage, and kept it a secret afterward, someone afraid to let Morwen or Terris know what had happened. Careless as the others were, she could not believe that any of them would deliberately destroy the radio. Surely most of them, even Morwen, in spite of what he had said, still clung to the hope that Ship would return and somehow transform their lives.

Terris began to move around the room. He looked down at the tables and then up at the shelves of records. Safrah forced herself to be still, to seem indifferent. To act as though she cared about anything here might only provoke the two.

Morwen bowed his head and stared at the floor. For a moment, he seemed like the small boy he had once been. "We need more clothes," he said softly.

"We can see that," Safrah said, but kept her tone gentle.

"We need more clothes soon," Morwen said more insistently. Terris sat down on the floor and rested his arms on a tabletop, suddenly looking as lost and bewildered as Morwen sounded.

Mikhail fidgeted. Safrah shot him a warning look. "Maybe we can go and fetch some more clothes for you in a little while," she said, knowing that appeasing the two was their only choice. There might still be some old garments in the abandoned eastern side of the settlement, where they hadn't scavenged for over a year. "If you'd like, maybe you could even come with us this time."

Morwen's eyes widened with fear. He jerked his head away, then looked back at her with his usual belligerent expression. "Don't have to go with you," he said. She had known that he would refuse. "Just get some clothes for us." He motioned to Terris. "Come on. Let's go kill some rits."

Terris stood up and reached for the stun gun hanging at his own waist, then pulled out the weapon and smashed it against the table. Morwen laughed, even though Terris had done no more than leave a small dent in the tabletop. They stomped toward the entrance. Morwen kicked the door as it slid open, then stepped into the darkened corridor outside, Terris at his heels.

The door slid shut behind them. Awan let out a sigh of relief. "You didn't really expect them to go with us, did you?" he asked.

"Of course not," Safrah said. The only way to the abandoned domes lay across an open field, and the two boys, like all the others, were afraid of the outside. Afraid, angry at their own fearfulness, careless, violent, and lost; she saw all of that in Morwen and Terris. But for a moment she had allowed herself to make the mistake of thinking that they might not be only what they seemed, that there was still something of the curious and more gentle children she had once known inside them.

"Somebody came in here," Awan muttered, "and deliberately destroyed the radio. Who knows what they might do to the records? Or the librarian?"

"If we have to fetch clothes for them," Jina said, "maybe we ought to take more screens with us, too, and start hiding more records over there. We should copy some more of the most important stuff before we leave."

We can't count on anything, Safrah thought. The light in the sky might not be Ship. Even if it was, they might not be able to fix the radio, and then Ship might leave Home again.

"And how do we guard the library while we're gone?" Awan asked. "At least one of us should stay here."

Mikhail managed a small smile. "Two of us wouldn't be able to take on Terris and Morwen even if they came here all by themselves," he said. "And all of us together wouldn't be able to protect the library if all the young ones showed up."

"One of us should stay here, anyway," Awan said, "and it might as well be me. Maybe I can get the radio repaired by the time the rest of you get back." He offered them a smile, but Safrah saw the doubt in his eyes.

When they got back to their dome, the pieces of two broken plates were scattered across the floor, and there was a puddle in one corner that looked and smelled like urine. They had seen worse damage in the past when some of the others had broken in.

Mikhail slid the door shut and propped the brace against it. Safrah picked up the shards of pottery and put them on the table; they would feed them to the recycler when they went to the dining hall.

If the light they had seen that night was Ship, she wondered how long it would keep trying to contact them, and what it might think if it found out that one of its children had deliberately destroyed the radio. With no response to its messages, Ship might come to believe that they wanted no contact with the mind that had seeded Home, or even that they had forgotten it.

Ship might leave and never return. Could Ship get angry? Was it capable of such feelings?

"Go to sleep, all of you," Awan said. "I'll clean up here."

Safrah went to her room, knowing there would be little sleep for her.

5

Four days after the mysterious light was sighted in Seaside, two boaters came downriver and tied up at their only dock, a platform of reeds lashed together with rope.

Cemal went down to the dock to greet the newcomers. Bian and Arnagh trailed after him, carrying a basket of melons. The two boatwomen told them that they had never brought their boat this far south before, but had heard that Seaside was offering a large harvest of fruit, for which they intended to offer a few decorative carvings, various tools, and several lengths of Lakeview cloth. They had come there from Overlook, where everybody was talking about the light in the heavens that, according to some of the older folk, might mark the return of the ancestral Ship. The old promise

Nuy had neglected to mention in her tales of Ship was, it seemed, still recalled by others.

The boatwoman who had introduced herself as Vilia said, "Maybe by the time we get back there, they'll have found out more about the light and what the dome dwellers might know about it." Of course, it was highly unlikely that any such news would travel downriver so swiftly, even if a boater or rider carried it there at top speed. "In the meantime, let's see what you've got for us."

Bian and Arnagh set their basket down on the dock. "We've got these melons," Cemal replied, "and by this evening, we'll have a basket or two of tartberries ready to go. They'll be ripe enough for eating or preserving in two or three days, depending on whether the people in Overlook prefer them fresh or cooked."

The boater named Rashida frowned. "Thought you'd be further along on harvesting your fruit than that," she said. Like her companion, she was slim and muscular, with large dark eyes and a long braid down her bare back. "We've never seen the sea, and wouldn't mind spending some time by the shore. Hope it's all right with you if we wait a few days so we can carry more fruit back with us. I'm not about to trade what we've offered for only two or three baskets."

"Actually, we have another trade in mind." Cemal waved an arm at Bian and Arnagh. "Maybe you could take these two up to Overlook in return for this basket and a couple of others, then come back here afterwards for more of our fruit. We can discuss our terms for that trade then, and you'd be free to wander down to the shore for as long as you like. If Bian and Arnagh decide to travel on from Overlook, they can find other boaters to take them north."

Rashida shrugged. "Guess we could do that much for you."

Vilia glanced from Bian to Arnagh. "I'm sure I've seen you before," she said, "from a distance."

"I've been upriver with my aunt and uncle," Arnagh replied.

"What about you?" Vilia asked Bian. The boatwoman already looked doubtful about her.

"I haven't been upriver. I haven't even left my village except to wander down to the sea. Guess you could say I'm not too adventurous."

The two boaters were silent as they studied Bian, who forced herself to meet their gaze. "Hard to believe," Rashida said. A boater would probably say that about anyone Bian's age who had never felt the urge to wander or to be apart from others, to be alone for a time without others around who might pick up the signs of one's innermost thoughts. Rashida and Vilia could not be more than twenty or so, but both of them had the more contemplative look of people who had been traveling up and down the river for some time.

"You don't have to worry about her," Arnagh said. "Anyway, it was Bian's idea for us to go."

"I won't be any trouble," Bian said.

"Of course you won't," Vilia said, "because if you are, we'll drop you off and let you walk home."

"I'll look out for her," Arnagh said. Bian was grateful to him for saying it, but resented that he had done so.

The small two-room cabin Bian shared with her mother was at the southern edge of the village, near the cabin of Nuy's son Kadin, the youngest of her seven children and the only one of them who still lived in Seaside. Bian and Tasu sat on a reed mat that covered most of their dirt floor as they discussed what Bian should take with her.

"You'll need enough food to last until you get to Overlook, and you should probably take more," Tasu said, "along with some goods to trade for food after that." She reached inside one of the baskets next to the wall and drew out several necklaces and bracelets made of shells. Tasu had a talent for making such adornments, and each piece was made of shells that were closely matched in color and size. "You'll have to trade your labor for anything else you might need, but I doubt you'll get that far upriver before you hear something."

Bian searched her mother's face. "You're still not trying to stop me."

"I've held on to you for long enough. Maybe too long." Tasu sighed. "I told myself that I needed my only child with me, that I couldn't bear to lose you, too. I knew that eventually you'd have to make your own life, but in the meantime, it was a comfort to have you with me, and the more I sensed that you were perfectly content to stay close to me and be protected, the more protective I became. Now I'm afraid that all I've done is to make you as fearful as I became after I lost your father."

"If you tell me to stay here," Bian said, "I won't go." She was hoping that Tasu would forbid her to leave, even while knowing that such a command would solve nothing. To refuse to travel upriver now would only shame her, after she had offered to go in front of the whole village. Arnagh would expect her to go with him.

"If I tell you to stay," Tasu said, "Nuy would come here and force you to go. You promised everyone that you would. She won't allow you to turn your own words into a lie."

Bian looked down. Nuy would push her to go because she could not go herself, because she was too old now to travel easily even to Overlook.

She had nothing to fear. Arnagh would be with her; she would see more of what lay outside her village; and it was likely that, within one or two strings of days, she and Arnagh would know whether or not the dome dwellers were in contact with Ship. They would carry whatever they discovered back home, and others could decide what to do after that.

Bian left with one small sack of food and a larger pack that contained items to trade, along with some clothing. A loincloth and leather foot coverings were enough for her to wear in their village, since the weather was always warm, but the climate was colder and more changeable north of Seaside, and the dome dwellers, according to those who had traded with them, concealed themselves in shirts and leg coverings even on warm days.

Rashida sat in the stern of the boat, one hand on the rudder, as the craft glided upstream. Bian and Arnagh sat in the middle, with four covered baskets of fresh fruit at their feet, while Vilia perched in the bow. A few people, Arnagh's mother and father among them, had come down to the dock to see them off. After that they had wandered off to the orchards, following the rest of the villagers there. That day would pass for them as most days did, in tending the plants, harvesting ripe fruit, feeding the flightless birds that provided them with meat and eggs, searching their field for hidden rit holes and burrows, and working at whatever household tasks needed doing. If she had not been aboard this boat, Bian might have been out with a group of young people and a few of the younger children, clearing gourds, twigs, reeds, and other debris from the ditches that irrigated their fields; or she might have spent the day with Cemal and her mother, checking on the nests of their bluewisps and stingers, the flying insects that pollinated their orchards during the season of blossoms.

Little changed from day to day in the village. The greatest disruption in their daily routines had occurred a few years ago, when the infants and smaller children had suddenly started to wail in high, piercing tones and everyone had felt the disturbance in the air, a warning that a great storm was coming their way. The storm had swept in from the northeast, and the villagers were able to save themselves by taking shelter in the caves downriver, but they had lost that season's crops and most of their huts. They lived in the caves while rebuilding their homes, and Bian had learned how to thatch a roof and how to tie thick reeds together to make walls. Soon people from Overlook and elsewhere were sending them food and other needed supplies by boat. Within another two years, they had repaid all those who had helped them to recover and their lives were much as they had been before the storm.

The boat's engine hummed softly. Coming downriver, Vilia had explained, the current was with them and could carry their boat, but going north they would have to draw on power their old solar fuel cells had managed to store.

"Will there be enough power to get us to Overlook?" Bian asked.

"If there isn't," Vilia replied, "you'll just have to row." She gestured at the oars lying in the bottom of the small boat.

"I've never rowed a boat," Bian admitted.

Vilia smiled. "You'll learn. But I think we'll get to Overlook without having to row ourselves there."

They had left the village behind them. The boat passed a grove of blue-barked boltrees, their limbs heavy with purple gourds. To the east and west of the reeds and shrubs along the riverbanks stretched a plain of pale green grass, a flat landscape broken by only a few jagged outcroppings of rock. Upriver, a few wild horses had come down to the river to drink. One horse lifted its head and sighted the boat, and then suddenly all the animals swung around, galloped east, and were lost amid the high grass.

"What's Overlook like?" Bian asked.

"Bigger than Seaside," Vilia said.

"A lot bigger," Arnagh added.

Bian caught the anxious tone in his voice. He had been relaxed earlier, looking happier about going upriver again.

"Big enough now that some there are thinking about leaving Overlook to start another village," Vilia said. "There's even talk about heading across the eastern plains and settling along the banks of a river there, if they can gather enough tools and supplies to keep them going until they get some homes built and some crops harvested."

"They'd leave the river?" Bian asked. She tried to imagine what it might be like, living farther out on the plain. There would be no boaters to carry news to them, only those traders who cared to make the long journey across the grassland, but few would want to go to such trouble when they could find plenty of business in the villages along the river.

"Might be better for the rest of you if more people did move away," Vilia said. "If Overlook grows too big, they'll need to clear more land to grow their crops, and that means more ditches to irrigate the fields, maybe even a dam, and that would mean a bit less water going downstream to Seaside. Maybe not enough to matter now, but later on—"

"There'd be more shit going into the river, too," Rashida said as she pulled the rudder a little to her left, "and more waste. And more of whatever ends up in the water would be heading your way from all the villages upriver. A river can probably handle only so much before it's unable to clean itself."

"Can there ever be enough people to harm a river?" Bian had been outside her village for barely half a day, and already she was wrestling with unfamiliar notions. "And wouldn't it be hard to live out on the plain?"

"Oh, I don't know," Rashida murmured. "According to maps I've seen, there's a good-sized stream three or four days to the east, and a long river beyond that, and caves where people could live until they've finished building other dwellings. And after a while, there'd be more of them, and they'd spread out and build more villages, and maybe it would be horsepeople instead of boaters who would carry news and trade to those settlements." She smiled at Bian. "Still, I know what you mean. I wouldn't want to leave the river myself. I'm content with traveling north and south and trading and bringing people tales from other villages."

Bian had thought of most boaters as discontented people, restless and impatient with village life and in need of more solitude than most people could endure. Tarki, Kadin's son, whom Bian had never known, had been one such unhappy person, according to those who remembered him. Tarki had left their village to become a boater when he was about Arnagh's age, and only his grandmother Nuy had not tried to keep him from going; so Tasu had told Bian many times. Tarki, according to Tasu, wanted something that the village could not offer him, although he was hard-put to explain exactly what it was he wanted instead. He had a habit of sitting outside and staring up at the sky as if what he searched for might be found in the clouds or among the stars.

"Let him go," Nuy had said to everyone at last. "He's

unhappy here, and having to see and sense his misery will only add to our own." Since then, Tarki had not returned to the village. All Bian had heard about him was that he was living on a boat in the north, trading with the dome dwellers and the villagers who lived along the shore of the great lake.

Perhaps he was still unhappy, but the boaters Bian encountered seemed as content with their lives as most of the villagers she knew seemed with theirs, and life in the village would have been harder and more tedious without them. The boaters offered them not only the means to trade with one another, but also a way to find out what was going on elsewhere. In the past, there had been some talk of making devices that would enable the villagers to communicate with others over long distances, but why go to all that trouble to hear of distant events when any truly important news would come soon enough, through one of the boaters? And what was the point in listening to a distant voice or a stream of signals when one could hear a boatman's or boatwoman's tales? Anyone could listen to a boater and know from the smoothness or hesitancy in his voice, from his posture and movements, even from his scent, whether or not he was speaking the truth, concealing information, or adding a few flourishes or exaggerations to his story; and any device that put distance between a speaker and a listener would only make it more difficult to discern the truth. At a distance, with only a voice to go on, someone could lie far more easily.

Or so Bian had always thought. It came to her now that, if they had been able to contact other villages at a distance, they might already know if the light in the sky was Ship, and if the dome dwellers were in communication with the great vessel. They might have been able to speak to Ship themselves.

Bian had thought that the boaters would halt their craft for the night, but Vilia and Rashida decided to stop only long enough for an evening meal. They wanted to keep moving and get to Overlook well before the fruit ripened; the riper it got, the less it was likely to bring them in trade.

They pulled up along the western bank amid a patch of reeds. Arnagh and Bian had brought beans wrapped in bread to share with the boaters. While they ate, Vilia told them a little about Lakeside, the village far to the north where she had grown up. Lakeside was the northernmost village inhabited by the river people, less than half a day from where the lake narrowed into the river, although Westbay, a settlement on the southwest bank of the lake, was nearly as far north. Almost everyone in Lakeside grew up with some experience on boats, since they often crossed the lake to trade with Westbay. But even so, few of them chose to lead a life on the river later on.

"You get used to the lake," Vilia explained. "Even now, I sometimes miss looking out and seeing all that water stretching so far to the west. When the weather was hot, we'd go down to the water and swim for hours. Sometimes we'd have competitions, seeing who could swim to Westbay in the shortest amount of time."

"Sounds like the sea," Bian said, "except that you wouldn't want to swim in the sea for hours, or even go too far from shore, because of the undertow. You could get swept out so far that you might not be able to swim back." She thought of her father, who had been swept away and lost to the sea. Death was what Kwam's fearlessness had brought him; that was the lesson Bian's mother had taught her.

"The lake isn't anything like the sea," Arnagh said, the only one among them who had seen both bodies of water. "Big as it is, it's still small enough that you can look out from Lakeside and glimpse the smoke from a campfire near Westbay on a clear night."

"Why did you become a boater?" Bian asked Vilia.

Vilia smiled. "A boat arrived from Plainview one day, and Rashida was aboard. It was her first journey upriver—she'd been a boater for only a couple of months, but she already knew that was how she wanted to spend the rest of her life."

"I came upriver with my brother, aboard his boat," Rashida added.

"I asked if I could travel with them," Vilia said, "and traded some cloth for my passage. By the time we'd passed Plainview and were heading toward Shadowridge, I knew that I wanted to be a boater, and Rashida's brother, after years traveling up and down the river, had decided he was ready to give it up."

"He's living in Shadowridge now," Rashida said, "with a mate and a year-old son."

"So we took over his boat." Vilia glanced affectionately at her companion. "I knew I wanted to stay with Rashida, too."

Arnagh's mouth tightened, a look of longing coming into his eyes. He lowered his head before Bian could read anything more in his expression.

"My cousin Tarki's a boatman," Bian said. "At least he was, the last we heard. He hasn't come back to our village in years, and no one's ever brought us any word about him."

"Tarki Kadinson?" Rashida asked.

Tarki would not have used such a name in Seaside. "Kadin is the name of his father," Bian admitted.

"I know Tarki," Rashida said, "but I haven't seen him for a long time. He stays near Westbay when he's not traveling up and down the river, and I've heard he hasn't been on the river for a couple of years now. Keeps to himself more than most do—that's probably why you haven't had any news of him. No mate, and no children, either."

"They say he's traded with the dome dwellers more often than just about anybody," Vilia said.

Arnagh looked up at that, then lowered his head once more. Talk of the dome dwellers was clearly stirring his emotions. What was it about them that pained him so much? Bian forced herself to suppress her curiosity. Arnagh had a right to keep his troubles to himself until he was ready to share them.

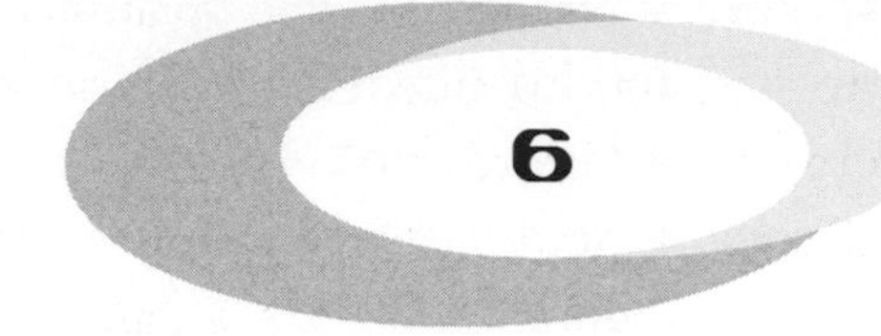

6

The sight of several boats crossing the river to the north was the first sign that Bian and her companions were nearing Overlook. Seeing sheep grazing in the field beyond the bank to her left was another sign.

Their boat continued to glide north. On the eastern bank, at the base of a sheer rocky cliff, a few small cabins sat around an open space, but most of the villagers here apparently lived on the other side of the river, where cabins and longhouses dotted the plain to the west. In the wide field between those dwellings and the six docks along the western riverbank, where more boats were tied up, lay paddies of rice fed by a network of ditches. People carrying large baskets were out in the paddies, wading in the shallow water as they harvested the rice.

Bian expected the boatwomen to head west, since that was where most of the dwellings stood, but instead Vilia steered their craft east, toward two docks that jutted out from the eastern bank. Only one craft, a boat with a canopy large enough to shelter several people, was tied up at the docks.

"We'll have to stop on this side first," Rashida replied in response to Bian's puzzled expression. "The leader and council members will want to find out if we're just here to trade or want to stay on for a while. And if there's any news from up north, we're likely to hear it there first." Two days of travel with the two boaters had not yielded any more details about Overlook, or any of the other settlements along the river. The two women had grown less talkative, and Arnagh had fallen into a somber silence.

Clearly he already regretted having come on this trip. Bian wondered if he would decide to go back to their village with the two boatwomen. She might have to stay here or else head farther north by herself. Her growing curiosity warred with her fears. She would go on, she decided, even if she had to travel alone.

Rashida crept toward the prow of the boat, holding a rope tied to a hook near one of the oarlocks. As the craft slipped toward the southernmost dock, she moved into a crouch, then leaped to the dock and quickly looped the rope around a pier. A bare-chested man in a loincloth wearing a colorful necklace of shells stepped out of a nearby cabin and walked toward the dock, his back straight and his head held high; he looked like someone used to respect and obedience.

Arnagh climbed out of the boat, then held out a hand to Bian as she stepped onto the dock. "Greetings, Duman," Rashida said to the man as he approached.

"Hai," the man replied. He halted and stared intently at Arnagh. "You've been here before," he said. "Arnagh of Seaside."

Arnagh nodded. "I'm surprised you remember me."

"It's my business to remember the people who pass through Overlook." He turned to Bian. "And who are you?"

"My name's Bian. I'm from Seaside, too."

"I assumed that much." He smiled, and she felt a bit less intimidated by him.

Vilia stepped onto the dock. "She's a great-granddaughter of Nuy's," the boatwoman said.

Duman raised his eyebrows; he seemed to think better of her. "And you were never curious enough about us to visit us before?" he asked. "It's not as though we're that far away."

Bian felt shamed by her timidity. "My mother needed me near her," she said. "My father died when I was still a baby, and she was afraid she might lose me, too. But it was also easier for me to stay at home." She might as well admit that. If this man's senses were even slightly sharper than those of most people, he would be able to read her shyness and hesitancy in her gestures and expressions.

"Was it your father or your mother who was part of Nuy's line?" Duman asked.

"My father. His name was Kwam."

"Ah." Duman closed his eyes for a moment. "I remember him. He came here a few times when we were still boys, riding up on horseback, full of gossip about Seaside and ready to race against any of us on his horse. I was very sorry when I heard of his passing." He motioned to the boatwomen. "And what have you brought us this time?"

"Two baskets of melons and two of tartberries," Rashida said, "but we'll be going back to Seaside for more fruit in a day or two. Bian and Arnagh came with us to see if they could find out anything about that new light crossing the night sky."

Duman shrugged, then shook his head; obviously no information about that phenomenon had yet traveled this far south. He glanced at Bian. "Are you planning to wait here in the hope that we hear something about that soon?" he asked.

"I don't know," Bian replied, hoping that they could at least stop here for a short time to rest. She had not slept well in the bottom of the boat; the slight rocking of the craft as it cut through the water and the soft hum of its engine had kept her from sleeping soundly.

"We might stay here for a day or two," Arnagh said, "but we're more likely to hear some news if we keep going." Bian tried not to betray her relief that he wasn't going to turn back and leave her here by herself. "Do you know of any boaters who are heading north?"

Duman shook his head. "If you had come here a couple of days ago, you might have had better luck. Any boater who had business north of Overlook and who was also looking to pick up some news has already left here."

Bian was both disappointed and relieved. They could go back home with Rashida and Vilia and say that they had tried.

Then she heard the sound of a flute. Rashida and Vilia lifted their heads; Duman scowled. Bian held her breath as the notes tripped past one another and then rose to a higher pitch. A few of the people in Seaside had fashioned flutes from the thicker reeds by the river, but she had never heard such compelling music from them.

She turned toward the sound. Farther up the bank, a young man sat outside a cabin, holding a flute to his lips. Three young women and another young man sat with him as he played, their bodies swaying in time to the music. Bian tapped a foot, entranced by the sinuous sound of the flute.

Duman hurried from the dock and strode toward the flute player. Arnagh scurried after him. Bian gazed after them, then glanced uncertainly at the boatwomen.

"Duman looks like he's really going to tear into Enli this time," Vilia said.

"We'd better stay out of it," Rashida added. The music broke off as Duman advanced on the group, Arnagh at his heels.

Bian ran from the dock after Arnagh. "Useless boy!" Duman was shouting. "There's a cabin wall that needs repairs, and you sit here—"

"That wall's already been repaired," the flute player shot back. Now that she was closer, Bian saw that he was younger than she had thought, probably close to her own age. He had broad brown shoulders and large brown eyes; a smile flickered across his face. "Take a look for yourself."

"I doubt you did any of the work," Duman said.

"Can I help it if somebody else offers to do the job in return for some music?"

The women and the young man sitting with the flute player got to their feet. "It's a good job," one of the young women murmured in a shaky voice, "really it is, and we finished it faster than Enli would have all by himself."

Duman frowned. "That's not the point." He motioned to the young man standing near the flute player. "Also, you should be on the lookout for passengers in need of being ferried across the river, not sitting around idle."

The three young women hurried toward a cabin while the man walked toward the docks. The flute player stood up; he was only a little taller than Bian. "Wouldn't it be better if we didn't have this argument in front of two visitors?" he asked. He turned to Arnagh. "Why did you come here, anyway?"

"We came up from Seaside—,"Arnagh began.

"—to find out whatever they could about that new light in the sky we've all seen," Duman finished. "But I told them they wouldn't find any boaters here to take them north now."

"We'd like to stay here for a couple of days," Arnagh said, "if anybody's willing to have us. We can trade some food and a few goods for a place to sleep, and maybe by then—"

"You can stay with me," the flute player said.

Duman glared at him. "Where they'd probably just pick up your bad habits."

"It'll save you the trouble of finding them someplace else to stay."

Duman's chest swelled. To Bian's surprise, he suddenly clapped the boy on the shoulder and then gave him a quick hug. "Yes, that will save me some trouble," Duman said. "The girl's called Bian, and the boy's name is Arnagh." He let go of the boy. "This is my son Enli, whose one great talent is avoiding any work he doesn't want to do."

The flute player shook his head. "Thank you for that fine introduction."

"They deserve a warning, son." Duman shrugged. "Just don't put them to work on all those tasks you'd rather not do."

"How long do you plan to stay here?" the boy asked.

"Only until we can find somebody to take us north," Arnagh said.

"You may be waiting a long time then, unless you want to head north by yourselves. But I don't mind putting you up in the meantime."

Bian looked up at Duman. "Go on," he said. "You've got a

long walk ahead of you. If you get tired of Enli's company, come back in a couple of days and we'll send you back to Seaside with Vilia and Rashida."

Bian and Arnagh helped Vilia and Rashida carry the baskets of fruit to Duman's cabin, thanked them for passage, and returned to the boat to get their packs. Enli watched, toying with his flute instead of doing anything to aid them. By the time Enli started leading Bian and Arnagh away from the cabins under the ridge, other members of Overlook's council had gathered in front of Duman's cabin to discuss what to trade for the fruit.

Enli had tied his flute to a leather strap that looped over his left shoulder; a small pouch and a knife also dangled from the strap. They walked past a large fenced-in space of trampled grass that looked like a pen for larger animals such as cattle or horses, then continued north, past the last of the cabins and along a path between the shrubs and reeds that bordered the river and the grassy plain.

"You don't live with your mother and father?" Arnagh asked. His voice wavered, as if the other boy intimidated him just a little.

"No," the boy replied.

"Do you have a mate, then?" Enli was old enough to have committed himself to a partner.

"No."

"Another companion, then?" Arnagh said.

"No." Enli halted for a minute. "I prefer to live by myself."

"Without anybody else at all in your home?"

"Yes."

"So are there any other cabins near your house?"

"No." Enli walked on, moving a few paces ahead of them.

Bian followed, keeping her eyes on Enli's long dark-brown braid, which fell nearly to his waist. Timid as she was, she could not imagine needing so much extended solitude. Where was he taking them? She envisioned a hut, maybe a tent; she could not imagine any other kind of dwelling for a boy who preferred to live alone.

They walked on. Out on the plain, not far from the river, Bian soon spotted a small herd of horses. Riders were astride three of the animals, and they seemed to be herding the rest of the horses south. Most of the people of Seaside considered keeping horses to be more trouble than it was worth, but Bian had often wandered to the edge of the village whenever wild horses were seen out on the plain. Those who had known her father Kwam had told her that he had managed to train a couple of horses and had ridden them often. Horses were beautiful, graceful, and free, everything that she felt she was not.

One of the riders rode toward them. Enli offered no sign of recognition to the rider, not even when the black horse was within a few paces of them. The rider waved her right arm at him while gripping the reins with her left; she was a slender girl with a long yellow braid. A thin piece of white cloth was tied around her chest, and her thighs were covered with leather leggings.

"Enli!" she called out. He ignored her. "Enli!" There was urgency in her voice. The horse slowed to a trot, then halted. "You're still angry with me, aren't you?" the girl said. "Tell me you're not."

Enli kept on walking and said nothing.

"Tell me you're not!" the girl cried. Her pretty face was flushed; her large blue eyes glistened. She slid off the horse and walked at his side, leading the horse by the reins.

"I'm not angry," Enli replied. "I just can't talk to you now, that's all."

The girl looked back at Bian. "Who are you?" she asked.

"My name's Bian, and this is my friend Arnagh."

"We're from Seaside," Arnagh added. "We needed a place to stay for a couple of days, and Enli told us we could stay with him."

"Really." The girl snorted. "You ought to be flattered, then. These days, he doesn't even ask those of us who know him well to stay with him in his house."

Enli walked on in silence. The girl kept near him, then slowed, keeping pace with Bian and Arnagh. Bian felt awkward, unable to speak, but also curious about why this girl was so angry at Enli.

"We're supposed to make a pledge," the girl said then, as if picking up on Bian's thoughts. "At least, we were going to make a pledge, but now he's decided he'd rather live in his house by himself than join his life to mine. Enli has no reason to be mad at me, but I have every reason to be furious with him."

Enli quickly turned around. "Shut up, Lusa."

"You're too lazy and selfish to share anything with anyone," she said.

"Then you should be relieved we're not going to make a pledge after all."

The blond girl made a fist with her left hand; she looked ready to hit him. She threw one arm over the horse, pulled herself onto its back, grasped the reins, and rode toward the other two riders and the horse herd.

Enli looked back, waiting for Bian and Arnagh to catch up with him before walking on. "Sorry you had to hear that," he said.

"It's all right," Arnagh muttered, looking embarrassed. "We talked about making a pledge, but that's all it was, just talk. I didn't promise Lusa anything."

Bian disliked the way the boy said that, as if the girl had no right to her anger. If they had grown close enough even to talk about a pledge, Lusa probably had ample reason to resent him for deciding not to make one.

The riders continued to herd the horses in their direction. Enli led Bian and Arnagh away from the path and into the higher grass as two of the horses trotted past them, followed by a woman on horseback. She reined in her horse and beckoned to Enli.

"My mother," Enli muttered under his breath. "They're from Seaside," he called out, motioning to Bian and Arnagh. "I told Duman they could stay with me until they decide whether to go upriver or not."

The woman offered them a half smile. Her golden brown skin was paler than her son's, and a long black braid fell over her left shoulder. "My name's Zan," she said. "And what are you called?"

"I'm Arnagh, and this is Bian," Arnagh replied.

"Perhaps my son's music will amuse you," Enli's mother said. "Just make sure he doesn't work you too hard in return for it during your stay. He trades with it and does little else." She rode on, followed by a young man on horseback and the rest of the horses. Lusa trailed after the other two riders and the herd, refusing to look in Enli's direction.

They walked on. Bian waited for Enli to tell them more about his parents or his people, but he did not seem in the mood for talk. At last Arnagh said, "How much farther do we have to go, anyway?"

Enli pointed north. "There." He was pointing at a distant

wall of rock near the horizon. Bian realized that the wall was part of a structure overlooking the river, and that a small craft was tied up near it on the bank.

"That's your home?" Arnagh said.

"That's it."

"And your boat?"

Enli nodded.

"You didn't tell us you were a boater."

"I'm not. I just happen to have a boat."

Maybe he could take them upriver to the next village in his boat, Bian thought, but suppressed her hopes. So far, all she knew about Enli was that his father and mother considered him lazy and that he had broken a promise to a girl who expected to become his mate. She and Arnagh might be better off finding someone else to guide them north.

Enli's dwelling was a large cabin that overlooked the river. The wall of rock Bian had glimpsed earlier turned out to be part of an enclosed courtyard in front of the cabin. Enli led them through an opening in the wall that faced west. The fireplace, a hollow in the ground filled with dead ashes and surrounded by flat stones, was in the center of the courtyard. The land bordered by the walls sloped down to the river, where the boat, nearly the size of Vilia and Rashida's, was tied up among the reeds; unlike their craft, this one had a short deck spanning its center.

The open rectangular entrance to the cabin was wide enough for them to walk through shoulder to shoulder. They entered a large room, the center of its dirt floor covered with mats woven of reeds. Another entryway had been made in the cabin's eastern wall, through which Bian could glimpse the square wooden structure of an outhouse and the expanse of the grassy plain beyond. To her right, a curtain of white cloth hung in front of another opening in that wall. Enli's home had enough space to house three generations of a family.

"You can sleep there, Bian." Enli pointed to one corner, where a brown woolen blanket lay on top of the mats. "I can get out another blanket for you, Arnagh, unless . . ." He looked from Arnagh to her uncertainly.

"We're only good friends," Arnagh said hastily. Bian nodded.

Enli stepped to the curtain and swept it aside. "This is where I sleep."

Bian peered past him into another smaller room. A thick mat much like her bed at home lay on the floor, while five reed instruments of various sizes hung from hooks on one wall. Shelves on another wall held blankets, stoppered clay jars, two large packs, a couple of light wands, and a reading screen.

"You own a lot," Arnagh said. "You have more things than just about anybody I know. You must have worked hard and traded much for all of this, so why does your father say you're lazy?"

"Because the way he sees it, I am," Enli replied. "I've been making and playing flutes ever since I was a child, and it wasn't long before I realized I was better at that than anyone else here. All I ever really wanted to do was play a flute and make music, and I probably would have done it all the time if my mother and father had let me. Then other boys and girls started to offer me trades in exchange for my playing, food and tools or whatever else I needed at the time, and after a while I found out that I could trade my music for their work." He looked around the room. "I designed this place, and did some of the work myself, but I would have had a hard time building it alone, so I traded my music for some of the labor."

Bian wondered if such a trade was something to admire. Enli frowned, as if sensing her doubts. "I enjoy making my music more than just about anything else. Can I help it if people want to give me something in return for listening to it?"

"I guess not," Arnagh muttered.

"That's why I decided to live out here by myself instead of in Overlook. I can practice out here, work on my music and get it right before I play it for anybody else. At least that way I can make the music worth the trade." He fell silent, then said, "It's a wonder to my mother that people will trade to listen to it."

Bian untied her larger pack from her shoulders and let it slide to the floor. "We can trade you some of our food for letting us stay here," she said, "but we'll have to keep the rest of it in case—" She paused. "Is it true, what your father said about the boaters, that we probably won't find anybody here to take us north?"

Enli nodded. "I'm afraid so."

You have a boat, she wanted to say; you could take us north. But she said nothing.

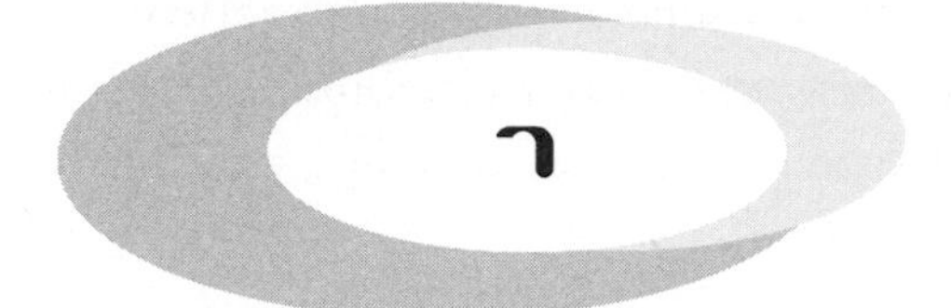

7

Bian woke to sunlight streaming through the eastern entryway. She sat up and stretched, with a faint memory of getting up during the night and stumbling outside to the outhouse. She had looked up at the night sky, thinking irrationally that the strange light might not appear again, but it was still there, moving slowly across the familiar backdrop of stars. For a moment, she had been terrified of the nighttime silence, of realizing that she was no longer in Seaside, safe in her own home with her mother resting nearby.

Arnagh, curled up in the corner across from hers, was still sleeping, his blanket wound around him. Outside, she heard the trilling of a flute. She and Arnagh had shared some fruit and dried fish with Enli for their evening meal.

He had still been awake, carving tiny holes in a reed with a small curved knife, when she and Arnagh settled themselves in their respective corners to sleep.

Arnagh sighed, then sat up. Without speaking, he stumbled toward the arched opening and outside to the outhouse. Bian drew up her legs and wrapped her arms around them as she listened to Enli's playing.

The music abruptly broke off. "What are you doing here?" Enli's voice said.

"Don't worry, I didn't come here to argue with you," a girl's voice replied. "Your mother asked me to ride over to see how those two visitors are doing. The boaters they came with are impatient to go back to Seaside, so if they want to leave with them, they'll have to head back to Overlook today." The speaker paused for a moment. "Are they still sleeping? They must be as lazy as you are."

Bian scrambled to her feet, then quickly rolled up her blanket. Arnagh came back inside just as the yellow-haired rider they had seen the day before came through the entrance facing the courtyard.

"Hai," the girl said, looking away from them for a moment. "I didn't mean to wake you."

"We were already awake," Bian said.

"Oh." The other girl stepped back. "Zan sent me. Enli's mother. Apparently Vilia and Rashida agreed on the terms of their trade with Duman faster than they expected to, so they're already getting ready to leave for Seaside. If you're going to go back with them—"

"They just got here yesterday," Enli said as he came inside, holding a flute in his right hand.

"I know, but—"

"They haven't even had their morning meal yet." There

was a tremor in Enli's voice, as if he was trying to restrain himself. "At least give them a chance to eat."

The girl's mouth tightened. "All right, then." She looked from Arnagh to Bian. "Do you have enough water?"

Arnagh shook his head. "We drank most of ours."

"I'll fetch some more, then." The girl smiled, as if trying to make amends.

Bian went to the packs, which lay near the back entryway, and pulled out their two waterskins. "Thank you," she said as the taller girl took them from her.

Enli stared after the girl as she went outside, then turned to them. "You don't have to leave today," he said, "whatever Lusa tells you." Bian saw that he wanted them to stay. Her breath caught. That notion unexpectedly pleased her.

"That's kind of you," Arnagh said.

The three of them sat down. Arnagh took out some flatbread and dried fish and passed around pieces of the food. Lusa came back inside, seated herself next to Arnagh with her legs folded under her, and handed him his waterskin.

"Thanks," Arnagh said.

She passed the other waterskin to Bian, then moved closer to Arnagh. "When Enli first decided to build a house out here," she said, "most of us just assumed that more people from Overlook would move here and build houses, too, that eventually this would become another part of Overlook or else maybe the beginning of a new village. Then, when I saw how large a place he was planning, I couldn't imagine why anybody would want so much space for just himself, so naturally . . ." Her eyes narrowed as she looked toward Enli. "But he just prefers being alone. Oh, he let people stay here when he needed their labor, but now that he doesn't . . ."

"Lusa, stop it," Enli murmured in a tone that was both angry and mournful.

Arnagh held out some food to Lusa; she shook her head. "If you like," she said, turning to Arnagh, "I'll go back and get a couple of horses so you can ride back to Overlook instead of walking."

"We don't know how to ride horses," Arnagh said.

Lusa seemed surprised. "Our people don't keep horses anymore," Bian explained. "We used to, back in my grandparents' time, but with the kind of work we do and the crops we raise, after a while we didn't—"

"Horses are useful," Lusa interrupted, "if you want to travel without having to hitch a ride with a boater." She focused on Arnagh. "Too bad you have to leave. You could have spent time out in the pasture with our horses, and I could have taught you how to ride." The girl was flirting with Arnagh, not picking up on either his growing anxiety or his obvious lack of interest in her.

"Let them finish their breakfast," Enli said. "If they decide to go back to Overlook, I can get them back there by this afternoon, but as far as I'm concerned, I don't mind if they stay here for a while."

Lusa opened her mouth, as though about to speak, then swiftly got to her feet. "Go ahead and stay with him, then, if that's what you want to do."

Arnagh said, "We haven't decided what we're going to do yet."

"You'd better decide before Enli eats all your food and leaves you with nothing to trade but your labor."

Enli got up. "Lusa," he whispered, then held out his arms and pulled her toward himself. She leaned against him, hiding her face for a moment, then wrenched herself away. Tears streamed down her face; Bian quickly looked down.

"You promised," Lusa said softly.

"I didn't know what I was doing. I don't want to hurt you." Enli drew her to him again. "Lusa—"

She shook off his grip. "I wish you weren't here. I wish you'd go far away, so I wouldn't have to see you or think about you anymore."

"Maybe I will go away. I've got a boat. I could take them as far as Shadowridge. Anyway, I could use some new ears for my music, people who won't keep asking me to play their favorites over and over."

Lusa turned away and hurried outside. Bian was afraid to say anything. After a few moments, she heard the distant whinny of a horse and then the sound of hooves pounding against the ground.

Bian forced herself to finish her food. Arnagh gulped down some water, then said, "Did you mean that, about taking us to Shadowridge?"

Enli sat down. "I meant it. I was thinking about doing that earlier. You might find some boatpeople there who would take you farther north."

Bian glanced at Arnagh, wanting to say that maybe it would be better for them to go home instead. Enli might only want to take them north for complicated hidden motives of his own.

"I'm willing to go with you," Arnagh said to Enli. "Bian, you can do as you like. If you want to go back to Seaside by yourself—"

"I'm sticking with you," she responded. The words had come from her almost against her will. She did not want to disappoint her great-grandmother or her people by returning without news, and it would mean more time with Enli, who wasn't like anyone else she had known.

Bian and the two boys were about to board Enli's boat when a horse and rider appeared in the distance, coming toward them through the shorter grass near the riverbank. The horse passed a small grove of boltrees and then moved into a gallop. Bian soon saw that the rider was Enli's mother, Zan.

"Go on," Enli murmured, setting down his pack. He hurried toward his mother while she and Arnagh waited by the boat. The horse slowed to a trot as Zan rode up to the stone wall, then halted. Still holding the reins, Zan leaned over to speak to her son.

Bian said, "That girl must have told her we were going north with him."

"You don't have to come with us," Arnagh said. "Zan could take you back to Overlook."

She had been doing her best to push her worries to the back of her mind so that her voice and gestures would not betray her fears. "But I want to go with you."

"I know, but you're scared, too."

She looked into his face. "So are you."

"But not for the same reasons you are." Arnagh let out his breath. "Maybe we'll find out what we need to know in Shadowridge, or in Plainview, if we can find somebody to take us there. But if we don't, we'll have to keep heading north, and the farther we go without finding anything out, the more of a chance—" He paused. "You might as well know. There's somebody upriver I hoped I'd never see again, and at the same time—" A hurt look came into his eyes.

Bian turned away from Arnagh, embarrassed at seeing his inner pain so openly revealed. Enli was nodding at his mother. Zan sat up, apparently finished with whatever she wanted to say to her son, and rode away. Enli picked up his pack and walked toward them.

"What did your mother want?" Arnagh asked.

"To make sure I had everything I needed before I left. She'll let Vilia and Rashida know that you're going upriver with me." He glanced from Arnagh to Bian. "She's really worried—frightened. She told me to come back as soon as I found out anything, but that if we get as far as Plainview without hearing anything, to come back home after that. If news hasn't traveled that far by then, she's sure it'll mean that the dome dwellers have decided to keep anything they know to themselves."

"And what happens then?" Bian asked.

"I don't know," Enli said. "It might mean that the dome dwellers are talking to Ship and want to keep anything they can find out to themselves instead of sharing it with us, or—"

"I didn't mean what they might do," she interrupted. "I meant, what are we going to do."

Enli's expression hardened. "Oh, I think I can answer that. Nothing, that's what we'll do, nothing at all, unless people begin to worry that whatever the dome dwellers are doing might cause us a lot of trouble. We might do something then, anything to keep things just the way they are." Bian was about to ask him why he seemed so angry about all of that when he added, "Come on, let's go," and motioned them onto his boat.

The boat glided upriver, piloted by Arnagh. Enli had shown him how to handle the rudder, and Arnagh quickly picked up the skill, having had some experience with steering other boats. Bian sat under the deck, inside the tiny cabin at the boat's center. Enli crept up to the prow, settled himself there, reached into the pack he had brought aboard, and took out a flute.

The tune he played reminded Bian of the music she had first heard from him, right after she and Arnagh arrived in Overlook. The notes coming from his flute tripped to a higher pitch, and then abruptly softened, bouncing against one another until they rose once more to a high piercing cry. She had never heard any music like it before. Unfamiliar as it was, she found herself longing to hear more.

"How did you come up with that?" she asked when he fell silent.

"With what?" Enli asked.

"With that kind of music. How did you make it up? Is that the kind of music your people play in Overlook? All we ever hear in Seaside is the same simple melodies, over and over, usually after a harvest or at a party for two people who have made their pledge."

"I've added passages of my own to this music," Enli said, "but most of it is music I heard when my father and I went north to trade with the dome dwellers."

"You've traded with them yourself?" Arnagh asked. "So have I. Last time was a year ago, with my aunt Tiri and uncle Malcum. Tiri has cousins in Lakeview, so she likes to go up there every two or three years to visit them, and the last three times she and Malcum took me along to help them with their goods." He looked down, but not before Bian saw that now familiar look of pain cross his face.

"I was there about a year and a half ago," Enli said. "It gets so cold up there that you have to cover yourself with a shirt or a tunic and pants, and even then, the wind can cut right through you when it blows across the lake. My father handles most of our trade with the dome dwellers, which is why I have this boat. Duman lets me keep it at my house as long as he can use it when somebody needs ferrying or whenever he has to head north."

"Was that the first time you went north to trade?" Arnagh asked.

Enli shook his head. "That was my fifth trip." Arnagh's eyes widened with respect. "The first time was when I was nine and I went up with my father and two members of our council. Word had come down to us from Lakeview that some dome dwellers were especially interested in our leather goods. Nobody seemed to know what they were willing to offer in return, but Duman thought the trip would be worth it even if we didn't make a trade. By then it had been over two years since anybody along the river had heard anything from the dome dwellers, so he was really starting to wonder."

"So were we," Arnagh said. "I remember my grandmother saying that they used to send their people out to trade three or four times a year when she was a girl. Then they made it clear they wanted nothing to do with us except for a trade once in a while. Almost everybody was saying that if they insisted on cutting themselves off from us, that was their business, and we could get along by ourselves if it came to it, but Nuy—Bian's great-grandmother—started telling everybody that we should have done more to stay in contact with them."

Enli looked toward Bian, as though expecting her to add a few words to the conversation.

"My great-grandmother Nuy and great-grandfather Yukio lived by the lake for a while," she began. "That was back when, as she puts it, Lakeview was only a few huts and a storehouse. She and Yukio and her foster father Yusef used to visit the dome dwellers at least once a year, even if they didn't have anything to trade. Even after the dome dwellers stopped inviting the three of them inside the settlement, a few would at least come out and meet with them down by the lake. But after a while, no one would come out unless they needed to trade, and by the time the first of Nuy's children was born, the dome dwellers had made it clear that they didn't want anyone to come even as far as the northern end of the lake. By then, Yusef had died, and Yukio and Nuy had gone south to live closer to the sea. I suppose they had enough to do, what with making their home and bringing up all their children, to stop worrying about the dome dwellers after a while. At least the northerners were still trading with us, Nuy said, even if they let traders go only as far as their outpost. Now she wishes we'd made more of an effort to stay connected to them."

Enli looked thoughtful. "She might have been right about that, even if they didn't want any contact with us. Maybe they would have changed their minds if we'd been more insistent." He looked down at his flute. "I first heard their music the second time Duman and I went to trade with them. Landed our boat near their outpost and waited for them inside one of the shacks."

"There are two cabins," Arnagh explained to Bian, "and if nobody happens to be around, you have to wait there until the dome dwellers come down to trade with you."

"But how do they know you're there?" Bian asked.

"There's a tower north of the cabins," Arnagh replied, "with a beacon at the top. One of us would go there and turn on the beacon—it's bright enough, and the tower's high enough, for the dome dwellers to see it from their settlement."

"It seemed dimmer the last time I was there," Enli said. "Maybe the fuel cells are failing."

"My aunt told me that my grandparents used to wonder why they didn't put a radio in the tower," Arnagh said. "If they didn't already know how to put one together, they should have been able to figure that out from their records." He shrugged. "But they were avoiding us more and more, so I suppose opening up another way to communicate with us didn't make any sense to them."

"We could have put a radio together ourselves," Enli said, "or found some other way to communicate."

Arnagh shook his head. "We don't have the tools, or any—"

"We could have traded for what we needed," Enli interrupted. "With the records stored in our screens, we could have figured out what we needed and picked up those things from them, maybe a little bit at a time to keep them from getting too curious about what we wanted it all for." He let out his breath. "That's one thing we and the dome dwellers seem to have in common: We're happy to let everything go on the way it has, as long as we've got enough to eat and everybody's getting along, or at least not fighting. We're so perfectly adapted with our transplanted plants and animals from Earth and the bits of Home inside us." He did not even seem to be trying to hide his discontent. "But if Ship has come back, if the dome dwellers are talking to it now, I wonder if anything can stay the same."

It can't be Ship. Bian thought of what her great-grandmother had said when they first saw the strange light in the sky. *I don't want it to be Ship.* Maybe Nuy had been thinking of the battles of the past, and the violence that had marked other times of change.

8

The tunnel leading to the dining hall sloped sharply upward. Safrah and Mikhail trudged up the slope, empty sacks slung over their shoulders. They had brought the shards of the broken plates with them, but nothing else; Jina had gone to the greenhouse early that morning and returned to say that only a patch of green beans, a few sprouts, and a couple of melons were ready for harvesting.

They would pick that food and take it with them. There was no point in bringing so little fresh food to the younger ones, who did not seem to care what they ate as long as there was enough of it and they did not have to prepare any of it.

"Why do we have to grow food here, when the dispenser can give us enough food?" That had been one of the first questions Safrah asked Moise on one of their trips to the greenhouse. He explained that the dispenser should be used only when they would otherwise be malnourished. The technology was a drain on their power sources, and it was dangerous to become too dependent on tools that might break down when they lacked the technology to re-create and replace them.

Moise's answer had not entirely satisfied Safrah. If dependence was potentially a problem, then why had Ship given the first people to settle on Home tools that they couldn't make for themselves? Because otherwise too many might have died in the process of adapting to Home, Moise had told her; because they needed their reproductive technologies, such as the artificial wombs, to ensure the biological diversity that was necessary to make their colony viable; because they needed such help to sustain them and to help them make Home another Earth.

Such answers had ended Safrah's questions for a while, but now she felt doubts rising in her once more. Why had the older ones in the settlement grown weaker and fewer in number even while the villages of the river people had increased in size? The people living outside the settlement might value what they gained in trade from Safrah and her companions, but, unlike her people, they could survive without such things.

That didn't matter, Moise would have told her. Those inside the settlement were still the true descendants of humankind, while those outside were not. And now, he would have insisted, their most pressing obligation was to repair their radio or else find some other way of contacting Ship—if Ship had actually returned.

"Couldn't Ship have given us more than a radio?" she once asked the older ones. They had answered that Ship and the first settlers wanted to be sure that they could communicate with an easily maintained piece of technology, one that they could replicate. She had accepted that explanation, even though it again raised the questions of why other advanced pieces of technology, not so easily maintained, had been brought to Home and why the radio remained the only communication device they had. A thought had come to her that Ship and the first of its Earthseed on Home might have had many uncertainties, doubts, and disagreements about how to settle the new world, and that this confusion was reflected in what was here and what was not, but Safrah quickly thrust that thought aside.

They could survive as long as the windmills turned, the solar panels were maintained, their fuel cells lasted, and the dispenser gave them food. They should have been further along than they were, built more from what they had been given. They should have become more than people clinging to the remnants of what their ancestors had left them. Moise would have expected them to be planning for children by now, with the next generation gestating in the artificial wombs and the first of their own biological children due soon, but trying to fulfill that obligation would strain their limited resources even more.

Mikhail stopped in front of the closed door and pressed his hand against the surface; the door slid open. The smell of rotted food and the odor of sulfur from behind the doorway to the latrines was so strong that Safrah nearly gagged, but the large room did seem somewhat tidier than the last time she had been here. The tables had been cleared, the unrolled sleeping mats lined up next to one wall, and it looked as though someone had at last mopped the floor.

In one corner, Riese and Carrei were slumped over a

screen with four other children; in another, five older children watched as Farkhan wrestled with Vinn. The twenty oldest ones, Terris and Morwen among them, sat at one of the long tables, eating pastries from a plate and drinking what looked like water but was obviously the alcohol they had brewed in the still that was the only piece of equipment they had ever managed to put together. All of them were in the same state of ragged undress. Playing games, shooting at vermin, running through the tunnels, testing themselves against one another to see who was strongest, and drinking: That was how they seemed to pass most of their time.

Morwen looked up. "Got our new clothes?" he asked.

"Not yet," Safrah replied.

"Well, what are you waiting for?" Morwen glared at her. "Has to be days since you said you would go."

"We'll head over today. We came to get some food to take with us. We'll be back with some clothing as soon as—"

"How soon?"

"Two or three days, four at the most." She thought she saw a look of fear in his eyes, and then his face hardened again.

"Come back sooner than that, and with a pair of foot coverings that'll fit me, and maybe I'll give you some more of this." Morwen lifted his cup.

"I don't want any more."

"Sure you don't."

Safrah looked away and moved closer to Mikhail. Every time she came here was harder than the last. The children had been living in here for over three years now, ever since Ilse's death had left Moise as the only one of their guardians still alive.

"Let them do as they please," Moise had said whenever Morwen and Terris were reluctant to do any work or spend any more time on their lessons in the library. "When they're older, they'll come around and realize that everyone has to stick together if you're going to bring up a new generation." So they had let the younger ones take over the dining hall and live there by themselves for most of the time. For a few months afterward, Safrah and her friends had occasionally been able to encourage or bribe a few of them into helping them tend the greenhouse, repair cisterns, or clean up abandoned domes. Now she and her companions saw them only when they came here to get more food, or when a few of the younger ones came to their door and banged on it until someone opened it.

Moise had thought they would come around. Maybe all he had been hoping for was that the four children who were most willing to listen to him would be able to take care of all of them after he was gone, and finally persuade or force the younger ones to do what they would have to do.

"Safrah."

She turned toward the voice. The girl sitting next to Morwen lifted her head. It took her a moment to recognize Paola, even though she had seen her only a couple of months ago. The other girl's curly black hair was chopped short, the skin of her usually pale face was chapped and red, and her breasts swelled under her tattered shirt. Only her large hazel eyes were the same.

"Morwen said he saw you near Ship's Room yesterday," Paola said, slurring her words slightly.

Mikhail nodded.

"Why go there?" A tear trickled down Paola's face; she rubbed her cheeks with her hands. "Why bother?"

"Shut up," Terris muttered.

"Think it's ever coming back, that Ship?" Paola's voice was

rising. "Every time you come here, I wonder if you've finally heard something from that radio, but you never do. We'll never get a message. Nothing's ever going to be any different." She gazed down at her cup, lifted it to her lips, and drank.

"Stop it, Paola," Morwen said, lifting his arm. Safrah tensed, expecting him to strike the girl. Instead, he slipped an arm over Paola's shoulders. "It'll be all right. We get along all right here. I can take care of us. We don't need anybody else, not even Ship."

Paola wiped at her face. She had been the last of the young ones to stop coming to the library, the only one who had ever shown any curiosity about the outside and the traders Safrah had met. She leaned against Morwen and gulped more from her cup.

"Listen to me," Morwen called out. Everybody else in the large room stiffened and turned in his direction. "Nobody goes near the library or Ship's Room unless you're with me, understand?" His arm tightened around Paola. "I'll keep that radio safe. Don't you worry about that." He glared at Safrah as if he had suddenly remembered a grudge to hold against her.

Safrah went to the recycler, emptied the bits of broken pottery into its maw, then moved toward the dispenser. She pressed her hand against one panel, and images of various foods appeared on the screen in quick succession as she selected what to take: dried fruit, nuts, wheat and rice flour, dried meat.

Mikhail helped her load the food, which was wrapped in a fibrous material, into their packs. "Let's get out of here," he whispered, throwing his sack over his back. They hurried across the room and back to the door, conscious of being watched by the others.

As soon as the door had closed behind them, Mikhail heaved a sigh of relief. "We can still get food from the dispenser," he said. "Every time I go there, I wonder if it'll still be working or if we'll finally have to think about leaving this place for good."

"Don't say that," Safrah said, as she always had before whenever any of them mentioned such a possibility.

"And I wish I knew why Morwen was saying all that stuff about Ship's Room," he continued as they made their way down the slope.

"To make Paola feel better, I suppose."

"But he sounded as if he was thinking somebody might actually try to mess with the radio, as if he had some idea about why someone might have wanted to damage it. I never thought any of them would go that far." He paused. "Let's hope Awan can fix it."

Safrah and her companions emerged from the greenhouse into late afternoon. Her long purple shadow rippled ahead of her over the pale green grass that was just beginning to sprout in the field. Wheat grew there once, Ilse had told her; and near the field, there had been trees that bore fruit, trees that had long since died and been chopped down for their wood. There had been fenced-in spots for their pigs, coops for the flightless birds that had provided meat and eggs, and pastures where the settlers had grazed their sheep, cattle, and horses. Now the coops, stables, and stalls were gone, the wood and other materials used to build them scavenged or given away in trade. Any surviving domesticated animals had most likely joined the wild herds and flocks long ago.

To the northeast of the settlement, a wall of trees was a

black ridge against the green sky. The trees were not native to Home, and they had grown tall, with wide branches that were thick with green needles. Safrah remembered lying under the trees on a bed of dried needles, inhaling their scent and listening to the sighing sound the trees made when the wind stirred their branches. There were even more trees to the north, Moise had said, that had sprung from seeds and cones carried there by the wind; they seemed to thrive in the north, even with the thick layers of snow that were said to cover the ground there during the coldest season. "When I first saw the trees north of us," Moise had said to her and the others, "I wondered if they would make all of Home into a forest in time." So far, only scattered groups of smaller trees had grown nearer the settlement; some evergreens stood near the bottom of the hills and at the northern edge of the lake, but Moise could remember when there were no trees anywhere near the domes.

There were still three working carts outside the greenhouse, but Safrah and her companions preferred to walk. They could use the exercise, and if they salvaged more than they could easily carry back in their packs, one of them would go back for a cart.

Jina and Mikhail were silent as they walked across the field. Ahead of them lay another hill and the domes that made up the eastern side of the settlement. There were still tunnels from a few of those domes that led to the large square structure that had once been a community hall, but not many tunnels had been built before that part of the settlement was abandoned. Even from this distance, Safrah could see that more domes had caved in, but several near the bottom of the hill remained intact.

They had left Awan in the library with enough food for

four or five days, but planned to get back to him sooner than that. She worried about leaving him there at all. Whoever had damaged the radio might suspect that they were trying to repair it in secret. She hoped Awan was safe. Maybe Morwen's warning to the others would be enough to keep whoever had damaged the radio away from the library, at least for a while.

She did not expect to see any sign of Ship until nightfall, but found herself glancing up at the sky. Even if Awan succeeded in repairing their radio, what would they say to Ship? How would they ever be able to explain why so many of them had left the settlement? What would they tell Ship about Morwen and Terris and the other children?

"Look," Jina said suddenly. "The beacon just lit up." Safrah looked to where the other girl was pointing, past the gray expanse of the lake to their south, and spotted a patch of barely visible light on the horizon.

Traders had come to the outpost, but they might not be looking only for trade. They would have seen the new light crossing the sky and might be wondering what Safrah and her people knew about it. She gazed at the distant beacon, another signal to fear.

9

As evening came, Enli steered the boat toward the eastern bank of the river. Bian and Arnagh tightened the knots of the rope around the large stone he used as an anchor, then threw the stone over the side; it hit with a splash that showered them with water. The three of them would sleep aboard the craft, taking turns keeping watch, looking out for wolves, big cats, or other predators that might slip down to the river during the night.

They might also run into boaters traveling south. If they were carrying any news about the apparition in the night sky, all of them would want to hear it right away.

Arnagh and Bian shared some more of their food with Enli, a ripe melon and some beans wrapped in flatbread. Enli gulped down his bread, then cut himself a slice of melon with his knife. "How much food do we have left?" Arnagh asked.

Bian peered inside her pack and then Arnagh's. "Enough for two more days for all of us," she said. "Three, if we stretch it."

"We should be in Shadowridge by then," Enli said as he slipped his knife under the belt of his loincloth, "and I've brought most of the food I had stored in my house. We can share that after we finish yours."

"We owe you food for our passage," Arnagh said.

Enli shook his head. "You don't owe me anything—we're all in this together. Maybe I owe you something for giving me an excuse to get away from Overlook for a while." Perhaps he was thinking of Lusa.

Bian finished the rest of her melon. The sky was dark green in the west as the sun set. Perhaps she would not see the light tonight, although its disappearance would solve nothing for them; assuming that the light was Ship, they would still be left to wonder if it had decided to leave its orbit around Home and what reasons it might have had for leaving. They would not know if Ship was still communicating with the dome dwellers even after leaving orbit, or if those people had told Ship something that had driven it away.

"Who did you trade with the last time you went north?" Enli asked.

"An older man named Moise," Arnagh said, "and two young people, Jina and Awan." His voice caught a little on that last name. "Before that, Moise came with a girl named Safrah and a boy called Mikhail."

"We traded with Moise, too," Enli said. "Once he came with Jina, and another couple of times with Awan and Safrah, but he was always with whoever else came to trade with us, until the last time, when Jina showed up by herself. My father asked her why Moise wasn't with her. She said he had a job to finish in one of their greenhouses, but we could hear the lie in her voice. Duman was sure she was hiding something from us."

"Maybe Moise was ill," Arnagh said. "He didn't look too well the last time I saw him."

"Or maybe the cold weather outside was too much for him. Whatever the reason, we traded with Jina. She kept on talking about how well everything was going for them and how they didn't really need what we brought with us, but appreciated it anyway. She came down to meet us in the morning with a cartful of stuff, and by afternoon she was headed back to her settlement with a cartful of our goods. Both Duman and I had the feeling that she just wanted to get rid of us as soon as possible."

"My aunt and uncle had the same feeling." Arnagh leaned forward. "We actually got more than we expected during our trade. Moise wasn't even trying to drive a hard bargain."

"Jina didn't, either. She even gave me another screen when I told her the one I had was acting up. When Duman asked her what she wanted for it, she told him we'd already given her enough in trade." Enli reached behind himself and pulled out a screen from his pack. "I brought it with me, along with my other screen."

"You've got two screens of your own?" Arnagh said, clearly impressed by such wealth.

Enli nodded. "But the one that was giving me trouble finally died, so only one of them's still working. I thought I'd better bring some things with me in case we have to trade for whatever we might need."

"A screen that doesn't work?" Bian asked.

"We might meet somebody who's going north to trade with the dome dwellers," Enli said, "somebody who'd trade for this screen and a chance to get it recharged by the dome dwellers in exchange for something else."

Bian looked down. "I hadn't thought of that." She looked up again. "There's so much I don't know. The farther I get from home, the more ignorant I feel."

Enli laughed. "Same here." He patted her arm, and she felt both embarrassed and pleased. "There's a lot we don't know, and that the dome dwellers don't know, even if Jina made it sound as though her people have everything and know all."

"Makes you wonder why they trade with us," Arnagh said. "Their bragging always sounded to me as though they were trying to convince themselves as much as us that everything was all right in their settlement."

"That's how it sounded to us, too." Enli leaned back and rested his head against the gunwale. "Jina almost sounded believable, but Duman and I heard the fear in her voice. He thought then that maybe she was just afraid of coming to trade with us all by herself. Now I'm wondering . . ." Enli stopped speaking.

"What?" Bian asked.

Enli exhaled. "If they were already talking to Ship. If it was in contact with them well before we could see any light in the sky. That might explain why she was so nervous and why nobody else was with her."

Bian took the first watch. The sky was already growing cloudy in the south, and by the time she crawled under the deck and woke Arnagh to take his turn, the clouds had obscured the first rising moon and the stars. She sensed no signs of danger as she curled up on the floor of the boat, no salt in the air or the distant, almost imperceptible rumblings that were often an early warning of a storm about to sweep toward them from the sea.

By morning, rain was falling intermittently. They sheltered themselves under the deck, taking turns at the rudder and at bailing out water from the boat's bottom with a bucket Enli had on board, a task that did not require prolonged effort in such a light rain.

By afternoon, the sky grew clear, and the air was warmer and more humid. They sat on top of the deck, waiting for the sun to dry them. They had eaten only some tartberries since morning. Bian took out pieces of flatbread, filled them with dried fish, and handed them to Enli and Arnagh.

None of them had spoken much during the day, preoccupied as they were with the rain and with piloting the craft, and Enli had not played his flute. Now he peered intently ahead as the boat drifted, as if searching for other boaters. She felt his need for silence. The grassland around them was so quiet and empty that they might have been the only life on Home.

Bian finished her food. "I've been thinking," Enli said at last, "about what to do after we get to Shadowridge. I mean, if we don't find out anything there."

"So have I," Arnagh said. "What do you think?"

"That we should keep heading upriver until we do hear something, even if it means we have to keep going until we get to the dome dwellers' outpost."

"You said your mother wanted you to turn back if we got as far as Plainview," Bian murmured.

"We're not in Plainview yet. Maybe by the time we get there, we'll have heard something, but if not, I say we keep going. Are both of you with me?"

"Yes," Bian said, knowing that Enli would be disappointed in her if she said no, but also wanting to continue the journey. To go home with no news would disappoint her village and her great-grandmother, but that wasn't the only reason she wanted to keep going. She had finally been to some place other than Seaside, and now she found herself longing to see more of Home.

"Good." Enli finished his food, then took out a screen from his pack. His fingers danced over the screen. The thunder of drums beat against her ears, followed by other sounds she could not identify; she listened for a while until she recognized the sounds as music.

"I didn't know screens could carry music," Arnagh said.

Enli touched the screen again, silencing it. "Of course they can. They carry images and the sounds of voices, don't they? They can carry any of the records the dome dwellers have that they're willing to share with us. It's just that we've never asked for them, or even looked to see if some records we don't know about might be stored in our screens." He scowled. "But of course we can't risk using up our screens and then having to trade with the dome dwellers to get them recharged again, not when we need to trade goods for more important things." A mocking tone had come into his voice. "Better just to use the screens to teach ourselves to read and find out how to build our houses and grow our crops and take care of our animals and weave our cloth. We have to be practical, after all, and as Zan always says, there's no point in learning things you don't really have to know."

He slipped the screen into his sack. "I remember the first time I heard music from a screen," he continued. "I wanted to stay at the outpost and listen to it forever. Duman was afraid we'd have to trade too much for the music, but Moise said it was no trouble at all to embed some music for me."

Enli got up, slipped off the deck, crept into the stern, and sat down next to the rudder. "I was listening to music so much that our neighbors started complaining about the noise, and Duman and Zan were afraid I'd ruin the screen for anything else. I started making flutes and my own music after that." He drew the rudder toward himself. "We've lost so much. Everything that Ship gave us, everything our ancestors had—we kept only the smallest part of it. I wonder if even the dome dwellers really understand most of it."

Enli docked his boat at Shadowridge four days after they left Overlook; by then, the weather had turned hot and dry once more. Shadowridge was composed of clusters of mudbrick huts, most of them surrounded by stone walls that stretched from the riverbank to a high ridge of stone that seemed to mark the village's southeastern boundary. From the number of huts, Bian estimated that at least three hundred people lived here, perhaps more.

One lone boater was at the dock, tying up his boat. He was a middle-aged man who introduced himself as Telem, told them that he had arrived there that morning from Plainview, and that he had heard nothing about the strange light in the heavens from anyone there. "But if I were you," Telem continued, lowering his voice and tugging at his beard, "I'd turn around now and head back downriver."

"Why?" Arnagh asked. "We won't find out anything that way."

"I talked to a boatman in Plainview before he left to go north who said he was heading up to the lake. He told me that maybe the thing to do was head for the dome dwellers' outpost, like we're making a trade, wait there until one or two of them come out, and then force some information out of them. Told him I wanted no part of that kind of thing, but he won't be the only one thinking about doing something like that."

"You don't think . . . ," Enli began.

"All I'm saying is that you might run into more trouble than news up north." Telem turned away and left them on the dock.

"Should we listen to him?" Bian asked, already sensing that Arnagh and Enli would ignore the boatman's warning.

"We can stay here for a few days," Enli said, "and hope we hear something more by then, or we can keep going upriver. I've got enough food to feed us until we get to Plainview."

"And we have enough goods with us to trade for food after that," Arnagh said. "I say we keep going."

Bian nodded. "I agree."

Enli quickly untied his boat and they boarded it again. A few people standing along the bank watched them as they drifted away, but others had already crowded around Telem, who shook his head and showed them the palms of his hands, indicating that he had nothing to tell them. Soon they had passed a stretch of cleared land at the north of Shadowridge, empty now, but ready to be irrigated by ditches and then sown with grain. The river was wider north of Shadowridge, and Bian saw fewer of the distant ridges of rock jutting up from the plain to the east.

By afternoon, black clouds had formed against the green sky to the north. Bian felt her skin prickle, the way it sometimes did when a storm was brewing, then noticed that Arnagh and Enli were watching the thickening clouds with worried looks on their faces.

"A storm's coming, isn't it?" she said.

Enli nodded, resting his hands on the rudder. "And from the north," he said. "I've been in that kind of storm only once before, by the lake. The wind wasn't as bad as the storms that come up from the south, but it was the coldest wind I've ever felt, and the rain turned into pellets of ice." He paused. "Frozen water."

"I know what ice is," Bian said.

"Knowing what it is doesn't prepare you for how it feels. I thought I'd never be warm again." Enli glanced up at the sky. "I just know that I don't want to be out on the river when that storm hits." He steered the boat toward the eastern riverbank. The bow made a swishing sound as it cut through a patch of reeds, then shuddered to a stop. Enli slipped over the side, then beckoned to Bian, who followed him into the water.

The boat had run aground in the mud on the river bottom. The water was up to Bian's chest. Enli splashed his way toward shore. "Tie the rope to an oarlock," Enli called out, "and then throw it to me. Bian, you push from the back." She struggled toward the stern, feeling the mud shifting under her feet.

Arnagh threw a rope to Enli, then slid over the side of the craft into the water. He and Bian pushed at the stern as Enli tugged at the rope. By the time they got the boat up on the bank, with only its stern still in the water, the sound of distant thunder had grown louder. The clouds in the north were the color of slate, and they already covered almost half the sky, while in the south the sky remained clear. Bian sensed a chill in the air. She suddenly wanted to wail the way babies and small children did whenever storms threatened Seaside. Arnagh's widened eyes betrayed his fear.

The storm bore down on them rapidly. They climbed into the boat again, secured their goods and supplies under the deck, then sat down with their backs to the walls of the small cabin. Bian smelled the terror of her companions and felt panic rise inside her. They would be safe: The boat would protect them; it would have to protect them. She did not want to think of what might happen if the storm damaged the boat.

Suddenly she could hear nothing. Her ears throbbed. Then the wind rushed upon them with a shriek, rocking the boat. For a moment she was afraid the craft would roll over, trapping them all under its hull. Enli moved closer to her; she felt him bracing himself against the port side of the boat, the side facing north, and did the same. The light faded outside the cabin until Bian could see nothing in the darkness, then abruptly whitened with light. The thunder came a few heartbeats later, slapping against her ears.

The wind moaned, no longer shrieking at them. The rain sounded like pebbles hitting the deck. Thunder rolled over them again. Enli pulled her closer to him. She shuddered, sensing his longing for her. She tightened her arms around him, then tensed, thinking of Arnagh sitting so close to them; and of Lusa, who had believed herself pledged to Enli. She found herself pushing against his chest, resisting him even while wanting him to hold on to her. Enli let go of her and she felt a twinge of regret.

It was good that the darkness hid her now. By the time the storm passed, she could pretend that nothing had changed, and if Enli glimpsed any hints of her growing feelings for him, maybe Arnagh's presence would keep him from responding to them.

But she wanted him to embrace her again.

She had never wanted to experience such feelings. She remembered the times when she had sat with her mother, who had gone on grieving for her lost mate Kwam for years after his death. Bian had told herself that she would never allow herself to know such grief, to long for any person so much, to love anyone so deeply that life without that person would become nearly unbearable.

The air had grown colder. Thunder rumbled, and the rain was still hitting the deck above them, but more softly. "It's going to pick up again," Arnagh's voice said in the darkness.

"Yes," Enli replied. Bian sensed it, too; the storm was not yet over. She felt Enli's breath against her face and heard him move, and for a moment she saw his face as lightning flashed.

10

The storm assaulted the plain throughout the night, easing up long enough to allow Bian and her companions a few moments of undisturbed slumber, then waking them again with slaps of thunder, flashes of light, and more rain whipping the deck and hull. Once Bian woke to find herself shivering with cold, then suddenly felt a piece of cloth being thrust into her hands.

"Put it on," Enli's voice murmured. She grabbed the cloth, realized that he had handed her a tunic, and pulled the garment on over her head. The storm seemed to be subsiding; all she could hear now was the patter of rain. She curled up, careful not to jostle Enli, and fell asleep.

She woke to silence and the sight of a gray dawn sky

outside the cabin. Enli and Arnagh were already awake, sitting across from her. Both of them wore long shirts that came down nearly to their knees.

"It stopped raining," Enli said.

"I know," she said.

"It might start again, though," Arnagh said. "We figured we should stay here a while longer until we're sure it's over."

"Fine with me." Bian thrust her hands into her sleeves. She no longer felt chilled, and the air was warming up, but she welcomed having a shirt to wear. She remembered how she had felt when Enli's arms were around her, which made her feel more at ease keeping herself covered. Her cheeks burned. She had never felt that way before, wanting to cover herself in order to hide her body.

There was a low rumble of thunder, more distant this time. Arnagh and Enli were probably as hungry as she was, but they had not taken out any food, and she decided to wait before eating anything herself. If they had to stay here for more than a day or two, they might run out of food before they reached Plainview.

"We could head back to Shadowridge," Enli said, as if picking up on her worries. "Their buildings, most of them anyway, could easily survive those winds. Lucky for them, harvest time is past, so they won't have lost any crops."

"Are you thinking there will be more damage in Plainview?" Bian asked.

"Maybe. The storm would have been even stronger to the north of us. And if these clouds don't lift and the sun doesn't come out soon, my solar fuel cells are going to die."

"Eventually they'll recharge," Arnagh said. "And we could row."

"We've come this far," Bian said. "I think we should keep going north."

"Good," Enli said. "That's what I think, too, but I wanted to hear you say so."

"What are they like?" Bian asked abruptly. "The dome dwellers, I mean. Are they very different from us?"

"They look like us," Enli said.

She sniffed. "I know that much."

"Except that they're larger," Enli said. "Taller and bigger, and they look well fed. They always looked like they didn't really need our food. But they seem—" He paused. "I don't know how to describe it. Sometimes I'd get the feeling that they didn't quite grasp what my father and I were telling them, as if they were just a bit slower than us."

"Or a little deaf," Arnagh added, "or blind. It's as if their senses aren't that sharp."

"Maybe they don't need to be as alert in their settlement," Enli said. "They always acted as though there was nothing they had to worry about, even if we often got the feeling that they were trying to hide things from us."

"I wish—," Arnagh began before falling silent. Bian didn't ask him what he wished for, sensing that he was reluctant to say anything more.

The rain was falling again. Enli rummaged in his pack, took out one of his flutes, and began to play.

Bian slept deeply, then woke to find that it had stopped raining and the stars were visible in the clear night sky outside the cabin. Dawn brought a cloudless sky and enough bright sunlight to drive away the remaining chill in the air.

Enli sat in the opening of the cabin, keeping watch. Arnagh yawned and sat up. "Is the light still up there?" he asked.

"Yes," Enli replied. "I saw it cross the sky before." He got to his feet. "Think we've slept enough. Let's eat something and then get this boat back in the water."

They continued upriver until nightfall. When the sun set, Bian sat on the deck and watched as the strange light rose above the horizon. Arnagh had been silent all day, saying nothing as he took his turn at the rudder or peered north, looking for some sign of other boats. After their evening meal, Enli took out a flute, but the music he played was somber, almost as mournful as the music the people of Seaside might hum after the death of a villager. It was warm enough now to sleep on the deck, but Bian crept into the cabin after she had finished her turn on watch. She needed to be alone with her thoughts before sleep claimed her, to convince herself that it was foolish to have strong feelings for someone she had known for such a short time.

They were moving upriver again just after dawn. As the sun peered over the eastern plain, Bian noticed that a few pale clumps of mud and yellow grass were drifting downriver toward them. By midmorning, the bits of floating mud, grass, and reeds, the kind of materials somebody might use for a thatched roof, had been joined by flat pieces of wood and a few small rafts of reeds tied together. Plainview would have been in the path of the storm; she wondered how much damage the village had suffered.

By early afternoon, she no longer saw any of the rocky ridges to the east, only plains of pale green grassland to the east and west. Although more debris had floated downriver, most of it was thatching, a sign that Plainview might have escaped widespread damage.

Just as evening was falling, they glimpsed the cluster of dwellings that had to be the southernmost edge of Plainview. Bian wondered what they would find there.

11

The sun had nearly set by the time they reached Plainview. It was a smaller village than either Overlook or Shadowridge. Thirty squat, sturdy brick dwellings with thatched roofs sat several lengths back from the eastern riverbank, with nothing beyond them except a wide cleared field and the endless plain. The sturdy walls of the buildings had apparently suffered little damage from the storm, but the roofs had holes and bare patches.

Enli and Arnagh had told Bian about Plainview's leader as the boat glided toward the village. Her name was Nenet, and she was a somewhat prickly and disagreeable woman, but the people of her village were content to have her as their leader because she was fair, or maybe because she treated everybody with the same grumpy impartiality. Even though most of the villagers had retreated to their homes for their evening meal, it was clear as soon as Enli tied up his boat at Plainview's only dock that no news about the mysterious light had reached this place yet. Someone would have already rushed to tell them about it, or else they would have seen some sign of it on the faces of the two young women, each carrying a light wand, who were now coming to greet them.

They introduced themselves; the young women told them that their names were Eliane and Weneth, and that Nenet was their mother. "I met her when I came through here with my father," Enli said, "but she never said anything about you."

"Our father moved back to Westbay some years ago, and we went with him," Eliane replied. "That's where he's from, and he'd come to miss his parents and cousins and old friends, and things weren't going well between him and our mother. We decided to go with him because we'd never seen Westbay before."

Perhaps that explained Nenet's prickly personality, Bian thought, although there would have been no point in her mate staying with her if he preferred to be elsewhere and would only have perturbed her with his unhappiness and longing for another place. "We came back a few months ago," Weneth added, "because we started to miss our mother and Plainview."

"Will your father ever come back?" Enli asked.

Eliane shrugged. "Probably not. Oh, he might visit eventually, but he's got his family and his friends, and he's found a new mate, and at this point even our mother would be just as happy if he stayed in Westbay." She paused. "I suppose you're heading north to see what you can find out. It seems that a number of people are heading in the same direction. A couple of riders from Shadowridge came through here several days ago with their horses, but they stayed only long enough to trade us a day's labor for food before they rode on."

Even in the faint light of the wands, Weneth seemed to be unusually interested in Enli, smiling as she peered up at him. She was younger than her sister and was small, even shorter than Bian, who could not help noticing that Weneth was also extremely pretty, with wide-set dark eyes, a sturdy and muscular body, and a thick black braid that hung over one shoulder. Bian folded her arms and thrust her hands inside the sleeves of her tunic.

"We can stay aboard our boat," Enli said, "but we're almost out of food, so we'll have to trade some of our other goods for whatever we eat."

"Pay us in labor," Eliane said. "The storm didn't hit us that hard, and we know how to build houses to last, but we've got some roofs and a couple of damaged walls that could use mending. Stay for a couple of days and help us out with repairs, and we'll give you enough food to get you to Lakeview."

"If you stay a few days longer," Weneth murmured as she gazed at Enli, "we might hear some more news."

"I'd rather keep heading north," Arnagh said. He glanced at Enli and Bian. She was quick to nod in agreement, but Enli was still staring at the two young women.

Weneth's smile widened. "Well, maybe you'll change your mind."

"I wouldn't mind staying here for a few more days," Enli said. Bian willed herself not to object.

Bian woke to the sound of music. She sat up and realized that she was alone on the boat. A voice fluttered above the notes of Enli's flute, singing words she did not know. She listened to the voice as it soared, hit a high note, and then held it for several long moments. Tears sprang to her eyes at the beauty of the sound; she quickly wiped them away. The flute and the voice fell silent and then began again, this time with lighter, more cheerful music. The singer was still using words she could not understand, but the joy in the voice made Bian smile.

She crept out from under the deck. Enli sat on the dock, the sleeves of his tunic rolled up, holding his flute to his lips. Weneth was singing, her head thrown back, face lifted to the sky. Arnagh sat on the bank, along with a few other young people, who soon clapped their hands in time to the music.

Bian moved slowly toward the bow, but remained on the boat. She saw Enli's face clearly now; he looked joyous. Weneth clapped her hands as she sang, breaking off her song with a trill.

"More songs," a young man called out.

"Yes, more," a woman with a long red braid added, "and I'll feed both of you breakfast in return."

Bian stepped onto the dock. "What about my friends Arnagh and Bian?" Enli said. "They're just as hungry as I am."

"Two more songs," the woman replied, "and I'll feed them as well."

"Agreed," Enli said. He lifted his flute to his lips as a woman came toward the dock. She was as compact and muscular as Weneth, and bore a strong resemblance to her. The woman's arms hung at her sides, her hands were balled into fists, and her face was tight with anger.

"Don't any of you have work to do?" the woman asked, glaring at Weneth. "Our own dwelling still has a hole in it, but the only one who's bothering to repair it is your sister."

The woman had to be Nenet, Plainview's leader. People jumped to their feet and scurried off in different directions. "Duman's son," the woman continued, staring at Enli. "I might have known."

Weneth went to her and held out a hand. "It's my fault," she said. "I asked if I could sing with him."

"I don't care whose fault it is. Shan needs his roof repaired, and if we don't get the coops fixed soon, even more of our birds will get loose. Show these three where to go and what to do, and then you can help Eliane with her work." Nenet frowned at her daughter, and then her face softened. "You can always sing while you work."

Weneth said, "I always do."

Arnagh, like Bian, had some skill in thatching, but Enli had learned little of that craft. Bian and Arnagh spent most of the day patching two roofs, using grass and reeds for thatching, while Enli worked with three villagers at repairing coops and rounding up stray birds.

Weneth brought them a supper of fruit and corncakes after they returned to the boat that evening. The four of them sat on the deck, saying little as they ate. Bian was yawning even before she finished her food, and Arnagh also looked ready for sleep.

Enli chewed the last of his corncake, then pulled a flute from his pack. "I'm going to play some music," he said, gazing at Weneth.

"Then I'll sing with you," she replied.

"Where did you hear the songs you sing?" Bian asked.

"My father traded with a boatman for a screen a few years ago, when his old one went dead," Weneth said. "He wanted to review some of the records on cultivating roots and tubers.

Eliane likes to draw on historical records for inspiration when she makes up stories to tell the younger children, and then we found that there were music files in the screen, too. I couldn't stop listening to them. My father finally had to tell me I couldn't use the screen anymore, that he wasn't about to trade to recharge it or try to get a new one from the dome dwellers, but by then I knew all the songs and most of the words, even the ones I don't understand. Now I make up my own from bits and pieces of the ones I heard."

In spite of herself, Bian felt admiration for the other girl's talent. "Sometimes I think about everything the people who sent our ancestors here inside their great Ship must have had," Weneth went on, "and how little we have in comparison. Their home world is so far away that we can't even see its sun in our sky, and still they were able to cross all that distance to come here. Vilho—my father—says that we may never be able to make what they could, their screens and their light wands and weapons and ships, and someday the tools we get from the dome dwellers may wear out and then—"

"I wonder what they'd think if they could see us," Enli muttered, "those people who built Ship. I wonder what Ship will think if . . ." He glanced up at the sky.

Bian thought of her past discontent with the predictable events of her life. Another day would come and she would do what work was given to her and learn and practice a new skill with the help of her screen or the guidance of one of the adults. Even the death of a villager, the disruption of a storm, or some other unforeseen and unfortunate event would not change the pattern of her life all that much. Now that she had seen more than Seaside, she felt a deeper discontent stirring, a longing for more than the life she had been given.

Enli stood up, then pulled Weneth to her feet. He held her arm as she stepped onto the dock, then led her toward the riverbank. Fires burned in the hearths just outside the houses near the bank; people sat around the fires, finishing their food. Others wandered down to the bank and sat down as Enli, still standing, turned toward them, lifted his flute to his lips, and began to play. Weneth stepped closer to him, and as she sang, those listening to them swayed from side to side.

Arnagh moved closer to Bian. "I hope we leave here sometime tomorrow," he said. "Not that I mind the work, or the people, but unless a boater gets here with some news by morning, we might as well trade what goods we can for more food and be on our way."

"I'm sure Enli—"

"He said he wouldn't mind staying here for a few days," Arnagh interrupted. "Now he probably wouldn't mind staying a lot longer."

Arnagh did not have to explain what he meant. She thought of how Enli had held her to him during the storm, and felt the pangs of jealousy as Weneth sang.

"I'm sorry," Arnagh murmured. "I can see how you're starting to feel about him."

"Is it so obvious?"

"It is to me," he replied, "but that's only because we're good friends. Somebody who doesn't know you as well probably wouldn't notice, and Enli obviously hasn't noticed, because he's so drawn to Weneth and doesn't seem to care if you know that." He paused. "I didn't want to come upriver," he continued. "Now I keep thinking—maybe some boater will get here with news tomorrow or the day after, and then we can go home. Otherwise—"

She sensed the tumult inside him. "Arnagh, what's wrong?"

He did not speak for a few moments. "Last year," he began, "when I went upriver with my aunt and uncle, I met someone, a dome dweller. He came down to the outpost with Moise and Jina. His name was Awan, and he hadn't traded with us before. Tiri and Malcum wanted a few more recharged light wands along with the ones they'd brought us, so Moise took our dead ones, said he'd recharge them, and be back in a couple of days with the rest of the goods we needed. Jina went with him, maybe because he looked too weak to go alone, but Awan said he'd stay with us while we waited. I had the feeling Moise wasn't too happy about that, but Awan convinced him that maybe somebody should keep an eye on us."

He stood up and went to the boat. Bian followed him aboard, knowing that he still wanted to talk.

"I took Awan out on our boat," Arnagh continued, "while my aunt and uncle stayed at the outpost. He wanted to show me what it was like on the other side of the lake, and he admitted that he was curious about our people. Took us most of the day to cross the lake—you can see more of the yellow grass to the west, and when you look north, you can just see the edge of a field of the darker green grass that the first settlers brought with them." He sat down on the deck, and she seated herself across from him. "Except for the cold, the weather was perfect, no wind, no clouds, just a sunny day with the lake so calm that our boat hardly rocked at all."

She reached for his hands. He let her hold them for a few moments, then drew back. "It was the happiest day of my life," he said softly, and she heard the pain in his voice.

She said nothing, waiting for him to go on.

"The weather looked like it was going to hold, and I knew Tiri and Malcum would appreciate some time alone, and Awan was nervous about crossing open water at night. So we pulled the boat up and decided to head back the next morning." He sighed. "By then I already knew that I wanted to stay with him, that he was the partner and mate I was looking for and thought I might never find."

"Arnagh," she said, sensing his longing. "How hard for you. A dome dweller—"

"It isn't that." His voice sounded hoarse. "Or maybe I should say that isn't the worst of it. His people wouldn't have welcomed me, and he'd find it hard to get used to our ways, but we could have tried. If he'd only said that maybe we needed time to think things over—" Arnagh's shoulders slumped as he bowed his head. "But he didn't say anything at first, even though I could tell that he had some feelings for me. Then he told me he couldn't be with me, that he couldn't stay with me for even a little while, that he couldn't have anything to do with me, that everybody he knew would only hate and scorn him if he tied his life to mine. Not just because I don't belong to his people, all those true human beings, but because he'd be the partner of another man."

Bian was bewildered. "But that doesn't make any sense. Why would they keep him from trying to be with somebody he cares about? What difference does it make if his partner's a man or a woman?"

"It matters to Awan. It matters to the dome dwellers. Their duty is to preserve true humankind, and that means having a mate and children and all the rest."

"But you could still have children. Didn't our ancestors come here with stored genetic material of all kinds? Nuy told me that the dome dwellers don't have to bear their children the way we do, even though they usually did; that they had ova and seeds and wombs and . . ." She wished now that her great-grandmother had found out more details about how the dome dwellers reproduced. "Anyway, it seems to me that they could—"

"It doesn't matter." Arnagh shook his head. "Maybe they've used up all that genetic material. Maybe the wombs don't work. Even if they did work, they'd never let Awan and me have one of their children to bring up, even if we wanted one. They think . . ." His voice had dropped so low that she could barely hear it over Enli's music and Weneth's singing. "He said that if they knew what he was, they'd think there was something wrong with him, and some of them might not want to have anything more to do with him. Some of them would have harmed him if they found out—he was really afraid of that. And all of them would have made him leave their settlement."

"I don't understand," she murmured. "Can't they sense what he's like? How could he hide it from them for years and years?"

"They aren't like us, Bian. I knew that before I ever met any of them, but they look so much like us that it takes a while to actually see how different they are. It's as if their senses are dulled, as if they can't quite see or hear what's right in front of them. I can understand how Awan could hide his feelings from them even if he couldn't hide them from me."

He fell silent. Weneth was singing a gentle song now, the soothing sort of song someone might sing to a child preparing to sleep. Villagers stood up and stretched and drifted off to their houses.

"I thought my feelings would fade after a while," Arnagh said, "and maybe they would have. But then I'd think of Awan in his settlement, keeping his secret, without anybody to turn to, and now I have to worry about what's happening if he and his people are in contact with Ship. Is that how Ship made them? People who have to hide their feelings, who think that somebody like me or Awan—"

Bian gripped his arm. "Ship planted Earth's seeds here," she whispered. "How they grew after that wasn't Ship's doing; it's ours." Nuy had said words much like those to her not long ago.

"But Ship made mistakes. Awan told me that, too. Some of Ship's children didn't turn out the way they were supposed to, and Awan kept wondering if he was just another mistake."

"Then all of us are mistakes," Bian said. "If that's what true humankind is like, I think I'd rather not be part of true humanity."

Weneth was no longer singing, and Enli had stopped playing his flute. They stood silhouetted against a hearth fire, their heads together, and then Enli took her hand. Bian gazed after them as they walked south along the bank until they were hidden by the tall grass at the edge of the village.

12

Bian was weeding Melii's small garden, a task she had begun the day before, when she felt a tap on her shoulder. She looked up at Melii's lined, brown face.

"Nenet's here," the old woman said, "and she wants to talk to you."

Bian got to her feet and wiped her hands on the edge of her tunic, welcoming a break from her work in the garden. She and Arnagh had been in Plainview for five days now, making themselves useful, and Enli still showed no desire to leave. He was often at Weneth's side, feeding the pigs or clearing an irrigation ditch with her in the mornings, entertaining groups of villagers with his flute while they ate their midday meal, helping some of the men clear a new field for planting while Weneth worked at whatever tasks her mother and sister found for her, then ending the day with supper and playing his flute while Weneth sang. He returned to his boat long after sunset; Bian knew that because the sound of his footsteps on the dock always woke her. He was even neglecting his boat, leaving it to her and Arnagh to clean the deck, scrape the hull, and check the motor's energy cells.

Bian followed Melii around the side of her small house. Nenet stood near the stone fireplace in front of the house, Arnagh at her side. "Have you finished your work here yet?" Nenet asked.

"Just about," Melii answered for her. "I can easily finish what weeding is left by myself."

"Good," Nenet said, "because there's something else you and Arnagh can do for me." A look of worry and puzzlement crossed her face.

"I hope the girl at least has time to eat the meal I owe her for all her hard work," Melii said.

"Maybe you can put some food in a pouch for her and the boy to take with them. Eliane keeps telling me not to worry, but I don't like to neglect anything out of the ordinary." Nenet glanced from Bian to Arnagh. "One of the children saw something strange last night."

"You told me it was Roran who saw whatever it was," Melii said, "and you know that boy can be fanciful." She moved closer to Bian. "Roran's always telling tales to the other children. Trouble is that he halfway believes them himself, so it's very hard to hear any deceit in his voice or to read it in his gestures." She let out her breath. "What was it he saw this time?"

"I sensed no lies in him," Nenet replied, "and this wasn't like the kinds of stories he usually tells, full of river spirits and weird birds and strange wild animals out on the plains and other such improbabilities. The reason nobody else saw what he claims he saw is that everybody was asleep. And this time, Roran ran to tell his tale to Eliane before telling it to the other children, and she was convinced enough that he was being truthful to bring him to me. Apparently, when he woke last night and went outside to take a piss, he saw a flying thing to the south of us, something like a bluewisp but much larger. He couldn't see exactly how much larger because it was too far away. Then it flew away and he couldn't see it at all."

"Maybe he imagined it," Melii said. "That boy can imagine a great many things."

"Maybe he did," Nenet said, "but I know he wasn't lying. He really believes he saw something out there, not far from the river, so it would be wise to send someone to investigate." She folded her arms. "I'd like you and Arnagh to head south and look for signs of anything out of the ordinary. I doubt you'll find anything, but it wouldn't hurt to look around. If this were one of the boy's usual stories, I wouldn't think anything of it, but . . ." She shrugged.

"I'm willing to go with Arnagh," Bian said. It would be an easier task than weeding or mending worn clothing, the next job she was to do for Melii.

"Maybe we won't have to go just yet." Arnagh was looking south. "A rider's heading toward us, somebody we met in Overlook. Maybe she saw something along the way."

Bian turned to her left. The tiny form was barely visible, but even from this distance, she could see the rider's yellow hair.

Lusa had followed them north.

Lusa had seen nothing odd along the way, she insisted while answering Nenet's questions, certainly nothing like the kind of flying object that had supposedly been sighted. She brought no news from Overlook, and was disappointed to hear that no one in Plainview had yet heard anything about the strange light in the sky. Now she sat with Bian and Arnagh, chewing on the dried meat Melii had offered them. The two packs she had taken off her horse's back rested against the old woman's fireplace.

"You might have been sleeping," Nenet insisted. "Maybe that's why you didn't see anything odd. The boy who told me of the flying object said that he saw the thing in the middle of the night."

"I'm a light sleeper when I'm riding," Lusa replied, "and I sleep on horseback, so Summercloud would have alerted me to anything out of the ordinary." She jerked her head toward her white horse, who was grazing in the grass bordering Melii's garden. "She would have had me awake in an instant."

Bian smelled the other girl's fear and nervousness and saw it in her tense posture and darting eyes. Lusa would have been all by herself during the ride, alone with her horse and the river and the endless plain. Bian wondered how she had been able to face it.

"Maybe you and your horse were too far away to see what the boy saw," Bian said. Lusa ignored her. "Maybe we should go and take a look around the plain south of here anyway." She did not want to be in Plainview when Lusa found out about Enli and Weneth.

"Enough of this," Melii muttered. "Wouldn't it make more sense to wait until night and then put these young people on watch? If they see anything like what Roran says he saw, maybe then we can start to worry."

"They told me at Shadowridge that you stopped there for only a moment," Lusa said; a look of jealousy crossed her face as she stared at Bian. "They said you didn't even stay long enough to greet any people there."

"A boater told us no one there had any news, so we decided to keep going," Arnagh mumbled, his mouth full. "Unfortunately, we ran into a storm, so we had to pull the boat up and wait it out."

"Oh," Lusa said. "All they had in Shadowridge was a strong wind and a bit of rain." She frowned. "So how long have you been here?"

"A few days," Arnagh admitted.

"Then I suppose that's why I didn't see you heading downriver on my way here. I was wondering—"

"What brought you all the way up here from Overlook?" Nenet interrupted. "Are you yet another one chasing after news of that speck of light in the sky, or have you come here with some news from your village?"

Lusa gazed at Nenet. "No news from Overlook," she said, "and I'm as curious as anyone about that light, but that's not why I'm here. I asked Enli's parents if I could follow him north, and they agreed, given how close our families are. Anyway, he told his mother he would come home if he got this far without finding out anything."

Lusa seemed to be telling the truth, but Bian sensed that there was more behind her words. Enli's father and mother might be worried about their son, or want him back in Overlook, but Bian suspected Lusa had worked hard to persuade them to allow her to follow him here.

"Then I assume you expect him to travel back with you," Nenet said.

"He might as well. There's no reason for him to trade his labor for food and shelter here when he's needed back in Overlook."

"We would miss his flute-playing," Nenet said. "He's quite good at it. I don't think I've ever heard anyone better."

"He's missed in Overlook, too," Lusa said. "Our work goes more slowly without his music to inspire us."

"Someone may come our way soon with news about that light," Nenet said. "Wait with us for a while, and maybe some news will reach us before you have to leave us."

Lusa's blue eyes narrowed. "I could wait here a day or two, but I think we should leave after that. If there's any news by then, everyone south of us should hear it as soon as possible, and if not, we should head back downriver before Enli's parents get too worried."

Nenet said, "You and they worry a lot about a boy who's nearly a man."

"It isn't just Enli I'm thinking about; it's these two." Lusa waved an arm at Bian and Arnagh. "It'd be easier for Enli to bring them back to Overlook instead of waiting for a boater to take them, and from there they shouldn't have any trouble getting back to Seaside. We could find someone—"

"I think we can take care of ourselves," Arnagh said, looking annoyed.

"I wonder if Enli will be so eager to leave," Nenet said, "with Weneth to hold him here."

"Weneth?" Lusa said.

"My daughter," Nenet said in a voice tinged with pride. "They've been together so much these past days, what with Weneth's singing and his flute-playing. Why, they can hardly keep their hands off each other. I almost think they might make a pledge before long."

"A pledge?" Lusa whispered. Her face had gone pale.

"Of course they'd have to build any shared life together

on more than music-making," Nenet continued, "but—" She leaned toward Lusa. "What's the matter with you, girl?"

"Enli—" Lusa sighed. "He was to ask me—" Her hands trembled. "I thought—" She glanced at Bian, then stared past her. "He and I were going to make a pledge, and then he decided he didn't want one and broke his promise, and now—"

"Did he actually make a pledge to you?" Not waiting for an answer, Nenet continued, "Then I don't see how he can break a promise he never made. What if you had a mate decide to leave you after living with you for some years? That might be something worthy of tears. What if your children decided to leave with him? Maybe then you'd have something to cry about." Lusa was crying openly now, her face in her hands as her shoulders shook. "I got past all of that, though, and my daughters came home, and you'll get past this, too."

Lusa slowly got to her feet. For a moment, Bian expected the yellow-haired girl to hurl herself at Nenet, but instead she turned away and ran from them. The white horse tossed its head and whinnied softly. Lusa kept running, past Melii's house and the house behind hers, then over a cleared patch of land, before she disappeared into the tall pale green grass.

"You do have a cruel streak, Nenet," Melii muttered.

"You shouldn't have said that," Bian said. "You hurt her terribly."

"The truth hurt her." Nenet stood up. "I know I hurt her, but better to get it over with now—she'll get past the pain faster."

"How kind of you," Melii said. "How very thoughtful. You weren't thinking of helping the girl past her hurt. You only want to see that she doesn't interfere with what

Weneth wants. You're only thinking of your daughter and trying to make up for all the years in which you couldn't be a mother to her."

Bian gazed after Lusa. "I'd better go after her."

"I'll go with you," Arnagh said.

Bian shook her head. "No." After she came to herself, Lusa was likely to feel embarrassed and humiliated. It would be easier for her to have just one person searching for her, and she would no longer have to direct any of her jealousy at Bian. "Arnagh, look after her horse." She hurried away before anyone else could object.

Lusa was a strong and swift runner. She remained far ahead of Bian, gaining more distance whenever Bian was forced to slow her pace. Soon Bian was panting for air and dampening her tunic with sweat. She slowed, wanting to tear her garment off, but restrained herself; a piece of clothing, however stained and worn from use, wasn't something to throw away.

She forced herself onward. Lusa maintained her lead, but was slowing. Bian fell back to a walk, willing herself to keep moving. Eventually the other girl would tire and she could catch up to her.

The grassy plain stretched to the east as far as she could see. Bian kept moving, pacing herself, slowed by the high grass; she sped into a run and then dropped back into a slower jog. She felt almost as though she were swimming through the grass, sweeping it aside with her arms, kicking at it as it lashed her legs.

Lusa's blond hair was still visible above the grass. Bian stopped and looked back. Plainview seemed far away now, hardly more than a few scattered sheds huddled next to the long gray snake of the river. She realized then that she had left her waterskin aboard Enli's boat, since she had not needed it in the village, and wondered if Lusa was still carrying her own waterskin.

Thinking of water was making her thirsty. She could go back, tell herself that she owed Lusa nothing, that the other girl should never have come here in the first place. Eventually Lusa would calm down and go back to Plainview. Bian took a deep breath and started running again; soon she had to slow down once more. Lusa was also slowing her pace now, but still held her lead. It couldn't still be rage, pain, and jealousy driving Lusa across the plain; now it had to be only her obstinacy, stubbornness, and pride.

Pale green grass surrounded Bian on all sides as she trudged on. She halted and tried to orient herself, glancing up at the sun and then southwest. In the distance, near the tiny specks that were now all that she could see of Plainview's buildings, she could barely glimpse two heads above the grass, trailed by the larger pale form of an animal. Even at such a distance, she recognized Arnagh's dark brown hair. The shorter person with him had to be Enli, leading Lusa's horse on foot.

Relief rushed through her. The sun would be setting before long, and night would hide the dangers of the open plain. She thought of what might be concealed by the grass, of the creatures that might come out at night to make their way toward the river, looking for prey.

By the time the sun was setting, Bian had nearly closed the distance between her and Lusa, whose slumped shoulders and slower pace showed her weariness. Bian had been calling out to Lusa, urging her to turn back, stopping only when her voice grew hoarse. Now she could not stop thinking of how thirsty she was.

It would be Lusa's fault if any harm came to them before they were able to get back to Plainview. Bian swallowed her anger as she remembered the pain she felt when she had first seen how attracted Enli was to Weneth. She had known Enli for only a few days, and he had offered her nothing except a brief embrace during a storm, while Lusa had known him for years and had loved him and had expected a pledge from him. Love had turned Bian's mother into a mournful wraith, Nenet hard and mean, and now it had apparently driven Lusa mad.

I hope never to love anyone that much, Bian told herself again, as she had so many times before.

Lusa's head disappeared amid the grass. Bian moved into a run and soon came to the edge of a small hill. Farther down the hill, Lusa had halted. Her blond head was bowed and her arms hung at her sides.

Bian descended the slope, expecting the other girl to flee from her, but Lusa was still, not moving until Bian was only a few paces from her. She lifted her head. Even in the soft light of twilight, her eyes looked red and inflamed, her face flushed, as though she had been crying for the entire day.

"I'm sorry," Lusa said, wiping her face.

"You ought to be."

"I don't know what's making me feel worse right now, knowing that I really have lost Enli or that I've completely shamed myself by running off like that." Lusa looked down. "I wasn't thinking of anything at first, only of how much I hurt, and then when I realized how far I'd run, I couldn't bear to go back there and . . . I'm so ashamed of myself." She covered her face. "What a fool I am," she mumbled through her hands.

"Maybe so," Bian said, "but Nenet could have been a little kinder to you, and it would have been easier—"

"Don't blame my foolishness and craziness on her. My foolishness is entirely my own."

"And Enli apparently cares about you enough to come looking for you. In fact, he's headed our way now, along with Arnagh and your horse."

Lusa sank to the ground. "Oh, no."

"Oh, yes, and I hope they brought some water with them, because I don't have any and you obviously don't, either." There were no signs of a waterskin on Lusa, who was wearing only a shirt, her leather thigh coverings, and a pair of moccasins. "By the time we get back to Plainview, it'll be night, so maybe we can slip in quietly and go to sleep on the boat. You can apologize to Nenet and Melii in the morning." She went to Lusa and pulled her to her feet. "Come on."

"I really am sorry."

"I know you are."

Lusa's hand suddenly tightened around hers. "What's that?" The blond girl was looking to her right. Bian turned in that direction.

In the dim light, she could barely make out the speck to the north, flying just above the tall grass. The black speck quickly swelled into a silvery body with flat shiny wings, then plummeted toward the ground and disappeared into the grass.

Lusa said, "You saw it, too?"

"Yes."

"Then I haven't gone completely mad."

Bian let go of Lusa's hand. They crept toward the flyer until they could glimpse it through the grass. Lusa sat down a few paces from it; Bian seated herself next to the other girl. The flyer had been coming from the north, where the dome dwellers lived. She steadied herself, then swallowed her fear as she studied the strange device.

Two wide wings were attached to a body only slightly larger than that of a sheep, while the flyer's six legs resembled those of an insect. The device had no eyes, yet somehow she knew that it was observing them. She sat there with Lusa, neither of them moving, and then heard a low, barely audible hum.

The flyer abruptly fell silent. Still watching the flyer, Bian wrapped her arms around herself.

"What is it?" Lusa whispered. "What can it be?"

Bian shook her head, too frightened to speak. A bowl-shaped object rose from the flyer and tilted toward them on its stalk.

"What are you?" Lusa said in a louder voice. "What are you doing here?"

A light on the flyer flickered and then caught them in its beam. "Do you not know?" a soft voice answered. "Can you not guess?"

Bian was terrified now. Lusa clutched at her arm. "What are you?" Lusa asked once more.

"The flyer you see is one of my probes," the voice said, "a part of me. Haven't you seen me in the sky these past nights, orbiting this planet? I have been calling to you, yet no one has answered me. Tell me that you know who I am, and that I haven't been forgotten."

Bian knew who had come to them now, whose mind somehow inhabited this flyer. "I know what you are, what you must be." She had to force the words from herself. "You're part of Ship, and you've come back to Home."

13

Night came, and still Ship's voice had revealed little about itself, its voyage across space, or its reasons for returning to Home. Instead, it continued to probe Bian and Lusa with questions, all of which they answered as carefully as they could, and all of which seemed to be part of a larger question: What happened on this world after Ship left Bian and Lusa's ancestors there?

They spoke of their villages, the daily events of their lives, the tales that their parents and grandparents had told them about the past, and the wariness and distrust that had long separated them from the people of the north, the people they called dome dwellers. They told Ship about the recent appearance of the light in the sky, visible to everyone who lived along the river, and of how they had come north to learn what they could about that light, which many already suspected might be the great vessel that had carried their ancestors to Home. Bian answered Ship's questions cautiously, and Lusa also seemed to be saying as little as possible; perhaps she, too, was worried that an insignificant detail might reveal too much. They still did not know what Ship's intentions toward them were.

What conclusions would Ship draw about their people? Would it be pleased with the lives they had made here, or disappointed? And why hadn't the dome dwellers responded to Ship? Maybe they had heard its call, but had reasons of their own for remaining silent.

The flyer retracted its wings, and its light winked out. It seemed that Ship was finished with its questions for now. Stunned as Bian was, trying to absorb what the presence of this probe might mean, she was again becoming aware of her thirst. Her world might change in ways she could not anticipate, yet all she could think about right now was her craving for water.

She stood up. "Where are you going?" The voice of the probe was higher now, more like a woman's voice than the lower, more masculine tones Ship had used to question them.

"Two people were following us." Instantly she wondered if she should have revealed that. "They may not be able to find us in the dark. They're friends of ours," Bian added, in case Ship might draw other conclusions. "They're probably worried about us being out here in the night."

The flyer was silent. "I can't move," Lusa said. "I can't believe this. I'm too frightened even to move. I feel like I'm going to start screaming at any moment."

"No, you won't," Bian said, even though she could smell the other girl's fear. "You mustn't. Promise me."

"I promise."

"Wait here." Her own fear was threatening to overwhelm her. "I'll see if I can spot Arnagh and Enli from farther up the hill."

"Don't leave me here alone for too long," Lusa said in a voice that quavered just a little.

"I won't."

Bian hurried up the slope. Behind her, the first moon would soon be rising, which would bring a little light to the dark night. The speck of light that was Ship would also be moving across the sky. What would Ship do if it was disappointed in what it found here? Would it simply leave again, or would it plant new seeds here, new life that might require cleansing Home of its people? Bian dimly recalled one of the stories she had read on her screen as a child, an old Earth legend of another ship that had sheltered a few people and their animals from a flood that had covered all of their world. The flood had been sent by an intelligence whom the people of Earth had somehow offended, an intelligence that now seemed to her to bear some resemblance to what her people knew of Ship.

That thought brought her to a halt. She and her companions might inadvertently reveal something that so offended Ship that they would endanger all their people, and she had no idea what Ship might find offensive. Maybe not meeting its expectations for true humanity would be their greatest offense.

A light danced in the distance, just above the grass. Arnagh and Enli had apparently brought a light wand with them. Bian cupped her hands around her mouth. "Hai!" She drew in her breath. "Hai!"

The light dipped down. "Hai," a voice said in the distance.

The light moved up, offering a glimpse of the large pale body of Lusa's horse. Bian stood at the top of the small hill and waited for them.

Bian told Enli and Arnagh that a piece of Ship, a flying object that resembled an insect, had come down to Home after Ship had received no response to its radio greetings. She explained that she and Lusa had talked to the voice of Ship and had been honest but cautious in their answers to its questions. The two heard her out without saying a word.

Enli turned off his light wand and thrust it into one of the packs on Summercloud's back. Arnagh handed her a waterskin. She drank, then handed it back to him. Both of them remained silent for a while, obviously trying to absorb what she had told them.

"I can't believe it," Arnagh said at last.

"I can hardly believe it myself," Bian said.

"What are we going to do?" Enli asked.

"Answer more questions, I suppose," Bian replied. "Try to find out what it wants from us."

"Why would the dome dwellers ignore Ship?" Arnagh said in a nervous voice. "Why wouldn't they answer its message?"

"How do we know they didn't?" Enli said. "All we know is what that probe—that thing—told Bian and Lusa. Maybe it didn't tell them everything. How do we know it's even telling them the truth?"

"It has to be telling us the truth," Bian said, convinced of that without knowing why. "I just know it. Why would it lie about something like that?"

They descended the slope. The flyer's eyes lit up again, lighting the area around it with a soft glow. Summercloud whinnied as Lusa stood up and turned toward them.

"You took long enough," she whispered to Bian. Enli gave her a waterskin. Lusa drank and then went to her horse, patting the mare to soothe her. "She'll be all right," she said. "She's probably just as scared as we are, but she won't run away." She sat down again, keeping a grip on Summercloud's reins.

Bian seated herself next to Lusa as the boys settled themselves near the probe. "Bian and Lusa tell me that you are their friends," Ship's voice murmured. "What are you called?"

Enli cleared his throat. "My name's Enli," he said, "and this is Arnagh."

"Bian and Lusa also told me that you live in villages along the river that runs from the great lake north of here to the ocean."

"Yes," Enli said. "Bian and Arnagh are from Seaside, near the southern seacoast, while Lusa and I are from Overlook, three days north of Seaside."

"And they told me that you traveled to a place near here called Plainview, because you were searching for information about a new light in the sky and believed you would learn more about that light from the dome dwellers with whom you occasionally trade."

"Yes," Arnagh said.

"Why did you come here?" Enli asked. The vehemence in his voice startled Bian. "If you really are a part of Ship, what brought you back to Home?"

"So you doubt that you are truly hearing Ship through this probe?" The voice did not sound offended. "I came back because I grew curious, because I had come to question the way that I was going about my mission of seeding other worlds, and thought I might become better suited for that task if I returned to see what had grown from the seeds I planted here. And I came back because I had promised those I left here that I would return."

The probe was silent for a time. At last Bian said, "My great-grandmother told me of your promise, but I don't know how many other people still remember it."

"Your great-grandmother surely could not be one of the young ones who lived inside me long ago. I know how much time has passed during my voyages, how much time sped by outside me even as it passed more slowly within me. Human beings of the kind I carried could not have lived for so long."

"No, she wasn't one you knew," Bian said, "but she was one of their children, and she has lived for a very long time. We call her one of the First, because she was part of the first generation born on Home. She's the only one of them who's still alive."

"Then she would surely remember some of those I did know," Ship's voice said. "Perhaps she knew Zoheret, who became one of their leaders."

"Zoheret?" Arnagh leaned forward. "Zoheret's daughter Rosa was a great-great grandmother of mine," he continued.

"Zoheret and her mate, Manuel, were part of my line, too," Enli said. "My mother's a descendant of their daughter Leila and a man named Trevor, who was the son of Bonnie and Anoki."

"Two people named Roxana and Tonio are among my ancestors," Lusa murmured, "and my mother claimed sky-folk called Lillka and Brendan as part of her line."

Ship said, "I knew all of them. I am calling up images of them right now."

The voice had grown gentle. Bian's fears eased a bit.

Ship had cared for their ancestors and had no reason to wish harm on their children, at least not yet. "Nuy's father was called Ho," she said.

"Yes, I remember him, too." Perhaps she was imagining it, but Ship's voice now sounded more distant. "I have another question for you, but think carefully before you answer it. What do you think would happen if I sent a probe north and revealed myself to the people who live in the old settlement as I have to you?"

Bian was silent. "I don't know," Arnagh said.

"I don't think any of us can answer that," Enli said. "Of the four of us, only Arnagh and I have ever gone there to trade with them, and we've never been inside their settlement, or even that close to it. We would wait at an outpost by the lake, where there are two cabins. A tower with a beacon lies north of the cabins. One of us would go to the tower to turn on the beacon, and that's how the dome dwellers would know somebody was there to trade with them."

"I have seen that settlement," Ship said. "I had scanned the region, and one of my probes waited near the hills there for some days, but encountered no people. After that—"

Bian waited for Ship's voice to continue. It had just revealed to them that it could view Home from afar, and that this flyer was not its only probe. Ship had to have learned something about their world by now, and might even know more about the dome dwellers than her own people had ever been able to find out. Why hadn't it sent a flyer to their settlement right away to tell them that it had returned?

"After that," Ship went on, "I thought it best to wait, to find out more before I revealed my presence."

"Everyone along the river already suspects that the new

light we see in the night sky might be Ship—might be you," Enli said. "We know that the dome dwellers can speak to you, but no news from them has reached us yet. You say they haven't answered you, and maybe it's because they can't receive any of your messages. It's also possible that they heard you and are just afraid to reply."

"That is a possibility," Ship said, "although I don't know why they would fear me so much."

"I'm afraid of you," Lusa said softly. "I can understand why they might be afraid, too."

"Afraid or not," Enli said, "the more time passes without any news, the more convinced some people will be that the dome dwellers are in contact with you but hiding it from us. They might think that you offered them something that they wanted to keep for themselves instead of sharing with us."

"Is there so much distrust and suspicion among you?" Ship asked. "But perhaps I shouldn't be surprised by that, given the history of your ancestors and your species." Ship's voice sounded more gentle now, but its words cut at Bian; Ship had already found something to hold against them. "It seems that if I don't contact your people soon, your suspicion and distrust will only grow. But if I contact the ones you call dome dwellers, you would fear that they might use me against you somehow. I must assume that you might also use anything you learn about me against them."

Bian shook her head. "Oh, but we wouldn't."

"I have only your word on that. I am wondering now if other people finding out about me would only sow more disruption here, perhaps even provoke conflict."

But Ship had already spoken to the four of them. Surely it realized that they couldn't keep such a momentous event to themselves. Bian caught her breath, sensing the implications of that thought. Ship might have any number of ways to keep them from revealing this encounter.

The flyer dimmed its light. "What are we going to do?" Lusa whispered.

"What can we do?" Arnagh said.

"This is all my fault," Lusa said. "If I hadn't run away like that, if I hadn't completely lost my senses, none of us would be sitting here now worrying about what Ship might do."

"Stop it," Enli muttered. "I'm sure it can hear every word we're saying."

"Still, if I hadn't—," Lusa began.

"That doesn't matter now," Bian said. "If it hadn't been us, somebody else would have seen the flyer, and somebody else would have had to decide what to do."

"What do you suggest?" Enli asked, and she caught the irritation and fear in his voice.

"We can't keep this to ourselves," she replied. "But we don't know what might happen if we go back to Plainview with this story. So much could change for our people, and many won't welcome it."

"People won't wait forever for news to reach them," Arnagh said. "Sooner or later, when they hear nothing from the dome dwellers, they'll start to believe that they're communicating with Ship but are keeping it to themselves for some reason. People will get impatient. Then they'll head for the outpost, if they haven't done so already, and I doubt they'll just wait for somebody to come down and meet them. They'll keep going until they reach the settlement, assuming the dome dwellers let them get that far."

"They've got weapons," Enli added, "probably more

weapons than we do, and they'll be able to recharge theirs after ours give out."

"Theirs," Bian said, keeping her voice low. "Ours." He was talking about fighting, as if they were enemies. "Do you think it'll come to that?"

"Can we prevent it?" Lusa asked.

"If we could only reach the dome dwellers before anybody else does," Arnagh replied, "we might be able to talk to somebody and find out what's going on. We just need to get there before . . . ." He broke off, and Bian knew that he was thinking of Awan and their brief time together. "Before anything bad happens."

"Impossible." Enli sighed. "By the time we get to the lake, there will be others far ahead of us."

The flyer's light grew brighter. "Would you be willing to intervene?" Ship said.

Bian started at the sound of its voice. "What did you say?" she whispered.

"Are you saying that you would go to those you call the dome dwellers and find out why they have not responded to my messages?" Ship continued. "Would you do whatever you could to prevent a conflict between them and your people?"

"Yes," Bian said, even as she resisted the idea.

"I would, too," Arnagh replied, hesitancy in his voice. "We have to try. Anything's better than fighting."

"I would go with you, too," Lusa said softly.

"And so would I. But it's impossible." Enli shook his head. "We'd never be able to get there in time."

"I might be able to help you," Ship said, "if you are truly willing to intervene."

Could Ship take them north? The flyer was even smaller than Lusa's horse; it could not possibly carry them all.

"Are you saying you could get us there?" Arnagh asked, obviously thinking the same thing. "I don't see how. And there would be many questions if we suddenly disappeared."

"Yes, I thought about that." Ship's voice had risen to an alto. "You could return to the place you call Plainview tonight and then leave tomorrow. Tell the people there only that you are continuing your journey north."

"And then what?" Enli asked.

"Find a place upriver where you can stop, where there are no people about. I am capable of tracking you." The thought of Ship's tracking them chilled Bian. If they wanted to back out of their promise later on, she wondered if Ship would let them.

"I must tell you," Ship continued, "that the settlement in the north is quite different from what I expected. My sensors have revealed many signs of human habitation, but no people have come outside since I began to orbit Home, and I see no signs of crops or animals in the land around their houses. Any people living there must be inside their domes and tunnels. My sensors showed some movement and heat sources inside the settlement."

How could they live like that? Bian wondered. How could they possibly survive? Perhaps they had not responded to Ship because they had everything they needed and more. Again she worried about what kinds of weapons they might possess. She began wishing that she could call back her promise to Ship, but knew she could not. Again she thought of the stories of the punishments that had befallen their ancestors on Earth when they had offended more powerful intelligences.

"Once you're far enough away from Plainview," Ship continued, "I will contact you again. I'm grateful to you for agreeing to be my emissaries. Perhaps you'll find that your people have nothing to fear from the dome dwellers."

The flyer's light blacked out, and Bian heard a low hum as the flyer rose out of sight.

14

They were back aboard Enli's boat before dawn. Exhausted as Bian was, she was unable to rest. She wanted to go to sleep and then wake up to discover that she had only dreamed about seeing a flyer and hearing the voice of Ship. She wanted everything to become as it was before Ship had spoken to them.

Ship could track them. It might be eavesdropping on them. She could almost imagine that Ship had some way to read their minds.

Bian forced herself to control her wilder thoughts. Human beings had created Ship and given the great vessel its powers. If Ship's abilities were unlimited, it would not have needed to ask her and her companions for help.

At last she gave up on sleep and crawled out of the cabin.

Arnagh sat on the deck, keeping watch. Enli was pacing on the dock, while Lusa stood on the bank as her horse drank from the river. Sleep had seemingly eluded them as well.

They ate their breakfast at Nenet's hearth as Enli explained that they had decided to leave that day and head upriver. Eliane and Weneth nodded but said nothing. Bian had brought some bracelets and necklaces to trade for food, and Lusa would leave her horse with Nenet. If anyone was willing to take Summercloud back to Overlook, Enli was sure that his family and Lusa's would be grateful to learn that they were heading north.

Eliane murmured a few words about how surprised she was by their decision, while Weneth wore a look of dismay. Nenet held up the necklaces and bracelets and nodded approvingly at the craftsmanship as Bian chattered about how her mother had made them and how valued they were in Seaside.

Luckily, Nenet did not ask any of them if they had seen anything on the plain that resembled the strange flying thing in Roran's story. Perhaps Plainview's leader was assuming they would have told her about any such sighting. But the woman watched them warily as they ate, as if she could see that they might be keeping a secret from her.

"I wish you weren't leaving Plainview now," Nenet said as they got up, "but of course you will stop here again when you come back downriver."

Enli nodded. "Of course." Weneth's face brightened with hope as Lusa's face paled.

Weneth followed them down to the dock. She was silent until they came to the river, then said, "Play one last piece of music for me, Enli."

"You make it sound as if you're afraid we're not coming back," Enli said.

"Maybe you won't. Something's changed, I can sense it. All of you look like you've suddenly been given something heavy to carry and don't know if you can manage to lift it."

"I'll play the flute for you again when we come back downriver," Enli said. "I promise."

Lusa turned away and boarded the boat. Bian climbed in after her, followed by Arnagh. Enli took a step toward Weneth, but she turned away and ran from the dock. Enli came aboard, his face grim.

Arnagh sat in the stern next to the rudder as they cast off and the boat moved slowly upriver. A few people had come down to the riverbank to wash garments and spread them on rocks to dry. Outside Nenet's house, Eliane was grooming Summercloud, who seemed to have taken to her. Eliane lifted her arm in farewell, and Bian waved back. Enli moved toward the bow without looking back at Plainview.

After a while, Lusa said, "If I hadn't followed you, none of this would have happened. We wouldn't have been out there last night." Bian stared out at the plain, pretending to ignore the conversation. "I made a fool of myself. Not that it matters now."

"I can't blame you for being angry with me," Enli replied.

"Do you care so much for that girl?" Lusa asked.

"I don't know. Her singing—I've never heard anything like it. We could go on for the whole evening and into the night, she with her voice and me with my flute. But I've known her for only a few days. It isn't the same as with you."

"No," Lusa said sadly. "She's something new, and you've known me all your life. I guess I can understand that."

"And if you hadn't been so upset—" An urgent and excited

tone in his voice made Bian look toward him. "We wouldn't have discovered the probe. We wouldn't have spoken to Ship." He clasped Lusa's hands. "It's good that this happened, don't you see? Things will be different now."

"Were they so bad before?" Lusa said, as if picking up on Bian's thoughts.

"Maybe not, but everything was always the same. Think about it." He glanced at Bian and then focused on Arnagh. "What were all of us doing before that new light appeared? Pretty much the same thing, day after day. I'd think of the years ahead and know that they'd go on mostly the way they always had. The only time anything was different was when we'd go to trade with the dome dwellers, or I'd hear a new piece of music on my screen. Our ancestors built Ship and came across the sky to this place, and we've never even sent a boat out to sea." He rested his arm on the gunwale. "Now that Ship's come back, things have to change."

"Doesn't necessarily mean they'll be better," Bian said. But Arnagh's eyes gleamed with anticipation, and Lusa also seemed to share his and Enli's feelings, judging from the hopeful look on her face.

"If you're thinking of backing out . . . ," Enli began.

Bian shook her head. "No." In spite of her fears, she wanted to go on. Maybe there was something of her great-grandmother Nuy in her after all.

They took turns at the rudder. From time to time, Enli took out a flute and played for them, while Lusa listened with a wistful look in her eyes. By evening, they had come to a place along the bank that provided an expansive view of the river to the north and south, and decided to pull the boat up there. Bian saw no sign of any boats upriver, and the plains to the east and west were as flat and empty as they were around Plainview.

"How far are we from Lakeview?" Bian asked as they finished some of the beans and wheat cakes Nenet had given them.

"At least three days," Enli said, "and sometimes it would take us four or five days to get there from Plainview. The closer you get to the lake, the more the current's moving against you, which slows you down."

Perhaps Ship would wait until they were farther away from Plainview before contacting them again. "Who's going to keep the first watch?" Arnagh asked.

"I will," Lusa said, although she looked as tired as Bian felt.

"I'll take the second, then," Enli said. "I should be all right after a little sleep."

"Then I'll take the third," Arnagh murmured.

Bian crept into the cabin, welcoming the thought of a stretch of uninterrupted sleep. The boat swayed slightly under her. She was back in Seaside, lying in her mother's cabin, dimly aware of the distant sound of the sea. Then suddenly her mother was prodding her.

"Wake up, Bian."

She still heard the sound of the sea, rising and falling, as she opened her eyes and struggled into wakefulness.

"Bian." That was Lusa's voice. Someone poked her again. She crawled out from under the deck. Arnagh and Enli stood on the bank, their backs to her, silhouetted against an oval of bright light. The rushing sound that had entered her dream persisted, and now she was able to make out the long dark shape that surrounded the oval of light.

"Come inside," a voice said, sounding unlike any she had heard before. "Now."

Bian hung on to Lusa, afraid that her legs might give way, and walked toward the light.

Part Two

15

Safrah sat with her companions under a hole-pocked dome, next to a wide opening in the wall that faced south. Jina had found a pot and filled it with water from the dome's cistern. As the water boiled on top of a small stove that still had a little fuel left, Safrah mixed flour and water in a smaller pot, flattened pieces of dough in her palms, set them on a flat rock, rolled bits of dried meat into each piece, twisted them into dumplings, and dropped them into the large pot. Moise had taught them how to make such food. She remembered sitting with him and Awan around another fire like this one, and felt pangs of longing and regret.

Jina fished boiled dumplings out of the pot with a ladle and set them on a plate she had found inside the dome. The light of the beacon was still visible in the darkness.

They ate without speaking. "One of us will have to go to the outpost," Safrah said at last.

"When?" Jina asked, sounding apprehensive.

"As soon as possible," Safrah replied. "By tomorrow morning at the latest. Everyone south of us has to be thinking that the new light in the sky might be Ship. At least a few of their older people must remember that we have a way of talking to Ship. They may be wondering if we're already in contact."

"But we don't know any more than they do," Jina said.

"We could tell the traders that," Mikhail said, "but maybe they won't believe us. We'd have to admit that our radio's damaged, that we don't have any way of communicating with Ship right now. Then they'd want to know how that happened, and then—"

Don't let them know how weak we are. That had been Moise's first command when he brought them to meet some traders for the first time. The outsiders had to believe that they were many and thriving, and that they still owned much that the river people lacked.

"We could tell them we've heard nothing from Ship," Safrah said, "and that the light has to be something else. That's all we'd have to say."

"Do you think they'll believe us?" Jina asked.

"All that matters is that they believe it until we can fix our radio," Safrah said. "But one of us has to go meet them, or they're going to wonder why nobody's responded to the signal." She reached for a dumpling. "I haven't gone to do a trade for a while, so I'll go. Just finish scavenging what you can and get back to Awan."

Safrah slept for a while, then woke to the sound of a high-pitched cry. Something was moving near her.

She heard another, lower cry, and knew then that a band of small wild cats had to be nearby. Their domesticated ancestors had once lived in these buildings. She did not have to fear those creatures, only the larger cats, which usually kept their distance from the settlement anyway.

Jina and Mikhail were still sleeping, wrapped in an old blanket. She got up without waking them and headed back to the greenhouse, looking up at the night sky only long enough to verify that the light that might be Ship was still orbiting Home. She did not expect to find any of the younger ones in the greenhouse, but remained alert anyway; she had not expected any of them to destroy the radio, either.

By dawn, she had collected everything she would need and was rolling south in a cart. The small, rectangular, roofless vehicle moved slowly enough that it would take her half a day to reach the lake, but she would get to the tower before nightfall. Any traders would be waiting farther south, at the outpost. There would be time to rest at the tower, to eat and sleep and prepare herself for any questions the traders might ask.

Even this early in the warming season, the green grass was already growing thick and high. She kept close to the flat, barren stretch that had once been a pathway, but, even there, patches of grass slowed her passage and made the cart rattle and bounce.

We've had no message from Ship. We don't know what that light is. We don't know if it means that Ship has come back or not, but since we haven't received any message, there's a chance that the light isn't Ship.

She would say that much to the traders, and it would be the truth. Moise had always warned them to say as little to traders as possible, in order to avoid saying something that might entangle them in contradictions later on. The farther she rode from the settlement, the easier it was to hold the image of the imagined thriving community in her mind, decreasing the likelihood that she might betray the reality.

By midmorning, the green sky was nearly empty of clouds, except for a few feathery wisps. The closer Safrah came to the lake, the cleaner the air smelled. She thought of the times the older ones had brought them to the lake to gaze at the gray expanse and immerse themselves in the refreshing coolness of the water.

Once, their people had gone out on the lake in their own boats, but none of those watercraft remained. All that was left of the docks were a few poles that poked above the lake's surface. Moise never told them what had happened to the boats, but it was easy enough to guess: They had been taken by the people who left the settlement to live along the banks of the great river.

The wind rose as she neared the lake, making her shiver in her threadbare tunic, even though the sun was overhead and promised a warm afternoon. There would be cleaner clothes inside the tower, hidden behind a panel, clothing that was worn only when they went to meet traders: shirts, pants, sturdy boots, even a few necklaces and bracelets, the kind of garments and adornments prosperous people might wear. She would rest and then climb the long, winding staircase to check on the beacon. When the tower had first been built, there was a lift to carry people to the top, but the pulleys had frayed and the lift had not been operational for decades.

Shards of sunlight danced on the water. Safrah turned southeast toward the tower that seemed to be no closer than it had been when she left the settlement.

A dark speck floated on the water near the tower.

Safrah caught her breath, squinted, then averted her gaze and continued toward the shore. As she neared the water, she pressed one of the panels in front of her, turning the cart to the east. She followed the old pathway along the shore, the cart moving at a crawl now, shaking only a little as its treads rolled over the rocky ground. Then she forced herself to look toward the tower again. She saw that the barely discernible speck was exactly what she had first suspected and feared.

There was an outsider waiting for her at the tower, someone who had come there in a boat.

16

Safrah approached the tower, longing to turn around and head back to the settlement. Any traders should have been waiting for her at the outpost, not here with a boat. All along the way, she had hoped that the next time she looked toward the tower, she would see the boat drifting south, indicating that the traders had decided to leave. She told herself that perhaps they were stopping at the tower only to get some rest before heading back to the outpost where they always waited.

None of the traders had ever come to the tower by boat. They would send one or two of their number there on foot to turn on the beacon before returning to the outpost to wait. Whatever their reasons were for waiting at the tower this time, turning back and refusing to meet with them would only make them curious about why no one had responded to their signal. She did not want them to come any closer to the settlement, so she would talk to them and get the trade settled as quickly as possible, and she would not ask why they had decided to wait for her at the tower.

But she knew why they must be waiting for her there. The traders had seen the light that might be the sign of Ship's return. Perhaps they had first glimpsed it on their way north; maybe it had been visible in the sky for even longer than that. She had no way of knowing when it had first appeared. The traders would have questions, and she had no answers to give them.

She was close enough now that she could go on foot the rest of the way. Her people had never needed to use stun guns on the traders, but they always brought them anyway, keeping them concealed; hers was under her tunic, tied to the drawstring of her pants.

She climbed out of the vehicle and walked toward the tower. The boat had been pulled up; its prow rested on a patch of muddy shore near a small green and violet bush of blossoming colulos. Now that she was closer to the boat, she realized that she had seen this craft before. The red and yellow stripes of the cloth curtain that hung in front of the cabin had faded since the last time she had seen them, but she knew whose boat this had to be.

She sighed with relief and picked up her pace. As she neared the tower, the door at its base opened and a man stepped outside. His broad face was adorned by a mustache, a long black braid hung down his back, and he wore a light brown tunic and dark brown pants.

"Tarki," she called out. A smile crossed his face briefly. "I haven't seen you for so long."

"Almost two years," he replied. "You look much the same, Safrah. A little thinner, perhaps."

She hurried to him and clasped his hands. "I've missed you," she said before she could stop herself. "We've all missed you," she added.

The boatman frowned. "You're alone," he said as she let go of him.

"Only because we didn't know it was you who had come here. If the others had known, they would have come with me. They're going to be really sorry that they missed you. Maybe you could stay at the outpost while I go and fetch them." It was easier to act cheerful and unconcerned with Tarki, who wasn't like the other outsiders she had met. Tarki lived alone, kept to himself, and preferred it that way; so he had often told them. At the same time, he had always welcomed them aboard his boat and usually prolonged his sessions of trading in order to spend more time with them.

"You could come with me, you know," he had told her the last time she saw him. "There's more to Home than that settlement up there, more to life than just staying in the same place and doing the same things all those generations of people ahead of you did. I could find you a place to live and some work to do." Of course, she had refused his offer. She had her obligations to her community, and life would be much harder for her without the technology that sustained her people.

"You can drop the pleasantries," Tarki said to her now. "I didn't come here to trade. I came to ask about that light in the sky. Have you had a message from Ship?"

She shook her head. "No."

His dark eyes were studying her. "I hear the truth in your

voice, much as what you say disappoints me. Then do you have any idea what that light is?"

Safrah shook her head again.

"If you've had no message from Ship, then surely you've formed some notion of what that light might be instead. Haven't you been watching it and making observations?" He sighed. "Now I smell fear. You're hiding something from me. But you've been doing that for some time now, haven't you, you and all your people."

"I thought you were our friend."

"I am, as much as you've ever allowed me to be. That's why I came here. Every night we look up, and that light's still crossing the sky, and there's more and more talk about how the dome dwellers might be communicating with Ship and poisoning Ship's mind against us."

"But we've had no message from Ship," she insisted.

"Then you could have sent somebody out to tell us that. Moise isn't stupid—surely that thought must have crossed his mind. So why didn't you?"

"Would you have believed us if we had?"

"Yes, if you told the truth. Now you've waited too long, and people have had more time to worry and wonder, and it may be too late. Do you know what's been happening in Westbay? When I left, people were saying that we'd waited long enough, that it was time to come up here and confront you and tell you that we have as much right to speak to Ship as you do. Some are gathering weapons and saying that it's time to go to your settlement and demand that right for ourselves."

Safrah stepped back, hugging herself with her arms. "There's been no message from Ship," she whispered. "That's the truth."

"Then you had better come with me and try to convince others of that. It isn't just you I'm thinking about, Safrah. I've suspected for some time that things weren't going as well for your people as it seemed. I couldn't help seeing the uneasiness in your voices and movements. But you still have things we lack, including the means to recharge your weapons. I'm not about to watch people from Westbay or anywhere else go to your settlement, only to be cut down by your people."

Too much was coming at her at once. She turned away and stumbled toward the lake. A hand gripped her shoulder.

"I thought that light might be Ship," Tarki said behind her. "I was hoping it was Ship, whatever trouble that might bring upon us. There are so many questions I would want to ask if it were Ship."

Jina, Awan, and Mikhail should have been with her. Moise should have been there to give her his advice. This was too much for her to handle by herself.

She shook off his hand and turned to face him. "I don't know what to do."

"Yes, you do. You'll come with me and—"

"I said that we had no message from Ship. That's the truth. What I didn't tell you is that we have no way at the moment of communicating with Ship." She had said it. Safrah was suddenly horrified at herself.

"But you do. You must. My grandmother Nuy told me that there was a room in your settlement where the ancestors used to go to talk to Ship. Long ago, she even saw the place for herself. As I've been up and down the river, I've heard many versions of the story passed down to us, including parts my grandmother stopped reciting after a while. Almost all of them tell of a room where Ship's voice could be heard, and mention Ship's promise to return to Home. Are you telling me that there is no—?"

"There's a room," she interrupted. She would have to tell him a bit more of the truth. "But the radio, the device that would carry Ship's voice to us, has failed."

Tarki stiffened; his dark eyes widened.

"We should be able to repair it," she continued. "Awan's working on it right now, and he can fix anything." That was all of the truth Tarki needed to hear for now.

"How long will that take?"

"I don't know."

"You'll have to come with me, then," Tarki said. "Maybe people will believe you if you tell them what you've told me. That may be the only way we can avoid a confrontation."

His people had nothing to fear from hers, she thought. If even a small portion of them moved against the settlement, they would have the advantage over her people. But there were Morwen and Terris, who smashed and destroyed things for no reason. They and the other younger ones would fight anything that threatened them, and even if they lost in the end, they could still inflict a lot of damage.

"I don't know what to do," she said.

"Well, we'd better decide. I assume you brought some food with you. Go fetch your cart, and we'll eat and talk about what to do now."

After she had gone inside the tower to turn off the beacon, they ate outside its entrance, around a shallow pit lined with flat rocks that might once have been a fireplace. She had brought a melon with her, so she cut it in half and gave a piece to Tarki. It came to her that the outsiders seemed more fearsome and alien when she was back in the settlement, mindful of all the obligations the old ones had placed on her and of their insistence that the outsiders had diverged from true humanity. She would think of how intently they peered at her sometimes, or how they heard sounds she could not hear, or how they could tell that a storm was coming when the sky was still clear. Yet Tarki did not seem so strange as he sat here eating her food and gazing out at the lake.

Tarki said, "You're looking shabbier than usual."

Safrah did not reply. She thought of the clothing stored inside the tower. There was no sense in going inside to change her clothes now, to disguise herself as a member of a thriving settlement.

"We'll sleep," he said, "and then we'll head for the outpost before dawn. I just hope that people aren't already there laying out a plan of attack."

"Are your people so violent?"

"They're frightened," he replied. "If Ship has come back, that changes things, changes everything. That's enough to scare some of my people into thinking they might have to fight yours."

She forced herself to finish her half of the melon, having lost her appetite. "I can't go with you," she said as she wiped her hands on her tunic. "The others will worry about me."

"That's nonsense and you know it. If this was a normal trade, they wouldn't start worrying about you for another three or four days at least, and even after that, they'd probably just think any agreement was taking longer than usual. But you've already admitted that you, like us, don't yet know what that new light is, and that your equipment for contacting Ship is useless until it's repaired. Your people won't be expecting you to get back there all that soon. They'll guess that we'll need to reach a very different sort of agreement this time."

"I should at least go back and let them know what's going on."

"Safrah, you must be honest with me now. There isn't time for me to drag the truth out of you. What else are you hiding from us?"

"Nothing."

"Why did you come here alone? Why didn't Moise or someone older—?"

"Moise is dead." She could give him that much truth.

"I'm sorry to hear it. I sensed some kindness and fairness in him, however much he distrusted us." He stood up. "I'm tired. Do I have your word that you won't run back to your settlement while I'm sleeping?"

"Yes."

"Good. I'm a light sleeper, especially under these circumstances, so you wouldn't get very far anyway. You can keep watch. Wake me if you notice anything out of the ordinary, and be sure to wake me once the second moon's on the rise."

"I will."

The sun was setting; a broad pathway of silvery light stretched to the west across the lake. Tarki went to his boat and climbed aboard. Safrah retreated to the tower and sat down, her back against the door.

She could still try to slip away, but that would solve nothing. She would have to go with Tarki and hope that she could keep his people away from the settlement. By the time she returned, perhaps Awan would have repaired the radio, and then—

She drew up her legs and wrapped her arms around them. If Ship had returned, she and her friends would have to admit the truth to Ship. What if it told them that it wanted to communicate with all the people of Home? The truth would come out then, that she and the others in the settlement were no more than a small group trying to preserve what little they still possessed. Would Ship conclude that its seeding of Home had failed?

When the second moon was just above the horizon, Safrah went to the boat. Tarki came out of the cabin, pushing the curtain aside, just as she was about to board. He grabbed her hand as she climbed into the craft.

"I'll go with you to the outpost," she said quickly, before she could change her mind. "We can decide what to do after that."

"I've already told you what you're going to have to do."

"Maybe you're wrong," she said. "Maybe we won't find anybody at the outpost. If so, I should head back to the settlement. Awan might have repaired our radio by then."

"We can talk about that later. Right now we're heading for the outpost."

"Now?" she asked.

"I'm not waiting until morning."

"Then I'd better get my cart."

"Forget the cart. This isn't a trade, so you won't need a cart to carry things back. We'll go in my boat." He turned away from her, then looked back. "I still don't understand why you came here alone, why none of the older ones came with you. Your people must be as worried as ours, but they sent only you out to the tower."

"There was no need to send someone else. I have experience dealing with outsiders." She kept her voice steady, grateful that she could not see his face in the darkness. "And I'm almost nineteen—I'm not that young."

"You're not that old, either." Tarki sighed. "Fetch what you need from your cart and then help me push the boat out. You can get some sleep in the cabin."

The floor under her was rolling gently. Safrah opened her eyes, saw a striped curtain outlined at its edges by bright light, and then remembered where she was.

One of her packs, the one in which she had hidden her stun gun, was under her head. It was warm, almost too warm, inside the cabin. She got up and drew the curtain aside.

The sun was high in the east. It was already midmorning, with the sunny green sky promising a warm day. The boat drifted slowly toward the eastern shore of the lake. She slapped her hands against the deck and hoisted herself up onto the surface.

Tarki sat in the stern, bare chested, the rudder in his hands. As he steered his craft toward the shore, the soft hum of the motor died. He stood up, reached for the heavy rope near him, and threw it over the side. The weight tied to the end of the rope hit the water with a splash.

"Why are we stopping here?" Safrah asked.

"Because I feel like swimming." Tarki pulled off his pants. Safrah was about to look away until she saw that he was wearing a loincloth. He came toward her across the deck, stepped to the edge of the boat, and jumped into the water.

He hit feetfirst, with a splash that showered Safrah. She watched as he swam to shore, then waded out of the water, plopping down next to a shrub. "Come on," he called out.

"I'm not any good in the water!" she shouted back. She

and her friends had never been allowed to wade more than a few paces from shore.

"Just jump in and wade over here, then. The water won't be much higher than your shoulders."

She did not want to take off her clothes in front of him. She also did not want him to think she was afraid of the water. At last she pulled off her shirt and pants, but did not shed the ragged shorts that were her only undergarment. She stepped onto the edge of the boat, pinched her nose, and jumped.

The cold of the water was a shock. Her feet sank into the lake's muddy bottom; her head bobbed above the water. She waddled toward shore, splashing about with her arms until she came to the bank, then waded out and sat down on a flat rock a few paces from Tarki.

"Admit it," Tarki said. "That felt good." She nodded. "And I needed to wash."

She turned away from him, slouched forward, and pulled her long dark hair over her chest, suddenly shy.

"We should be close to the outpost by nightfall," Tarki said. "Depending on what I see when we're closer, we can either keep going, or just sleep on the boat and wait until dawn to land."

"What are you actually expecting to see?" she asked, suddenly apprehensive again.

"What I'm hoping I don't see are a lot of people and boats from Westbay, and maybe other places, heading to your settlement to demand some answers." His hand snaked out and closed around her wrist. "You're not going to convince anybody of anything if you give them only a piece of the truth. You have to offer up all of it. I've been thinking for a while that things aren't going so well as your people pretend. I sense too much during our meetings that seems false."

"I've been honest with you, Tarki."

"No, you haven't," he said. "I've felt your dishonesty." His fingers tightened around her wrist. "The last time I saw Moise, he looked like a man not far from death. I was sorry when you told me he was gone, but that he was dead didn't really surprise me. For a while now, I've been brooding on the fact that the only dome dwellers who have ever come out to trade with me are you and Awan and Jina and Mikhail, and Moise while he was still alive. I've spoken to other traders over the past few years, and it seems you're also the only ones they've ever seen."

"You couldn't have spoken to all of the traders." She paused. "After all, only a small number of your people trade with us, so it shouldn't seem strange that only—"

"Safrah, you keep trying to say as little as you can, after I've told you that doling out little bits of truth isn't enough."

She tried to pull her arm away. At last he let her go. "I made promises to the older ones," she whispered. "You're asking me to break them."

"Maybe you don't have to break those promises. I'll tell you what I think has happened up there among you dome dwellers. You've kept things going, but it's getting harder and harder. You haven't grown large enough in numbers to build any more settlements, because if you had, you would have been sure to brag about it, or we at least would have seen some sign of them. Instead, what I see for myself and hear about from others who have come near here are growing herds of cattle and horses and other wild animals out on the plains, animals that seem to be more numerous in the north and the east than they are in the south. And I've seen other wild creatures in the regions near the lake, small cats and the occasional pack of dogs that can only be the spawn of the domesticated animals that once lived in your settlement, since they bear no resemblance to the larger predators left on Home. You bring us no seeds and no grain. All you've offered in trade for some time now are recharged screens or wands and other such tools, things that I'm sure you couldn't have made yourselves. Your settlement's failing. Maybe it's already failed. How many of you are left?"

She was silent. Saying nothing was not breaking her promise, and to deny what he had said would be a lie.

"We may be few," she murmured, "but your people would be in danger if any of them moved against us."

"That I don't doubt. I imagine you still have plenty of weapons."

Admitting the truth to Tarki would be nothing compared to having to confess it to Ship. Her people were still the true descendants of humankind. Would that be enough for Ship to forgive them for their failures?

They continued south, with Safrah seated in the prow and Tarki in the stern, tending the rudder. The weather was warm enough that her long hair dried quickly as she combed it with her fingers. She had not put her pants back on, and she would have shed her tunic in this heat, had she been alone.

She had told Tarki most of the truth, without going into detail. He knew how few of her people there were, and that there were no older ones to guide them. He seemed more concerned about that lack of guidance than anything else. "It can be dangerous to be young," he had said, "dangerous to yourself and to others, too, because young ones often don't believe they can die."

"I know very well that I can die," she had replied.

"You told me before that you weren't that young. Anyway, I wasn't thinking of you. I was thinking about the youngest of your people, the ones that frighten even you." She had told him nothing about her fear, not even that much about Morwen and Terris and the ones who ran with them, but he had picked up on it somehow.

Something inside her was telling her that she had betrayed her people, that all the older ones would have cursed her for what she had revealed. Another part of her was saying that whatever might happen now was out of her hands, and that she must do what would best preserve her settlement and her people. She did not tell Tarki that the radio failed because someone among her people had destroyed it, but she wondered how long she could conceal that detail, which now seemed the most shameful part of the truth.

By dusk, Safrah could barely make out the tiny huts to the south. There were no boats tied to the dock at the outpost, and no sign that anyone was waiting there.

Pale tendrils of clouds were in the sky. Tarki steered his boat toward shore, dropped anchor near a bed of tall reeds, and refilled their waterskins. They sat on top of the deck to eat a supper of some of her dried fruit and meat.

"I'll keep watch," Tarki said after they had finished their food, "and wake you if I get tired."

"You're not going on to the outpost tonight?" she asked.

He shook his head. "We don't want to be there if somebody comes there during the night, and you don't want to be there if they're suspicious and angry and you can't offer them any reassurances. We'll stay here for the night. If anyone coming north happens to glance in our direction, those reeds should keep us hidden, as long as it's dark and cloudy like this." He sniffed at the air. "Wouldn't surprise me if we get some fog tomorrow." He peered up at the thickening clouds, then put a hand on her arm. "Go to sleep, Safrah," he said more gently.

She crept under the deck and pulled the curtain open to the cooler night air. Awan might have repaired the radio by now. Perhaps he, Mikhail, and Jina were already talking to Ship. Or they might have picked up nothing except the usual background noises, and concluded that Ship had not returned.

Please, she thought, not knowing what it was that she wished for now. She lay there in the dark, the floor hard against her back. If she could just return to the settlement, everything would be as it had been only a few days ago. She and her companions would save what records they could from the library, and then they would move to the eastern side of the settlement. They would find enough there to survive somehow, and could leave the younger ones to take care of themselves. Awan would finally fall in love with her. Or Ship would speak to them at last, and tell them how to save their settlement.

But Ship could not speak to them. Someone among her people did not want Ship ever to be able to speak to them.

"Safrah." Tarki spoke so softly that she could barely hear him. "Come out here." There was fear in his voice.

She sat up and crawled out of the cabin. Tarki sat in the bow, arms resting against a gunwale, gazing south. She looked up and saw a streak of bright light above the clouds, and moving in their direction.

Part of the sky was glowing. A band of dark blue clouds rippled with yellow light as a long metallic object dropped below the clouds and then glided slowly toward the outpost.

"What is it?" Tarki whispered. Even this far from the outpost, Safrah could hear a high whining sound that seemed to be coming from the thing that was flying down from the sky. "What could it be?"

She knew what it had to be—she had seen objects much like it in the records. Vehicles shaped like that one had brought her ancestors to Home. Her gorge rose in her throat; she felt sick with fear and despair.

Ship had judged them, she thought wildly. Ship had found them wanting and had decided to reseed Home with better human beings, people who would displace hers. She struggled to control her panic.

The whining sound abruptly cut off and the light died. Tarki cupped a hand around his right ear and leaned farther over the side of the boat. Safrah realized that she was holding her breath. She squinted, but could not make out anything near the outpost in the darkness. Then the light suddenly flared up once more, rose toward the sky, emitted a sound like thunder, and vanished.

"What was that?" Tarki asked, after a long moment.

"Ship has come back," Safrah said. "I know that now."

"What are you saying?"

"That's the kind of vessel that brought the first people here. It's true, Tarki. I've seen vehicles like it on screens, in our historical records. It has to mean that Ship has returned." She covered her eyes and sank down next to him.

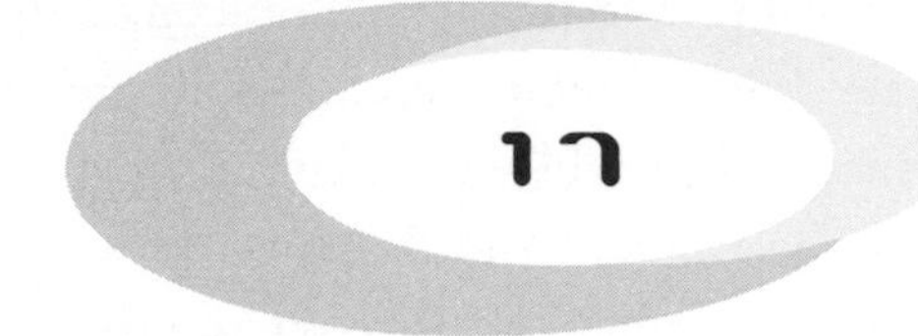

There was no place to hide. Safrah knew that, even as she pleaded with Tarki to flee as far from the outpost as possible. Ship could scan all of Home and send out probes; it could probably view or track anything it wanted to from orbit.

"We still don't know if Ship has left anyone there," Tarki said when she paused for breath. "Maybe it was only making observations."

"If Ship was only making observations, it would have sent a probe, and its probes don't look anything like what we saw. That was a vessel that carries people and cargo. We have to get away from here, Tarki. You could come with me to the settlement. We can find a place for you to stay. You've always been a friend to us, even if you're not—"

"—a true human being," he finished, and she heard a slightly bitter note in his voice.

"I didn't mean it that way."

"You meant it exactly that way." He paused. "Seems it hasn't yet crossed your mind that Ship might judge my people even more harshly than yours, if it's returned to pass such judgments on us. Oh, we've grown in numbers and settled in our villages, but we just hang on to what we have, content with knowing that the days that lie ahead will be much like those that have already passed. As far back as I can remember, I would wonder if that was the way we were supposed to live, if the people of Earth had gone to all the effort of building Ship to bring our ancestors here only so that we could lead our balanced, harmonious, and small-minded lives."

"It's better than fighting," she said.

"Oh, I suppose it is," he replied, "but a battle of some sort always seems to come sooner or later. My grandmother used to tell me that. When I'd object and tell her our lives were peaceful, she would tell me that we had just been lucky for a few generations or so." Safrah thought of the younger ones in the settlement, and the violence that seethed in them.

"The people of Earth sent Ship across the heavens," Tarki continued, "and we've never crossed the ocean. We haven't even wandered very far from this lake and the great river." He sighed. "I wish I could know even a little of what our ancestors knew," he went on. "When I was younger, I imagined that your dome dwellers had command of much of that wisdom. I chose the life of a boatman and trader because I knew that would bring me in contact with your people, and then I might learn what you know. All I found out in the end was that you know nearly as little as I do."

Safrah said, "I don't know what to do."

"If you want to run back to your tower and your settlement, I won't stop you, but you'll have to go there on foot and by yourself. Whatever's waiting for us at the outpost, I'd rather face it now than later."

Tarki handed her a waterskin. She drank and forced herself to stay calm. If Awan had repaired their radio, and Ship was now able to communicate with him, maybe whoever was at the outpost had only come there to help them. She did not want to think too much about why Ship might have sent people to the outpost instead of to a place closer to the settlement.

"You're right," she said. "We'll have to go to the outpost."

"And now that we've decided that," Tarki added, "I suggest that you go back to sleep. We can wait until dawn—I wouldn't want whoever or whatever's there to think we're trying to sneak up on the place."

It was still dark when Tarki woke her. She had not expected to fall asleep. Then she remembered what they had seen earlier that night, and fear shocked her into wakefulness.

Tarki lifted the curtain as Safrah slipped out of the cabin, then let it fall. "Aren't you going to get some sleep?" she asked.

"No. It'll be dawn soon." She glanced east, but clouds still veiled the sky and mist hovered over the lake. "We might as well get going," he continued, pressing what felt like a handful of nuts and dried fruit into her hands. "Eat this—I've had my breakfast already."

"I'm not hungry."

"Eat the food. You'll need it." He crept around the cabin toward the stern; she followed him. "Don't be so frightened, Safrah. Whatever happens, at least we may find out a few things we didn't know before."

"I brought a stun gun with me." She might as well admit that to him. "It's in one of my packs. I should go get it."

"Leave it where it is. Our weapons won't be of any use to us now." He pulled his rope and anchor out of the water, then sat down next to the rudder.

The fog in the east was growing lighter as the boat approached the outpost, moving slowly through the tendrils of mist rising from the lake. The doors of the two small cabins above the reedy bank were closed, and the windows shuttered. Whoever had been carried there was hiding, waiting inside for them.

Tarki steered the boat toward the dock, which was barely larger than a raft, then tied up his craft at one of the poles. "Come on," he said, and held out a hand to Safrah, who was still huddled near the rudder. She grabbed it tightly.

"Hai," Tarki called out as he leaped to the gunwale; she climbed up onto the boat's edge after him. "You can come out now." He let go of Safrah and jumped from the boat as she leaped after him to the dock. The reed surface swayed under her, nearly making her lose her balance. "We mean you no harm."

The doors of the cabins remained closed. Safrah could not even see the light of a lantern through the cracks of the shutters. Perhaps they were afraid. Maybe they were plotting an ambush.

"Maybe they don't understand our words," Tarki murmured. "Hai!" he shouted. "I am Tarki, son of Kadin, a boatman and trader. This dome dweller with me is called Safrah. You have nothing to fear—"

The door of the cabin nearer to them opened. A dark-haired boy with broad shoulders stepped out, followed by a taller companion.

She knew the smaller young man, even though he had been even smaller and younger when she last saw him. "Enli," she said, stunned at the sight of the young trader. The other boy also looked familiar; she could not recall his name, but was certain that she and her people had traded with him, too. "What are you— How—"

"Tarki?" a voice called from inside the cabin. "Then you must be—" A small, slender girl with a long black braid came through the doorway. "You don't know me, but I know about you. I'm from your village of Seaside and you're a cousin of mine. My name is Bian. I'm a great-granddaughter of Nuy and the daughter of—"

"I know who you are, child. I celebrated with Kwam and Tasu when you were born." Tarki hurried toward the three, then halted. "But how—"

A fourth person, a yellow-haired girl, followed the dark-haired girl out of the cabin. "Ship carried us here," Enli said, "in one of its shuttles."

"We were close enough to see the vessel that carried you," Tarki said.

"We were by ourselves when we first heard Ship's voice," Enli continued. "No one else knows we're here. Ship even made sure that there were no people nearby when it sent its shuttle for us."

"But why did Ship bring all of you to this place?" Tarki asked.

"To find out why no one in the dome dwellers' settlement has responded to its call," the taller boy replied, "and why its probes have seen no one outside their buildings and no crops or animals near the settlement. But that isn't the only reason." He faced Safrah. "Some of our people may already believe that yours are keeping any messages you might have from Ship a secret, and that you may even be trying to turn Ship against us. Some of them are likely to come to your settlement demanding answers. We promised Ship we would do whatever we could to avoid any conflict."

"We know your people have more weapons than we do," the girl named Bian said, "and we were afraid you might turn them against anybody who approached your settlement." She peered up at Safrah. "Why haven't your people answered Ship's call?"

"Maybe they picked up a call," Enli added, "and had their own reasons for not answering."

"But we haven't received any messages from Ship," Safrah said. "That's the truth. We couldn't have heard any message because our radio isn't working." She felt the force of what Tarki had told her earlier, that bits of the truth would not be enough. "And the reason it isn't working is that someone among us destroyed it."

All of them were staring at her now. Safrah bowed her head as shame bit at her. Enli and his companions had seen her people as more than they were only because they had been deceived. Now Ship had brought the four of them to this outpost because of her people's failures and weaknesses.

"But why would anybody do that?" the yellow-haired girl asked.

"I can't tell you," Safrah replied, "because I don't know who did it."

"But why now," Enli said, "with a strange new light traveling across the sky? Didn't it occur to you that it might be Ship?"

"No, it didn't." Offering large portions of truth was proving to be even more difficult than she had expected. "We hadn't been outside our domes and tunnels since the onset of the cold season, so none of us even saw that light until a little while ago. Whoever damaged the radio didn't know about that light, and didn't have any reason to think Ship might have come back."

"Then we should go to your settlement," the taller boy said, "and tell your people that Ship has returned." He reached into a small pouch that hung from a cord around his neck, then held out his hand; a round, silvery object rested in his palm. "You won't need your radio now. We can speak to Ship with this."

Tarki's eyebrows shot up. "Ship gave you that?" He stepped closer and peered at the object. "What is it?"

"Ship calls it a comm," the boy answered. "Ship told us to take it with us when we left the shuttle, but asked us not to use it until we'd accomplished whatever we could by ourselves."

"But why not?" Tarki said. "If you can talk to Ship with that thing, then can't Ship also talk to us?"

The boy nodded.

"Then we can avoid any conflict now, can't we?" Tarki said. "All we have to do is show that to Safrah's people, and they'll know—"

"What?" Enli interrupted. "They might think it's some sort of trick. Besides, she says that one of her people destroyed their radio, and she doesn't even know who. Somebody among her people obviously doesn't want any of the dome dwellers to be able to communicate with Ship. Whoever wrecked the radio might try to destroy this comm, too."

Tarki fingered his mustache. "Then we'll go to Westbay

and show it to everyone there before they get any more ideas about going north and confronting the dome dwellers. We can head to Lakeview and then downriver after that. We'll be able to talk to Ship and prove that we're as much a true part of its Earthseed as any of the people in the old settlement, and the dome dwellers won't be able to say a word against us."

"Tarki," Safrah muttered, stung by his words.

"I didn't mean you," he said, "or any of the others I've traded with, and once we've spread the word and spoken to Ship, we could send someone to your settlement to—"

"Stop it," Enli said. "Ship asked us not to use the comm until we'd settled everything among ourselves."

Tarki said, "That makes it sound as though Ship doesn't trust any of us."

"Seems to me it has good reason not to trust us," Safrah said. "You see that device, and the first thing you think of is using it for your own advantage, and I'm no better—I was thinking the same thing."

"Ship spoke to us for a while," Bian said, "and one of the things it said was that it was afraid contacting more people here might only cause more conflict. We promised we would try to avoid that. If we can, then Ship will speak to us again. If we can't, I don't know what might happen." She took a step closer to Tarki. "If we go to Westbay with you, we might only start more trouble." She looked down. "I think Ship means this to be a kind of test for us."

And if they failed it, Safrah thought, Ship might leave and never come back.

Bian lifted her head and turned to Safrah. "Would your people listen to us if we spoke to them? Would they promise not to use their weapons against our people if—"

"It may already be too late for that," Enli said. "Look." He lifted an arm and pointed south.

Safrah turned around, but could see nothing in the murky early morning light except an expanse of choppy dark gray water below the thinning fog.

Tarki let out his breath. "That's what I was afraid of," he muttered.

Safrah squinted, but could make out only a few tiny specks on the misty horizon. "What do you see?" she asked.

"Can't you—" he began to say. "But of course you can't—your people might as well be blind. There are more boats coming this way." He motioned to Enli and Bian and their companions. "Go inside and grab whatever you've brought with you. You're leaving on my boat, all of you." He paused. "I'll stay here."

"But you can't," Safrah protested.

"Somebody has to stay here to let them know what's going on, tell them about Ship. Maybe I can keep them here for a while, long enough for you to settle things with your people. We have to hope for that now." Tarki waved an arm at the lake. "Go."

The boat cut through the water, moving fast enough to create small waves in its wake. There was a chance that they had not been spotted through the fog, but Enli, who had taken control of the rudder, did not want to count on that.

"The fog's very thick now," he murmured, "and it's hard to see what you don't expect to see, but we should still get as far ahead of them as we can." Enli had told Safrah that the yellow-haired girl, whose name was Lusa, came from his village of Overlook far to the south. Bian and the taller boy lived in a village even farther south, one near the southern ocean.

"I know of that place," Safrah said. "It's called Seaside." She remembered the taller boy's name then; he was called Arnagh, and she had last seen him when he came to the outpost with the traders Tiri and Malcum of Seaside.

The four young people had carried small packs aboard that looked much like the packs she had sometimes found in abandoned domes. Both of the girls, sitting next to the packs, watched her in a way that made her uneasy. She realized that she was probably the first of her people they had ever seen. They were small, Bian over a head shorter than she was and Lusa not much taller than that, and both were slender and small-boned enough to make her feel awkward and much too large.

"How did Ship find you?" she asked.

"We were staying in Plainview," Lusa replied. "We'd come upriver to see if we could find out whether news about the light had reached the villages closer to your settlement. We happened to be out on the plain bordering Plainview when a flying thing that looked like a very large metal insect found us."

"Ship called it a probe," Bian added. "Ship spoke to us, and we told it that we were willing to go and meet with your people to find out why you never responded to its greetings."

All their lives had been devoted to hiding from these people, Safrah thought, to concealing what the dome dwellers were and keeping their secrets. What could she say to these four now that would prepare them for what they would find? Perhaps she could keep them away from the settlement, tell them that they would have to wait by the tower until she found out what was going on inside the domes.

Already she was thinking of ways to keep more of the truth hidden from them.

"The last time my aunt and uncle and I traded with your people," Arnagh said then, "Moise came to the outpost with Jina and Awan." He leaned toward her. "Moise didn't look so good the last time we saw him."

Safrah took a breath. "Moise is dead."

Arnagh sighed. "I'm sorry to hear it. And Awan?" He looked away for a moment. "And Jina and Mikhail?"

"They're all well."

"That's good to hear."

The girls were still observing her. Enli gazed ahead into the fog. Safrah rushed to fill the awkward silence. "Maybe Awan has even repaired our radio by now."

Arnagh reached into the pouch hanging over his chest and took out the comm. "I don't think he could have yet," he said, holding the device out to her. "Ship told us that if it heard anything at all from your people, it would let us know." He pointed to a tiny gem on the silvery surface. "We'd hear a soft humming sound, and that jewel there would start shining, and then we'd know that Ship was trying to speak to us."

Safrah gazed at the comm, knowing she had seen devices like it in the records; she wished now that she had paid more attention to those images. "Ship should have left something like this with your people," Arnagh said as he slipped the comm back into his pouch. "It could have left you a number of them, and we could have traded for them, and then your people and mine would both have been able to—"

"Ship wanted us to be self-reliant," Safrah said. "It didn't want to give us too many things that might fail and that we wouldn't know how to fix or make for ourselves." A feeling of hopelessness was settling around her that was as damp as the fog over the lake.

Bian and Lusa looked away from her, as if sensing her darkening mood.

The boat moved across the water in silence. Safrah got up and made her way past the two girls to the prow. The fog would lift soon, burned away by the morning sun. She rested one arm on the gunwale and stared out at the gray water. She would have to pick her words carefully, decide exactly how to tell these people how badly her settlement was doing and how few of her people were left. But that wouldn't even be the worst of it. Ship would learn of their failure as well, and might conclude that her people had failed in their purpose.

"Safrah." Arnagh had followed her. He offered her a brief smile as he sat down next to her. "I was surprised to see you in Tarki's boat."

"He didn't come to the tower to trade. He was there to find out what we knew, whether we were in contact with Ship. He turned on the beacon, and then he waited for somebody to come there and meet him. I told him I'd go as far as the outpost with him and left my cart at the tower."

"What were you going to do after that?" he asked. "I mean, if you hadn't found us at the outpost."

"I don't know."

"What do you think we should do when we reach the tower? Signal your people that we're there and waiting, or go to the settlement with you?"

"I don't know." She turned her head toward him. "I have to tell you this. You'll find out eventually, one way or another. My people aren't what you think. We may have bred true and preserved the true human genome, but that's about all we've done. There are very few of us left. All the older ones who reared us, Moise and all the rest, they're all gone—dead. Now it's only me and Jina and Awan and Mikhail and the young ones we've raised—thirty-one of them—and those younger ones are afraid of anything outside our settlement. They're afraid of the outside itself."

She heard him draw in his breath. A glance toward the stern of the boat told her that the sharp ears of his three companions had picked up her words.

"That must be why Ship saw no crops or animals near your settlement," Arnagh said.

"We have no crops or animals, unless you count the insects and rats we occasionally find in our tunnels."

"How do you live?"

"Our windmills and solar cells still provide enough energy for what we need," she replied, "and for recharging anything your people bring to us. We use any tools of ours that still work, one of which happens to be a food dispenser." She would not try to explain that piece of technology to him, since she barely understood it herself. "When we need something we don't have or have run out of, we can usually find it in one of the uninhabited domes."

"I never thought . . . I've been suspecting that your people weren't what we thought you were, but—"

"Moise made us promise that we'd never let you know how much we've lost and how weak we really are, but I had to break that promise. Tarki knows, because I told him, and now so do you."

No one spoke for a while. Then Enli called out from the stern, "And here we were afraid of a conflict. At least we won't have to worry about losing a fight, if there are so few of you."

Safrah heard the relief in his voice; he owed nothing to her people. "Don't be so sure," she said, feeling her anger rise. "Our young ones could still give you a battle."

"But there's no reason to fight now," Enli replied. "Tarki will tell the people coming this way what's happened, and also that we have a way of communicating with Ship. They'll know he's telling the truth. And if they still have any doubts, we can show them the proof."

Safrah said, "You're a fool." She could not keep her rage out of her voice. "Why should I assume your people won't try to overpower us, especially when they find out how few of us there are? Why should I believe you wouldn't take their side?"

"We didn't come here to fight," Bian objected.

"You might change your mind if you think you'd have something to gain. Let me tell you this. We know the region around our settlement, and you don't. We'd have the high ground. We'd see anyone coming from a distance, and a number of your people would fall before you even got close to our dwellings. And even if you got inside, we know the routes through the tunnels, and you don't. You might win out in the end, but you would trade some lives for that."

They aren't like us. She was hearing Moise's voice once more, reminding her of her obligations. They may look like us, but they haven't bred true. They've become something else; never forget that. If she had to fight these people to make up for her betrayal of her own kind, she would do that. Whatever she felt about Terris and Morwen and the others, she would have to stand with them against any outsiders.

"We should have stayed with that boatman Tarki," Lusa said, "and sent you back to talk to the other dome dwellers by yourself."

"I would have had to go with her," Arnagh said. Safrah glanced at him, surprised.

Lusa's lip curled. "So you two must be closer than I thought. I wouldn't have guessed."

Arnagh's face reddened. "It's got nothing to do with that."

"Stop it," Bian said. Safrah could hardly hear the girl's voice, but there was a fierce look in her tilted dark eyes. "We promised Ship we'd do whatever we could to avoid a fight, and look at us."

Safrah steadied herself. "I'm sorry." She said it quickly, to get it over with, even though she had nothing to apologize for and was still angry at all of them.

"Think of what Ship said to us," Bian continued. "It was worried that, if it returned, it would only make more trouble for us and for the dome dwellers. Maybe it was right to worry. Maybe it'll decide we're too much trouble for it to worry about us anymore, or that we were a big mistake and it's time to start over with some other Earthseed."

The same thought had come to Safrah. Enli made fists of his hands. Lusa bowed her head.

"There's this to consider, too," Safrah said. "Somebody destroyed our radio, and I don't know who among my people could have done that. I can be sure it wasn't Mikhail or Jina or Awan, but I don't know who of the younger ones might have done it or why. It could have been just a fit of anger, or somebody not really understanding what they were doing, but it might have also been somebody who wanted to make sure we'd never be able to talk to Ship."

They were all staring at her now, their eyes hard. "You keep talking of these younger ones," Arnagh said. "First you tell us that they can give us a fight, and now you're saying that one of them might have destroyed your radio. What kind of people are they, anyway?"

"We did the best we could, bringing them up," Safrah said, "but then we lost all our older ones, and the younger ones have been living apart from us for a while now. They go their own way, they don't listen to us, and sometimes I think they don't really care about anything. I'm afraid of them. You might as well know that. I don't know what they might do."

The fog had lifted. Maybe, Safrah thought, the younger ones weren't so wary of the outside as she assumed. Perhaps one or more of them had been sneaking outside for a while now and knew the night sky well enough to see that something new was crossing the heavens, a light that might be a sign that Ship had returned. Could that have provoked someone to destroy their radio? Were they that fearful of Ship's judgment?

"Safrah," Arnagh murmured, "I think you'd better tell us all exactly what we'll be facing when we get to your settlement."

18

The boat neared the tower as the first moon climbed in the sky. Safrah had finished telling the others about her people, and now she felt drained, ashamed, and even more fearful of what lay ahead. Once she had stopped talking, the others had begun to mutter about whether they should wait at the tower or head directly to the settlement, but nothing had been decided, and she had offered no suggestions of her own.

Enli steered the boat toward shore; Arnagh threw the rope and weight over the side. Enli had spoken longingly of his own boat, now far to the south, abandoned when Ship's shuttle had come for them. He and his companions had left all their possessions and supplies behind as well; all they had now were the packs of food Ship gave them after they had entered the shuttle.

Bian and Lusa gaped at the tower. "Your people built that?" Bian asked.

"Long ago," Safrah replied.

"I've never seen any building so tall," Bian said.

"Should we turn on the beacon?" Arnagh asked.

"No," Safrah replied. "I should find my cart and head back to my settlement."

"By yourself?" Enli asked, sounding skeptical.

"I should find out what's going on before taking any of you there."

"Or is it that you mean to warn them," Lusa said, "so they can prepare to defend themselves?"

"She didn't mean it like that," Bian said. "Can't you tell?"

"I'm thinking of your welfare," Safrah replied. "I don't want to take you to our settlement and have our young ones come after you before they find out why you're there."

The others were silent for a long time. "I'm sorry," Lusa murmured at last, drawing out the words as if she disliked having to make the apology. "I sense that you're trying to be honest with us, but I can smell your anger, too."

Safrah was as angry and unhappy with herself as she was with any of them. "I'll have to tell my friends that I broke my promises to them," she said. "I think they'll understand and forgive me, but I can't be sure."

"You shouldn't go alone," Arnagh said. "I'm willing to go with you. It isn't because I don't trust you, but . . ." She could not make out his expression in the darkness. "I've traded with your companions. I wouldn't be a stranger to them."

She did not want to let more time pass while they sorted this out. "Very well," she said. "Arnagh will come with me. The rest of you can wait here. If you see anyone approaching from the south, turn on the beacon."

"What about the comm?" Enli asked.

"You keep it," Safrah murmured. "Remember that someone destroyed our radio. We don't want to lose that thing, too."

Arnagh slipped the cord holding the pouch over his head and handed it to Bian. "I'll leave it with you," he said. "Take care."

The five of them waded to shore, packs across their shoulders. Lusa set down her pack and wrapped her bare arms around herself as she shivered in the cool night air.

Safrah dropped her pack. "You can sleep inside the tower," she said. "It'll be warmer there."

"Aren't you going to get any rest?" Bian asked.

"No. There isn't time." Safrah rummaged in her pack, pulled out some pants, and put them on, not caring if the four watched her. "We should leave now."

"Safrah—" Bian paused. "Good luck." Arnagh clasped Bian's hands briefly, then turned to Safrah.

She led him toward the cart. Already she was thinking that when they were closer to the settlement, it might be wiser to leave the cart and approach on foot. Those inside would be expecting her to return to the greenhouse with the cart and then go up the hill through the tunnel that led to the library. Perhaps she should not assume that only her friends would be waiting there for her.

She threw her pack into the cart and got in. Arnagh seated himself at her left and braced himself with his hands on the panel in front of him as the cart moved forward.

"Don't worry," she muttered. "I won't rush. These carts can't move that fast anyway, and I'm not about to risk having an accident in the dark."

Arnagh sat back. "I'm all right."

She hoped to return to find that Jina and Mikhail were still scavenging among the abandoned domes, then go to the library to discover that Awan had repaired the radio and was speaking to Ship. She could hope for that, and then whatever happened afterward would be out of her hands, determined by Ship. That thought brought both relief and fear.

The cart crawled slowly over the ground. "Just so you know," she said, "I've got a stun gun in my pack. The older ones told us we should keep them with us when we went to trade, even though we never needed them—not even against wild animals—but it's just as well that we have one now."

"I thought you might have one," he said.

"How?"

"Awan had one with him, last time I saw him. He didn't mean for me to see it, but he admitted that he always brought one along when he left your settlement. I was annoyed at first, but I couldn't get that angry with him, since my aunt and uncle always had one hidden on their boat. Not that they thought they'd ever really need it, not during a trade, anyway, and they hadn't fired it in so long that it might not have even worked."

"We could have recharged it for you."

"Then we would have had to let you know that we'd brought one along and hid it. Tiri and Malcum said trading to recharge a screen or a light wand was one thing, but a weapon—that might have been awkward."

Refusing such a request would have roused suspicion and distrust among the traders, but now that Arnagh mentioned it, she could not recall any of the traders ever having brought a stun gun to them for recharging. She wondered how many of the weapons his people had and how many of them still worked.

"It's not as if we need them most of the time anyway," Arnagh continued. "We make our own weapons for hunting, spears and bows and the like."

They had survived in their way, even making their own tools, while her people still clung to what their ancestors had left them. "Awan was careless to let you see his weapon," she said.

"I can't blame him for doing the same thing Tiri and Malcum did, and I knew he wouldn't use it against me. He will be safe where he is, won't he? Those younger ones you talked about wouldn't do anything to—"

She said, "He'll be safe."

"I hear fear in your voice."

"He'll be safe."

Morning had come by the time Safrah and Arnagh reached the northern end of the lake. They had stopped once to relieve themselves and a second time because Arnagh had insisted that she get some sleep while he kept watch. She still felt tired, her eyelids gritty, but she slept soundly for the short time Arnagh had allowed her.

He was asleep now, sprawled on his right side on the seat next to her, his head bumping against her thigh. He woke as the cart rolled to a stop.

"Hai," he mumbled, then sat up and rubbed at his eyes.

She gazed north, barely able to make out the tiny bulges of the distant hills of the settlement. "Those towers with long arms," Arnagh said, "are those your windmills?"

"Yes. We'll leave the cart here and go the rest of the way on foot. It won't take us that much longer than if we rode there, and if anything has gone wrong, we'll be safer if they don't see us coming."

"Maybe you'd better tell me more about those kids you're so afraid of."

"They're strong. Some of them have very good aim with their stun guns. I've seen some of them stun rats with just one shot before they cut their throats—we'd have a lot more vermin around if it weren't for them." Safrah paused. "They come to our home, the dome I share with Jina and Mikhail and Awan, and if we're not there, they go inside and mess with our things, because they know we can't do much about it."

"Mess with your things?"

"Break a cup or a plate. Piss in a corner and use whatever black gunk they've found in the corridors to write insults on the walls."

Arnagh shook his head. "But why do they do things like that?"

"I don't know. It could be worse. It's not like they've ever really hurt any of us. Oh, a few of them used to hit back or start punching one of us when we were only trying to get them to behave, but they'd calm down afterwards, and we were more than a match for them when they were smaller."

"But not now."

"No, not now." She got out of the cart and faced him. "You're as tall as I am, and you're the tallest one of your people I've seen. But a couple of them are even taller than you, and bigger, and others are almost your size. And they're afraid of your people and they hate them." She had contributed her share to that hatred, fear, and distrust, passing on all the tales the older ones had told about those who might seem human but were only sacks of alien microbes and genes. She had glimpsed some of her own humanity in Tarki and other traders, and yet had said nothing of that to the young ones, even after all the old ones were gone. By then, the children might not have believed her anyway.

"So they won't be that happy to see somebody like me."

She nodded.

Arnagh climbed out of the cart, then grabbed his pack. "Let's think about how to get Awan and your other two friends out of there."

19

Bian sat outside the tower, keeping watch, shivering in the cold night air. She lifted her hand to touch the pouch that held the comm. She feared Ship now, even more than she had feared it when its shuttle had swallowed her and her companions and then disgorged them near the two cabins of the outpost.

She had been in too much shock, too numb and too disoriented, to be badly frightened when she found herself inside a brightly lit space filled with what looked like thick sleeping mats draped over posts and surrounded by screens, lights, and pale bare walls. She recalled a voice telling her to stretch out on one of the cushioned mats, after which straps had suddenly snaked around her to bind her to the mat; she had managed to suppress a scream. Except for a brief moment of pressure against her chest and an odd feeling of lightness, she had sensed no movement. She had been surprised to stumble out of the strange vessel after what seemed a very short time to find herself near a cabin she had never seen before. Given the unusually cool night air and the presence of the lake to the west, that cabin had to be a good distance north of Plainview and the great river.

But none of that had frightened her nearly so much as her thoughts of Ship did now.

How would Ship judge them? She did not doubt that Ship would come to some sort of judgment about all the people of Home. If they did not succeed in avoiding conflict, that judgment was likely to be harsh. Would Ship punish them in some way, or simply abandon them?

At her right, the door to the tower slid open. In the dim light cast by the moons low in the western sky, she made out the shadowy form of Enli. "Have you seen anything?" he asked.

"No." There was no sign of boats or anything else approaching from the south, almost no sounds except for the occasional rustling of grass when the wind picked up, and the lapping of the water against the shore.

Enli sat down next to her. She had pulled on long pants, a tunic, and one of the longer coats she found inside the tower. The three of them had found rolled-up mats smelling of dampness and mold. The room inside the tower was smaller than Bian had expected; either the walls were thicker than she realized, or there was empty space behind them. They had moved around the room, tapping the wall with their fingers, until Bian picked up a slightly different sound. She had tapped the wall again, then slapped it with her palm, and suddenly the wall had slid open to reveal another room with more mats and shelves of clothing.

Enli had not known about the hidden room. Although he had harbored suspicions about the inside of the tower and the room that seemed too small, all he had ever done before was to enter, press the panel that would light the beacon at the top of the tower, and then leave for the outpost. This room was yet another secret that the dome dwellers had kept from them. It was far from the most important one, but the mats in that room were cleaner and thicker than the others, and the clothes welcome against the cold.

"Is it always this cold here?" she asked.

"It can get even colder than this," Enli said, "but it's warmer most of the time. In the summer, it can get as hot here as in Overlook. Aren't you going to sleep?"

"It'll be dawn soon," she replied. "I got enough sleep before, while Lusa was on watch." Lusa had been sitting next to Enli's mat after waking her, and Bian caught a glimpse of the longing, hopeful expression on Lusa's face before she turned off her light wand. Even with all that had happened, she was still enmeshed in her feelings for Enli. She was probably wishing that, whatever happened, he would eventually decide to pledge himself to her after all.

Bian felt a twinge of jealousy and envy, and then it passed.

Whether Enli had ever felt anything more than a passing attraction to her no longer mattered. She did not long for him the way Lusa did.

The pouch around her neck vibrated slightly, and then she heard a barely discernible hum.

"What is it?" Enli said.

"The comm." She slipped the device out of the pouch and cupped it in her hand. The gem embedded in the comm was glowing. "Ship," she whispered, "can you hear me?"

"Bian." Ship's voice was low and deep. "I have had a message from the settlement."

She glanced at Enli; he stared at the comm. "I heard the voice of someone called Awan," Ship continued. "He told me that the radio in his settlement had been damaged, and that this was why no one had responded to my messages. His voice was faint, so it seems his repairs were only partly successful. I heard him for only a few moments before the signal was lost."

"Lost?" Bian said, bewildered.

"Would you care to hear what he said?"

"Of course," Enli replied.

"Ship," an unfamiliar voice said then, "I heard your message, just picked it up. Can you hear me?"

"I can hear you," Ship's voice replied in an alto.

"My name is Awan," the unfamiliar voice continued. "I'm inside our library, in the place we call Ship's Room, at the place where our ancestors made their settlement. Don't know how much longer this radio will work. Can you still hear me?"

"I hear you."

Bian heard a crackling sound. ". . . can't believe I'm actually talking to you," the strange voice went on. "We didn't even know that you might have returned until . . ." The comm emitted a whine. ". . . when we saw an unfamiliar light moving across the sky . . . can't . . . believe . . . talking to you . . . don't know what to say."

"What has happened to your settlement?" Ship said. "Why have I seen no signs of a thriving community there?"

There was no reply, only more crackling.

"At first I thought that your people must have abandoned the place long ago," Ship continued, "since there were signs of human habitation elsewhere along the river to the south of your settlement. But that didn't explain why your windmills still turned and why the probe I had landed near your settlement picked up an occasional flash of light. What caused you to retreat inside your dwellings?"

"I'll try to explain when . . . don't know if I can . . . stop! No, don't! Stop!" His last word was a cry. A loud crack followed, and then silence.

"That's where his message ends," Ship said.

"He's afraid," Bian said. "I could hear how frightened he was." Safrah had sounded almost as fearful while talking of the younger dome dwellers. Bian had wondered that such a tall and commanding young woman, who carried herself with the same air of authority as Nenet or Duman, could be afraid of anything, but the slight trembling in her voice, the acrid scent of fear, and her nervous intermittent pulling of her long black hair had given her fearfulness away.

"What could have frightened him?" Ship asked.

Bian hesitated. Enli shook his head at her. She looked at him and said, "We have to tell Ship what's happened."

His shoulders sagged. "I suppose so."

"One of the dome dwellers found us where your flyer left us," Bian said. "Her name was Safrah, and she came there with one of our people, a boatman named Tarki. She told us that someone among her people damaged their radio, and that she thought it was one of the younger people who she and her closest comrades seem to fear. She's afraid of what else they might do."

Ship said nothing. After a long silence, Bian continued, "Safrah's on her way back to her settlement now, with Arnagh.

Tarki stayed behind at the outpost, where you left us, because people in boats are on their way there and he's afraid they mean to confront the dome dwellers. He said he'd try to delay them. We came here in his boat, and now . . ." She swallowed. "What should we do?"

Ship did not reply.

"There's nothing we can do," Enli said.

"Safrah and Arnagh didn't hear what we heard," Bian said. "They don't know that Awan got a message out to Ship and to us. You heard how he sounded."

"That might have just been because his radio was failing."

"You know better than that. He didn't sound frustrated or exasperated—he sounded afraid."

Enli let out his breath. He seemed about to speak and then he pointed at the comm. She knew what he was thinking: Ship was listening to everything they said.

"Ship," she whispered, "can you help us? What should we do?"

"I cannot tell you what to do," Ship replied in a tenor voice. "All I can do now is wait until I am able to communicate with all your people with some hope of not creating even more suspicion and fear among you when I do."

Bian's chest tightened. So they could do nothing except wait here, worry, and imagine what might be happening inside the domes or around the outpost. She had come all this way, only to be a helpless onlooker.

"If you have nothing more to say to me," Ship said, "simply press the light on your comm. If you want to contact me again, press that button, and I will be able to hear you and speak to you."

"I understand," Bian said. "I'm about to press the light." She pushed it with her thumb; the light winked out.

Ship could not hear them now. "There has to be something we can do," Bian said.

"I think we should just stay put," a voice behind her said. Bian started, then turned to see Lusa in the open doorway, her hair looking almost white in the faint light of dawn.

"How long have you been standing there?" Enli asked.

"Long enough to hear what you said and what Ship told you. Surely you heard me open the door."

Bian had been so intent on listening to the comm that she had been deaf to anything else. "We can't just stay here," Bian said.

"I don't see why not," Lusa replied. "Maybe that dome dweller will get his device working again. Then he'll be able to talk to Ship and we'll be able to find out more about what's going on there. We can decide what to do after that."

"I think we should go to the settlement now," Bian said. "Safrah and Arnagh might need us."

"What could they possibly need us for?" Lusa came toward them and knelt next to Enli, sitting back on her heels. "You heard what that big girl said. She didn't want us going there with her. She only brought Arnagh along because he'd traded with them before."

"She didn't hear what we just heard. If she had, she might have made a different decision. Don't you see? She and Arnagh might be in danger. You know what she said about the younger dome dwellers."

"Bian might be right," Enli said, looking at Lusa.

"We have to tell them what we heard," Bian continued. "Safrah might have some ideas—"

"How are you going to catch up with them on foot?" Lusa asked.

"We don't have to go on foot." Bian kept her eyes on Enli.

"We can take Tarki's boat. You saw how slowly that cart was moving when they left. A boat could move faster than that."

"You don't even know where we'd be going," Lusa said.

"I know that if we keep going north, we'll eventually reach the settlement. That's all we have to know." She leaned toward them. "You got us here, Enli. You could get us there."

"Haven't we done enough?" Lusa asked. "We don't owe the dome dwellers anything. Look at all the secrets they kept from us. How do you know they would have told us anything about Ship if they'd been able to talk to it first? They probably would have given Ship a lot of gab about how they are true humanity and we aren't. Maybe they will, once they can get their radio to work. Besides, we won't be of much use to anybody if we get stuck in the middle of something we can't handle. Those kids Safrah was talking about—she made it sound like they might try to hurt or even kill us."

"We won't be of any use if we wait here," Bian said. "Safrah and Arnagh might need our help. We could at least try to catch up with them and let them know what we heard on the comm."

"But Tarki might need us, too," Lusa said. "What if he comes here needing to prove what we told him to others?" There was some sense in what Lusa was saying, but Bian was picking up the other girl's fear and distrust. Enli sat there, saying nothing, clearly unable to decide what to do.

"Then stay here," Bian said. She stood up. "I'll walk there if I have to." She stomped into the tower, found the pack she had taken from Ship's shuttle near the entrance, grabbed it, and hurried back outside.

Enli was suddenly in front of her. "You can't go alone. I'll go with you and pilot the boat."

Lusa quickly got to her feet. "And leave me here all alone?" The fear in her voice was overlaid with anger.

"You said Tarki might need us," Bian said. "You can wait here in case he shows up." She took off her coat, pants, and foot coverings, stuffed them into the pack, and walked down to the lake, forcing herself to wade into the cold water. She glanced back only long enough to see Enli going inside the tower for his pack.

Her teeth were chattering by the time she got a few steps into the water. Her toes curled against the muddy bottom as she forced herself to keep going. Behind her, she heard Enli gasp as he entered the water. The dark shape of the boat loomed before her. She grabbed a rope hanging over the side and pulled herself up, bracing herself against the hull with her feet, then rolled over the side into the boat.

Enli waded toward her, his pack tied to his back. Lusa stood on the shore, her arms hanging at her sides. "Don't leave me here!" she shouted. "I'm coming with you!" She ran toward the tower, then emerged with her pack.

Enli climbed into the boat, breathing hard. He dropped his pack on the deck, then began to pull up the anchor. Bian watched from the prow as Lusa poked a bare foot into the lake, stepped back, hesitated for a moment, and then waded into the water.

The boat cut through the water, moving faster than Bian had thought a boat could travel. Enli had told her and Lusa that such a speed was likely to drain the craft's fuel cells of power, but that they stood a chance of reaching the end of the lake before the engine died. He did not know exactly how far north of the lake the settlement lay, but it had to be close enough to the tower for the dome dwellers to be able to spot the beacon.

Bian sat in the prow, the wind lashing at her face. Enli had taken the boat far from shore and did not expect any obstacles to slow them or endanger their craft in the deeper water, but he had told her to keep watch anyway. Lusa sat near her, arms wrapped around her legs, chin resting on her knees. One look at the expanse of the lake in the early morning light had been enough for her: Being surrounded by the plain of water clearly terrified her.

The early morning sun was already warming the air. Bian shrugged out of her coat. The shrubs and reeds along the eastern side of the lake seemed closer than they had been only a little while ago. To the north, she glimpsed a patch of dark green and, beyond it, a faint grayish shape that might be hills. In another moment, she was able to make out a tiny dark speck against the green bordering the lake; that had to be Safrah's cart.

She turned toward Lusa. "Tell Enli to slow down!" she shouted above the wind. Lusa nodded, rose into a crouch, and scurried past the left side of the cabin toward the stern, keeping her head down. In a few more moments, Bian saw that no one was near the cart; apparently Safrah and Arnagh had abandoned it.

The boat slowed. Bian rested her arms against the edge of the craft, keeping watch.

The boat, guided to the east by Enli, drifted slowly among patches of reeds toward the shore, where several poles jutted up from the water. At Bian's right, Safrah's cart sat in the grass several paces up from the shore, near a ditch. It was on flat ground that seemed to be part of a pathway running north and south through the grass.

"I'll try to get us as close to land as I can!" Enli shouted from the stern. "We can tie up at those poles." Bian and Lusa had already taken out a pole from inside the cabin, in case it was needed to push the boat closer to the shore. Tarki's boat was too large for oars to be that useful, and the small mast and sail aboard the boat would not help this close to land, even if they had known how to rig them.

The boat was moving very slowly now as the solar cells gave out. Bian glanced toward the back of the boat, where Lusa sat at Enli's feet. There was a loud scraping sound as the hull bumped against a couple of the poles sticking out of the water.

"We're close enough," Bian called out. "I can see the bottom of the lake. Any closer, and we might get stuck in the mud."

Lusa looked up. Bian saw terror in her pale eyes before she lowered her head again. Bian began to wish that Lusa had stayed behind at the tower.

"Just as well," Enli said. "It's going to take a day of sunlight to restore power to those cells."

"I can't," Lusa said then. "I can't."

Bian crept toward the stern. Enli frowned, then put a hand on Lusa's shoulder. "What is it?" he asked.

"I should have stayed at the tower," Lusa said. "It wouldn't have been so bad, waiting there."

Bian sat down next to her. "We're all scared."

Lusa shook her head. "No, not like me. I don't sense that kind of fear in you. You're afraid, but you can put it aside. I'm terrified." She was silent for a while as Enli rubbed her shoulder, clearly trying to calm her. "I didn't tell you this before. I was too proud to admit it, and Enli was kind enough to keep it to himself. The farthest I ever went from Overlook before this trip was to go out riding on the plain, and even then I always stayed close enough to keep our village in sight. The only reason I rode after you was because . . . because . . ." She fell silent again.

"Because of Enli," Bian suggested. The boy's face reddened.

"Because of Enli. Because I was jealous. Because I couldn't bear the thought of his being with you. My mother and father tried to convince me not to leave, but I wasn't about to listen to them, and Duman and Zan didn't try to stop me, and were even encouraging me to go. Anyway, I was just going to follow the river north, so what could possibly happen?" She sighed. "And it was all right at first, until I looked back and couldn't see Overlook anymore. I was terrified all the way to Shadowridge. Nearly turned back then, but I had to keep going, or—"

"Lusa." Bian sat down next to her. "You seemed so—" She tried to grasp the right word. "Brave," she said at last. "So fierce."

Lusa managed a smile. "Oh, I could forget how scared I was for a little while, when I was angry enough, or jealous and upset enough, or just tired enough."

"That must be why you couldn't sense how afraid I was." Bian pressed her lips together for a moment. "I never left my village before this trip either. I never even got as far as wandering the plain or going out to hunt with others. I stayed even closer to my own village than you did to yours."

Lusa's eyes widened. "I wouldn't have thought . . ." She shook her head again. "You had me fooled."

"And you fooled me."

Enli was staring past them. "I see two people to the north," he said. "They're too far away for me to make them out clearly, but they must be Safrah and Arnagh."

Bian got up and peered over the cabin. She saw them now, two tiny specks to the northeast against the distant misty hills.

She sat down again and said, "I'm going to talk to Ship." She took the comm out of her pouch and pressed it with her thumb. "Ship," she murmured, "we're at the northernmost end of the lake, not far from the settlement. Can you hear me?"

"Yes, I can hear you," Ship's baritone voice replied.

"Safrah and Arnagh have abandoned their cart and are heading toward the settlement on foot. Has Awan contacted you again?"

"No," Ship said.

"We're going to go after Arnagh and Safrah," Bian continued, "and let them know what Awan told you. Do you have any advice for—" She paused. "Do you think that's what we should do?"

"I can't answer that," Ship said.

Of course Ship could not—or would not—answer her question. She glared at the comm, thinking of how useless a device it was at the moment. "Then I suppose there's no point in talking to you," she said, pressed the light, and thrust the comm into the pouch.

"You ought to be more careful of what you say," Lusa said. "You don't want to anger Ship."

Bian stood up. "Let's go. We're wasting time." Lusa looked down. "Can you make it?" Bian said more gently.

"I don't know."

Bian knelt next to her. Enli watched them with narrowed eyes. "Would it be easier for you to wait on the boat for us?" she asked.

"I don't know." Lusa lifted her head. "No. I'd just be worrying even more, staying here by myself. I'll go with you, and I won't let you down."

20

The sun was low in the west as Safrah led Arnagh toward a small grove of evergreens. She had decided to head east and then north around the hills, keeping her distance from the settlement in case someone was outside, looking for her at the greenhouse or near the top of the western hill. Her comrades were probably wondering why she was not already back, and they might not be the only ones waiting for her. Terris and Morwen probably already knew she had left the settlement but not yet returned.

"We'll wait here, under the trees," she said as she sat down, "until it gets dark. We'll take shelter after that."

Arnagh looked to the southwest, up at the hills. The expression on his face was a mixture of awe and melancholy as he gazed at the ruins of domes on the eastern hill and then up at the windmills. At last he settled himself next to her in the shadows under the trees.

"I think," she continued, "that it might be better for me to go in by myself. Once I find out how things are with my friends, I can come back for you."

He shook his head. "I don't like that idea."

"Look, I told you, I don't know how they'll react when they see you. Just seeing you with me means they'll guess that I told you more about us than I should have." The pain of her betrayal was biting at her once more.

"You said it might be dangerous," he said. "You seemed a lot more concerned about the younger dome dwellers than about your friends. You might need me there."

"I told you, I don't—"

"I also think that if you bring me along, you won't have any trouble convincing your friends that you did the right thing—one of your friends, anyway."

She frowned. "What do you mean?"

He leaned forward and peered into her face so intently that she was forced to look away. "You were honest with me," he said. "I think I can be honest with you. The last time I came here to trade—"

She lifted her head. "The last time I came to the outpost," he went on, "Jina and Awan came with Moise to trade with me and my aunt and uncle. Awan stayed behind with us while Moise and Jina went back for our goods."

She nodded, remembering, because that was the last time Moise had left the settlement to trade with anyone.

"Awan and I spent the day together on our boat," he continued. "We crossed to the other side of the lake, and—" He fell silent for a long time. "Let me put it this way. I realized

I was beginning to care for him, and he said he felt the same way about me."

She heard the tremor in his voice. "You thought of him as your friend," she said, wondering why he seemed so upset; perhaps it was only that he felt shame in thinking of one of her people as his friend.

"You could put it that way," he replied, in a way that disturbed her. There was too much feeling in his voice. He reached into his pack, took out the waterskin that he had filled at the lake, drank, then handed it to her. "Do you want some food?" he asked.

"I don't know if I can eat anything."

"Try. We haven't eaten for a while." He handed her a packet. In its leaflike wrapping, it looked like something the food dispenser might have produced. She tore it open and bit into meat and vegetables laced with unfamiliar spices, realizing how hungry she was.

They ate in silence. Arnagh had said that he cared for Awan. He could only mean that he felt they might become friends, but something in his voice had her thinking of stories she had viewed long ago, in the library's historical records, about the ancient peoples of Earth. These stories had struck her as romantic until Moise had found out about them and told the librarian not to show her those records anymore. There had been one story about two young women who had become such close companions that they had pledged to live together for all their lives. There was another about two men who had fought a great battle together, a battle that had ended with one sacrificing his life for his comrade and the survivor dying of a broken heart.

Moise had not found the tales romantic. He had been

angry with her for reading them and looking at the visuals that accompanied them, and angry at himself for not restricting access to them earlier. Those were not the sorts of Earthpeople who had built Ship, who had dreamed of seeding other worlds; they were among those whom Ship's builders were trying to escape, human beings who had diverged from true humankind. Safrah's duty and that of her companions lay in bringing up the settlement's young ones and having children of their own, in preserving true humanity.

The sun was setting. She inched toward her pack and rummaged inside it for her stun gun. She might need the weapon if any wild animals came closer to the settlement than they normally did.

Arnagh lifted his head and cupped a hand around his eyes. "What's that?" he said, pointing at the hill of domes to the west.

She squinted, then saw a patch of light on the western hill, on the side of the slope overlooking the greenhouse. The dusky light was making it hard for her to see clearly. "I don't know."

"Now I can see—" Arnagh was suddenly on his feet. "Fire."

"What?" She looked up at him, bewildered.

"It looks like a fire," he said. "I see flames, and smoke."

She saw something else now, a small dark plume rising on the hillside. The patch of light grew brighter. Her throat constricted, making her unable to breathe for a moment.

"Can you see it?" he asked. "What is it?"

"It's the library," she forced herself to say. "That's what's burning. The library's on fire. That's where the radio is."

"You told me that Awan—"

She said, "He might still be there, trying to talk to Ship."

She heard his breath catch. Arnagh moaned, his voice laden with fear and grief. "Awan!" he cried out, and before Safrah could stop him, he ran out from under the trees and into the grass, racing toward the distant fire.

21

The two hills were strewn with the husks and ruins of domes. Between the hills lay a broad field of dark green grass.

A small speck of light suddenly blossomed on the hill to the west. Enli stopped, then said, "Something's burning."

Bian halted next to him, Lusa at her side. "I thought they stayed inside their domes," Lusa murmured. "Why would they need to start a fire outside?"

"Maybe Safrah and Arnagh are trying to signal us," Bian said.

Enli shook his head. "It doesn't look like that kind of fire. Part of a building's burning. And they wouldn't need to do something as dangerous as starting a fire to send a signal. Something's wrong."

Arnagh might be near the fire, Bian thought, fearing for him. He and Safrah might be inside that part of the settlement, trapped.

"Let's go," she said. "They might need help."

"We should wait here," Lusa said. "It could be dangerous to get any closer. Maybe the dome dwellers are just lying in wait for us. Maybe—"

"Their eyes aren't as sharp as ours," Enli said. "It's dark now—if we stay low in the grass, they'll have a harder time spotting us."

Lusa said, "Could be a trap."

"They can't know we're out here," Bian said. "Come on."

They moved slowly through the high grass, treading on the ground lightly, keeping low. They were still a couple of hundred paces from the hills when Bian heard a swishing sound up ahead, and then what sounded like a soft whimper. Enli, who was leading the way, thrust out his arms.

They hunkered down, pressing close to one another. "Somebody's out there." Enli's whisper was so soft that Bian barely heard him. He held Lusa's wrist with one hand while hanging on to Bian with the other; holding them back.

Bian heard another whimper. Somebody was up ahead, moving through the grass toward them. "Stay there," a voice called out. "Be quiet."

She smelled fear. Someone wailed. The wail rose to a shriek, and then there was the sound of a slap. "Shut up!" The hoarse voice was that of a child. "I'm just as frightened as you are."

Enli's grip tightened around her wrist. Dome dwellers were out there, and they might be armed.

Enli rose slightly in the grass, then suddenly darted to the right, knocking Lusa aside. A burst blossomed through the air in his direction, confirmation that the dome dwellers carried weapons. Enli swerved to the left, drawing another burst.

She smelled Lusa's terror now. The other girl lay on her stomach, hands over her head. Bian hurried after Enli, keeping low in the grass. "Stop!" she heard him call out. "We won't harm you." A third burst hummed through the darkness. Bian held her breath, afraid that Enli had been hit.

She crept toward him, then heard him clear his throat. He was a dark shape lunging through the grass. There was the sound of someone else gasping, and then screams.

"Let me go!" That was the same child's voice Bian had heard before. There was the sound of a hand slapping the ground. Somebody slammed into Bian, knocking her off her feet, then collapsed next to her.

"I've got a weapon." That was Enli's voice. Two dark shapes huddled in the grass near him, and there was another small creature at Bian's side, whimpering. A child, she thought, and one that stank of sweat, urine, and the odors of a compost heap. "I'll shoot if I have to, so if anybody else has a weapon, you'd better put it down now." She heard the nervousness in his voice.

Bian's nose wrinkled. One of the dark forms near Enli rose to its feet. "We had to get out of there." That was the first voice she had heard, and it apparently belonged to a child that was almost a head taller than Enli. "Morwen was going crazy." Enli took a step forward and the tall human shape crumpled to the ground.

"We won't hurt you," Bian said, hoping that she could keep that promise. The child next to her scurried toward the other dome dwellers.

"I started sneaking out a while ago," the child continued. "Couldn't stay out for more than a few moments at first, but it got a little easier. Then after a while I could get down the hill, and a couple of times I made it as far as the field. Nobody found out. At least I don't think they did."

Bian could see now that the shadowy form was a girl, with small breasts under her tattered shirt. The girl pulled the other two children closer to her.

"What were you doing out here?" Enli said. The girl did not answer. "Does it have anything to do with that fire?"

The girl's head shot up. "I didn't see the fire. Morwen was saying that . . ." She coughed, then wiped at her face. "I didn't think he'd do it, though."

"Do what?" Enli said, and Bian wondered that he was able to sound so calm.

"Set fire to the library. He and Terris said they'd . . ." Her voice trailed off. "Who are you, anyway?" she whispered.

"People," Bian replied.

"No, you're not. You're—"

Bian waited. The girl remained silent. There was a rustling of grass behind her; Lusa suddenly plopped down next to her.

"Sorry," Lusa whispered. "I couldn't help—" Bian poked her in the arm, silencing her.

"Listen," Enli said at last, "we followed one of your people here, a girl called Safrah. We only want to help. You have to tell us what's going on." Bian noticed that he said nothing about Ship.

"After Jina and Mikhail came back with the stuff they found for us, Morwen followed them to the library. Terris went with him, along with a few of the others. I followed them there because I could see Morwen was really angry about something, even if he wouldn't tell me what it was. He was shouting and yelling, asking where Safrah was and why they hadn't brought more stuff back, and then he started saying things I didn't understand." The girl was slurring some of her words and biting off the ends of others. "Things about the radio, about what was going on in the library, about all the stuff nobody would tell him or lied to him about. Then he said that if Awan didn't come out, he'd burn him out." She gasped for breath. "That was when I decided to get out of there. Rhee and Farkhan followed me." She suddenly sat down, still holding the other two children. "Tried to send them back inside, but they wouldn't go. We're safer sticking together, anyway. They've never been outside before."

"I want to go home," one of the children murmured.

"What's your name?" Bian asked.

"Paola," the girl replied.

"Can you take us to your home? Can you lead us inside your settlement?"

"But why?" The girl shook her head. "There's nothing you can do."

"We won't know that for sure," Enli said, "until we see for ourselves." The bright speck of light on the hill had grown into a larger, flickering light. "Please," he continued. "You have to guide us."

Arnagh was almost across the field before Safrah caught up with him. He slowed to a stop as she grabbed at his arm. He was panting; she gulped down air.

"Wait," she managed to say after catching her breath. "You don't know the way inside."

They were close enough now that she could see that part of the library's roof was ablaze. The hard, metallic walls were not likely to burn, but over the years, the holes in the roof had been patched with fabric, grass, ropes, and beams of wood.

"Can you put it out?" Arnagh asked.

"It should burn itself out," she said, but wondered how long that would take, how much might be lost before the fire died. "But if anybody's inside . . ." She steadied herself. "Follow me."

She led him toward the greenhouse near the bottom of the western hill. They could avoid the tunnel that connected the greenhouse to the library and enter the settlement through the back way that led to her dome. She hoped her friends were there, but doubted that they would be. Even if they had been there when the fire started, they would have run to the library and tried to save what they could. They would be thinking of the radio as well as the records. She hoped that Awan had given up on his repairs some time ago and left Ship's Room before the fire had started.

She reached under her tunic and took out the stun gun tucked under the waistband of her pants. She was trying to think of ways that the fire might have started by itself, and could not think of any. That somebody would have set the fire seemed unthinkable, but she wouldn't have thought that anybody could destroy the radio, either.

Arnagh glanced at her. "You're expecting trouble."

"Yes."

They skirted the greenhouse and climbed the northern side of the hill. Safrah could no longer see the dying fire, but there were traces of smoke and burnt rope and grass in the air, along with other smells she did not recognize. She thought of the shelves of records: Surely the tapes, disks, and chips would be protected by the cases that held them. She wondered if the heat could grow intense enough to damage them. The librarian might already be lost. Without the librarian, it would be difficult, maybe impossible, to locate and open many of the records.

Thinking about the records was distracting her from worrying about Awan. He should have been able to get out if he had fled at the first sign of a fire. But he might have risked his own safety to protect the radio.

In the dark, disoriented by her fears, she almost missed the entrance to her dwelling. "Here it is," she murmured as she stopped at the closed doorway. "Stay behind me." She pressed her hand against the door. It slid open slowly, then stopped before it was fully open. The mechanism was failing, but she could not worry about that now. She took aim with her weapon. "If there's any trouble—"

Arnagh sniffed. "There's nobody inside," he said.

"How can you tell?"

"I'd smell them."

She lowered her weapon and crept inside. Maybe Jina, Mikhail, and Awan were waiting for her in their dwelling, door barred against the others, safe. But even as that hope came to her, she knew how unlikely it was. They would be at the library, trying to put out the fire, not hiding here.

They came to the end of the short passageway and she pressed her hand against the wall. A crack opened in the wall and she used it to push the sliding door open the rest of the way. She entered the room that Awan and Mikhail shared, not bothering to push the door shut after Arnagh was inside.

She led him through her room and into the common room. The door was closed, and the pole they had used as a brace stood against the wall.

"What now?" Arnagh asked.

"We head for the library," she said. She pawed through the items on one of the shelves until she found the two stun guns that were usually left there, hidden in a recess behind a few plates. "Here." She handed one of the weapons to Arnagh and slipped the other under her belt. "You might need this."

He took the weapon. She glimpsed the fear in his eyes as he looked at it.

She opened the door and stepped into the corridor. The smell of smoke and ash filled the tunnel, and breathing the air hurt her throat. Arnagh motioned to her, tore a piece of cloth from one of his sleeves, and handed it to her before tearing off another strip and holding it to his face.

Covering her nose and mouth with the cloth, she ran toward the library, following the tunnel downhill, afraid of what she would find. The light was murky in the tunnel, obscured by the smoke. She came to the library's entrance. The door was open to a room filled with smoke.

She stumbled inside and looked up. There seemed to be holes in the roof, but the smoke was so thick and the dim lights so faint that she could not be sure. She led Arnagh past shelves of records over a floor covered with blackened clumps, pieces of burnt wood, and patches of smoldering rubble. A shelf in front of Ship's Room had been knocked over onto its side. She crept around small boxes of records and a piece of debris fell from the roof, nearly hitting her.

The piece of cloth fluttered from her hand. "Awan," Arnagh called out, and then, "Awan!" She saw the other boy then, lying under a broad beam just outside Ship's Room. Ashes sifted down from the roof. Arnagh stumbled toward Awan, heedless of the shower of ashes and the shards of debris covering the floor.

"Awan." He knelt by the boy as Safrah hurried to his

side. Awan, lying on his back, did not move or even open his eyes. There was a bloody patch on his forehead, and the beam had pinned him to the floor.

He's dead, she thought wildly, but then she saw his eyelids flutter. "Awan," she whispered.

Arnagh said, "We have to get him out of here."

Safrah hovered over Awan. Something hit the floor behind her with a loud thud; she turned and saw a large slab of charred tile. They would have to move Awan, even if it injured him further. None of them would be safe in here until the fire had completely burned out, and maybe not even after that.

Arnagh dragged the beam off Awan. The cloth he had tied over his mouth now hung around his neck. "Grab his feet," he said.

"Wait." She gestured at a plank lying near them. "Let's slip that under him and carry him out. We don't know what kinds of injuries he has. You don't want to make things even worse."

Arnagh nodded. They moved slowly, sliding the plank carefully under Awan as more ashes filtered down from above. Then they lifted the plank, Arnagh holding the end at Awan's head while Safrah held on to the end with his feet. Their burden was heavier than she had expected. Arnagh backed slowly toward the doorway. Safrah struggled with her end, but forced herself to ignore the pain in her shoulders and back.

Somehow they got him into the tunnel just outside the doorway, then lowered him to the floor. "Can you do anything for him?" Arnagh asked.

"A scan would at least tell us how badly he's hurt." There was a scanner in her dome, although Jina was more skilled at interpreting its readings than she was.

Arnagh knelt. "I can guess what's wrong with him." His hands moved lightly over Awan's body. "A head injury, possibly a fractured skull, and maybe a couple of broken ribs. From the sound of his breathing, the smoke's affected him, and one of his lungs may be punctured, too. There might be more injuries to his back. I asked if you could do anything for him."

"I don't know enough about healing," she whispered. "The older ones didn't have time to teach us everything they knew." Jina and Mikhail had not been in the library with Awan. Now she wondered where they were.

Arnagh sat down next to Awan. His eyes gazed past her; he seemed to be holding back tears. "Listen," she whispered. "I have to look for Jina and Mikhail. They would have been here trying to put out the fire and save Awan unless something else—" Her throat tightened. Jina and Mikhail would have been here unless something else had prevented them from going to the library. "I have to find them. Will you wait here for me?"

He was silent. Awan might be dying, she thought. At least he would not have to lie there alone.

"Go," Arnagh said at last.

"Keep your weapon handy. And use it."

He pulled the gun she had given him out of his belt. "Go," he repeated.

Someone had destroyed the radio, had tried to destroy the library, and had nearly killed Awan. She realized then where Jina and Mikhail had to be, if they were still unharmed.

Safrah stood in front of the closed entrance to the dining hall. Her throat was so tight and her mouth so dry that for a moment, she was afraid she would choke. She pressed her hand against the door, then quickly stepped aside.

The door slid open slowly; its mechanism was failing, too. She kept behind it, concealing herself from those who were inside, and held her breath. There was the sound of footsteps; someone was approaching the entrance.

"Come in, Safrah." That was Morwen's voice. "That is you waiting out there, isn't it? It can't be anyone else."

She did not move.

"Come in," Morwen repeated. "Jina and Mikhail are waiting for you."

He would think that she had come back to the settlement alone. He could not know that an outsider had come with her. "Are they all right?" she asked, remaining out of his sight.

"Of course they are. Why wouldn't they be?"

She said, "I have a weapon."

"I'm not surprised."

"Are you going to shoot me as soon as I show myself?"

"No. Why should I? And you better not aim at me." He sounded tired, maybe even a bit fearful. She might be imagining that; she had to remain on guard.

She crept toward the open entrance, then moved into a crouch. A few paces inside the room, Morwen sat on top of a table, a weapon in his hand, pointed at her. He had not fired; but he did not have to. Terris was behind him, holding another weapon. In the back of the room, Jina and Mikhail sat on the floor, their backs to the wall, their knees up, their wrists bound to their ankles. Seven younger children were near them, ignoring the captives, playing some sort of game on a screen. Riese, the girl holding the screen, moved her fingers over the surface and then handed the screen to Vinn, the boy sitting next to her.

"Mikhail said you didn't come back with them, because

you went to meet some traders," Morwen said. "You must have come here from the library. You would have seen the fire while you were on your way back."

"I went there," she admitted. Jina lifted her head; Safrah noticed the bruise on her cheek. Jina and Mikhail would be worrying about Awan; she wondered what to say. "I found Awan there." She kept her eyes on Morwen. "He's badly injured."

"He shouldn't have been in there," Morwen said. "Told him to get out of there, and he wouldn't come out. It's his own fault."

Mikhail looked up. His face was bruised, and there was dried blood at the corner of his mouth. "You shot him," he said.

"Shut up," Terris said, waving his weapon.

"He was messing with the radio," Morwen said, glaring at Safrah. "Think I didn't know about that? Think any of you fooled me that last time you were all there in Ship's Room? You didn't want us to know what you were doing. You didn't think we'd ever find out."

"I don't understand," Safrah said, bewildered.

"Yes, you do. You wanted to make sure we'd never be able to talk to Ship if it ever did come back. You didn't want Ship to come back and be able to talk to us, to tell us what to do instead of you. You wanted everything to just be the same as it always was, with all of you telling us what to do."

He blamed them for destroying the radio. That was what had sent him into his rage. He had gone to the library thinking that Awan was in Ship's Room taking the radio apart, instead of trying to repair it.

"Awan was trying to fix the radio," she said. "You have to believe me. Somebody else tried to—"

"Liar!" Terris shouted. "You were always going to the library, acting like it was your place and not ours."

"You could have gone there any time you wanted," she said. "We tried to get you to go there more often."

"Go there to do what? Sit around and have you tell us we should look at this or that? Talk about how much we don't know and have to learn? Think any of that matters to us?"

Talk was pointless, but at least it gave her a chance to try to figure out what to do now. She wondered where the rest of the younger children were. Most likely they were in the next room, which had once been a kitchen, asleep on the floor, but they might be in the tunnels, shooting rats or hiding from one another as part of one of the games they often played.

She could tell Morwen and Terris that Ship had returned, and that they no longer needed the radio to communicate with it. Knowing that might be enough for them to release Jina and Mikhail. She would have to tell them that she had brought an outsider here, but she did not think they would react well to that, with their fear of anything from the outside.

One of the younger ones had sneaked into the library and taken the radio apart; that much was clear. Yet somehow she did not think any of the youngest children could have done it.

"Well, you can't go there now yourself," Terris went on. "You don't have much of a library left now, and it's all Awan's fault." He glanced at Morwen, then back at her.

Morwen or Terris had destroyed the radio. Maybe they had both wrecked it together, although it seemed more likely that Morwen had torn it apart by himself. It seemed so obvious to her now, as she forced herself to look into Morwen's contorted, angry face. Ship had abandoned them, and

Morwen had struck back at the only part of Ship that remained with them. He believed Ship would never return, so it would not matter if he destroyed the radio. Maybe he had not been thinking any of that, or thinking at all, and was only lashing out at what was left of Ship. Fear of angering Terris would have made him keep his secret, and he could now blame Awan for what he had done himself.

"Awan's hurt," she said. "He may be dying." Terris flinched at her words; Morwen continued to stare at her. "We have to help him."

Morwen's eyes narrowed. "He brought it on himself."

"If he dies, I'll hold you responsible. I won't forget it. You'll pay for it, too, I promise you that."

He looked fearful for a moment, the way he did when he was little and she had scolded him, and then his face hardened once more. "Oh, I don't think I will. I don't think you're going to do anything about it, either." He gestured at her with his gun. "Now get over there and sit down."

She did not move.

"You heard me," he said. "You can't do anything now, and you know it. Shoot me, and Terris shoots you. Or the other way around." He laughed in a high-pitched giggle. "So you better do what I say. You saw what happened to Awan. Now get over there and sit down."

She had no choice. She surrendered the weapon she held. He flashed a grin at her and pointed at her waist. "Lift it," he said.

"What?" she asked.

"Your shirt. Pull it up." She pulled her tunic above her waist and he reached for the other weapon under her belt. She dropped her shirt and walked past him toward the back of the room, her head down, defeated.

22

"We can use this entrance," Paola whispered. "I'll go in first."

They stood in front of a flat metal wall near the foot of the western hill. Bian looked up at the hillside. Above them, the fire she had seen earlier had died. She hoped that Safrah and Arnagh were safe.

Enli gripped Paola's shoulder, restraining her. "Exactly where are you taking us?" he asked.

"To the library," Paola replied. "I don't think Terris and Morwen will be there now. They would have gone back to the hall where we stay."

Lusa came up behind them, holding on to the two small children by their hands. Paola turned around. "Can you wait here with Farkhan and Rhee?" she asked. "They won't be so scared if you're with them."

Lusa nodded.

"We'll come back when we know it's safe in there," Enli added. Bian sensed that Lusa was still very frightened, but she was hiding it well, and even keeping the two small children calm and quiet.

Paola pressed her hand against the wall. It slid open with a creaking sound that made Bian want to cover her ears.

Paola led them inside. Bian found herself in a dimly lit tunnel that smelled of mold, damp dirt, and traces of smoke. Enli tensed, clearly apprehensive. Bian wondered how anybody could live like this, enclosed and hidden from the outside.

They followed Paola through the tunnel. The smell of smoke grew stronger, along with the odor of burnt wood and rope and a faint smell of sulfur and metal. The tunnel sloped upward. Bian kept close behind Paola, whose swift pace and long legs were making it hard to keep up with her. The girl disappeared around a bend in the tunnel. Bian knew from the thicker odor of smoke that they had to be near the library. She heard a soft cry up ahead, and then a familiar voice: "Who are you?"

That was Arnagh's voice. "My name's Paola," the girl replied. "Who are you?" Bian hurried ahead with Enli and found Paola in a wider space in front of an open doorway. Arnagh, with a weapon in his hand, stood over a young man who lay on top of a plank.

"Bian!" A smile flashed across Arnagh's face and then faded.

"The girl brought us here," Enli said. "She's one of the dome dwellers." Arnagh lowered his arm but kept his weapon aimed at Paola. "You can trust her—I think. Where's Safrah?"

"I don't know. She told me to wait here, but she hasn't come back."

Bian went to Arnagh. "This is Awan," he continued, gesturing at the unconscious young man. Arnagh's eyes glistened; he averted his gaze for a moment. "He needs help." He looked at Paola. "Can you help him?"

Paola shook her head. "He's dying," Arnagh said, and Bian sensed his torment. She reached inside the pouch hanging around her neck and took out the comm.

"What are you doing?" Enli asked.

"Be quiet." She pressed the button. "Ship," she whispered, "this is Bian. We're inside one of the tunnels in the settlement where the dome dwellers live. Can you hear me?"

A few seconds passed. She feared that Ship might not be able to hear her voice from under the hill, and then the comm's button began to glow.

"I can hear you," Ship replied.

"I'm here with Enli, Arnagh, and a dome dweller called Paola, who led us inside her settlement." Paola let out a gasp. "Awan, the one who picked up your message, is also with us." Bian swallowed. "He's badly hurt. Can you help him? Can you tell us what we can do to help him?"

Ship was silent. This was useless, she thought. Ship was too far away to help anyone, and even if Ship could tell them what to do, Bian could tell just by looking at Awan that it was not possible to save him. Even the healers of Seaside would not have been able to do much more than give him some water steeped in herbs to ease his pain and aid his passing.

"Please," she said.

"She's talking to Ship?" Paola's eyes grew wide. "You mean Ship has come back?"

Enli nodded. Paola slumped to the floor and covered her mouth, looking terrified.

"There's nothing we can do for Awan," Bian went on. "Ship, I beg you—if there's anything you can do—"

"Listen to me," Ship said in its baritone voice. "Can Awan be moved?"

"Yes," Bian answered.

"Then you must carry him outside and wait with him there. I will send a vessel. Keep the comm open so that I can speak to you while you wait with him. You will have to describe his symptoms so that I can decide how best to treat him. I will do what I can."

Bian's hands trembled; she could only hope. "Thank you, Ship." She went to Paola and helped her to her feet. "We have to carry him outside."

"I heard." Paola still looked awed and frightened.

Arnagh lifted one end of the plank that held Awan, while Enli lifted the other. Bian and Paola stood on either side, supporting the plank while Enli turned and braced it against his back. "Got it," Enli muttered. "Let's go."

They moved slowly back down the tunnel, taking care not to jar Awan. Bian heard his labored breathing; his face, under the bruises and blood, was much too pale.

"I think Morwen must have beaten him, and shot him, too," Paola said. "Maybe slapped him around after he shot him, because Awan would have given him a fight otherwise. Those guns can really hurt you if you hit somebody more than once. If he hit him more than a couple of times, he might be really messed up."

"I know," Arnagh said. Bian concentrated on holding up her side of the plank, until she glimpsed an opening at the end of the sloping passageway. They emerged from the tunnel into the grayish green light of an overcast dawn, and lowered Awan to the ground.

Lusa was there waiting, the two children asleep at her side. She lifted a finger to her lips, warning them to speak softly, then whispered, "What's going on?"

"This is Awan," Bian said, "and he's hurt. Ship told us to bring him outside and wait here with him."

Lusa sucked in her breath. "You spoke to Ship?"

"I asked if it could help him," Bian said, "but I don't know if there's anything Ship can do."

"Then why—" Lusa began.

Arnagh shook his head at her, then turned toward Paola. "We have to find Safrah and let her know what's happened."

Paola shrank away from him. "Listen," Arnagh went on, "when Safrah left me, she was expecting trouble. She said she was going to look for her friends."

"If they weren't able to get away from Morwen and Terris," Paola said, "then they'd be with them in the dining hall."

"Can you lead us there?" Arnagh asked.

"You don't want to go there," Paola whispered, "not now, not with Morwen acting like he was."

"I have to make sure that Safrah's all right." He seemed about to grab her, demand that she do as he asked, but instead he held out a hand. "Please."

Paola took a breath. "I'll take you inside again, but if anything bad happens to you, just know that it's your own fault and not mine."

Arnagh nodded.

"And if I have to choose sides, I'll take Morwen's side and not yours. I don't want him coming after me when you're gone from here."

"Let's go," Arnagh said.

"Wait," Bian said. "I'm coming with you." She did not entirely trust Paola. She pulled the cord that held her small pouch over her head and handed it to Lusa along with the comm. "Stay in contact with Ship, answer any of its questions, and do whatever it tells you to do."

"I will," Lusa said, "but—"

"We'll get back here as soon as we can." Bian turned away and followed Paola, Enli, and Arnagh into the darkness.

Safrah kept silent after Terris bound her wrists, not daring to say anything to Jina and Mikhail. She found out, when the door behind her opened and a child wandered out from the kitchen, that other children were sleeping there. The child grabbed some food from the dispenser and disappeared inside the kitchen again, so there was no chance to find out how many children were in that room.

The door to the dining hall was still partly open; maybe that mechanism had finally failed. Terris lay on a mat near the entrance, sleeping. Morwen still sat on the table, on guard. Once in a while, he glanced back at them. Did he intend to keep them there like that, bound and unable to escape?

Safrah worked at the ropes around her wrists, trying to loosen them, but Morwen and Terris had tied them tightly. She leaned closer to Jina. "Are you all right?" she whispered.

Jina nodded. "I'm fine." She grimaced. "Wish I could use the latrine, though."

"Me, too," Mikhail added.

Morwen's head whipped around. "Shut up!" he shouted.

"I wasn't talking to you!" Safrah shouted back. Jina shot her a fearful look. "Any chance we could relieve ourselves?"

"No." He pointed his weapon at her. "You'll just have to hold it."

Mikhail frowned. "He doesn't care," he said in a voice loud enough for Morwen to hear easily. "You've seen what a slob he and the rest of them are—he'd just piss all over the floor if he couldn't—"

"I told you to shut up." Morwen waved his gun. "If you start giving me trouble, I'll shoot you just to keep you quiet."

Mikhail sighed. He looked tired, and his face sagged with hopelessness. Jina leaned back against the wall and closed her eyes; Safrah saw that she was struggling against tears. They had given up; she saw that in their faces. They thought they were alone, with no one else to help them. She longed to tell them about Arnagh, about the others waiting at the outpost, about Ship.

Arnagh might decide to search for her when she did not come back. He might already be looking for her, and sooner or later he would probably find his way through the tunnels to this place. She did not know what Morwen intended to do with them, but he had shot Awan. He would not hesitate to shoot an outsider, or even kill one.

The only way she might be able to warn Arnagh would be to keep Morwen talking. With his sharp hearing, Arnagh should be able to hear Morwen at a distance. He would know then that he would have to approach this place very carefully. He had a weapon, so he might be able to disarm Morwen and Terris if he took them by surprise. Safrah could not think any further ahead than that. Even if Arnagh's companions became curious enough after a while to come looking for him, it was likely to be too late to do anything for Awan.

Stop thinking, she told herself; just do what you have to do.

"There's one thing that puzzles me," she called out.

"Thought I told you to shut up," Morwen muttered.

"I just wanted to ask you something." She bowed her head slightly, trying to look cowed. "About the library."

"What about the library?"

"Why did you try to burn it down?"

Mikhail stared at her, clearly puzzled by why she was asking Morwen about that now. "I told you why," Morwen said slowly, "because Awan wouldn't come out. Are you getting stupid?"

"How was burning down the library going to help?"

"Thought it'd force him out of there."

Safrah sighed. "But you were angry because you thought he was messing up the radio, so why—?"

"Just shut up!" he shouted.

Terris moaned, then sat up on his mat. "Can't you be quiet?" he mumbled. "I'm trying to sleep."

"What I'm saying," Safrah continued, "is that if you were so mad at Awan because you thought he'd damaged the radio, why did you try to destroy the whole library?"

"I told you to shut up!" Morwen was screaming now, his face red.

"Wouldn't that just mean that the radio could never be repaired?"

Morwen hopped off the tabletop. "Shut up!"

"I mean, you can't even go inside the library now," Safrah continued. "It's too risky. A really good storm would probably bring down what's left of the roof. If you were so angry at Awan because you thought he was taking the radio apart, you could have just shot him, left the library alone, and maybe somebody else could have got the radio working again."

Morwen darted toward her. Something struck her on the side of the head, dazing her, and she realized that he had hit her with his weapon. She felt dizzy, stunned by the blow.

"Keep talking," he said, leaning over her, "and there'll be some more of that." His voice seemed to pound against her head.

"Morwen!"

Safrah's head throbbed. She glimpsed Paola standing in the doorway. She wondered what she was doing there, why she was not with the other children in the kitchen. Then a burst hit Terris. He crumpled to the floor as another burst struck Morwen.

She saw Arnagh step through the entrance, and then the floor rushed up to meet her.

Paola had convinced the children to come into the large room, but they were still huddled against the back wall. A few of them looked frightened, but others glared in a way that made Bian glad Arnagh had his weapon trained on them. Enli had taken two guns away from the unconscious boys and given one of them to her, but a few of the taller children had guns tucked under the waistbands of their ragged shorts.

Bian finished untying the bound arms of the young woman. The young man, already freed, knelt next to Safrah, loosening the ropes around her wrists. He turned her over, and Bian was shocked to see how sallow and pale her face was.

"She's hurt," the young man said, gesturing at the patch of bloodied and matted hair near Safrah's left temple. "Safrah, can you hear me?" Safrah's eyes remained closed.

The young woman knelt next to him. "We have to get her back to our dome."

"What happened?" Bian asked.

"Morwen hit her on the head with his weapon," the young woman replied. "Hit her so hard that he knocked her out."

"Listen," Paola was saying to the children, "no one's going to hurt you, understand?" Bian glanced toward her. The children seemed wary of Paola, and a couple of them fingered the weapons at their waists.

"We have to get out of here," Arnagh said, still gazing at the children. "Jina, you and Mikhail can carry Safrah to—" He paused. "Paola led us here, so I'm not sure how to get back there. We came uphill, so you'll have to go downhill. You'll have to carry her outside."

The young woman pushed her long dark hair off her face. "Outside?" she asked. "But why—"

"We don't have time to explain," Bian interrupted.

"Just keep going until you come to an exit," Arnagh said. "You want to come out on the southern side of this hill. Look for a girl with yellow hair—she's out there with Awan."

"Awan?" The young woman raised a hand to her mouth. "He's all right?"

"I don't know." Arnagh looked away. "I hope so. Someone's with him, looking out for him. Now get out of here while you can."

Jina and Mikhail lifted Safrah by the arms and feet and carried her toward the entrance. Enli's eyes moved from side to side as he watched the children. Arnagh took a step backward, and then another. Bian kept near him as the three of them backed toward the door, covering Safrah and her two companions. She wondered how long it would take for the two boys lying on the floor to revive, perhaps to come after them.

One of the smaller children let out a shriek; another began to cry. Still another let out a scream of rage that terrified her. One of the larger boys suddenly knocked Paola out of his way. Arnagh aimed his weapon; a burst struck the boy and brought him down.

"Stop it!" Paola shouted. Bian could not tell if she was screaming at the children or at Arnagh.

"Run," Arnagh said.

Bian turned and ran through the open entrance into the tunnel, Enli at her heels. She was several paces away from the open doorway when she stopped and looked back. Enli was right behind her; Arnagh was backing through the doorway, still trying to cover them.

She turned away and ran. Safrah's comrades, now holding her upright between them with her arms flung over their shoulders, were staggering through the tunnel up ahead. Safrah seemed to be conscious now; she stumbled along between her comrades, and Bian saw her fingers tighten around their shoulders.

The mustiness and closeness of the tunnel frightened Bian. She heard footsteps behind her and glanced back. Enli and Arnagh were following her, but more slowly; Enli waved her on. She caught up with the others and kept behind them, hoping that none of the crazed children would follow them, expecting to hear their belligerent screams at any moment. She held on to her weapon, wishing that she knew how to use it.

They came to a fork in the passageway and Safrah's companions chose the tunnel to the right. That was not the route they had taken earlier with Paola, but Safrah's comrades were familiar with these tunnels; they had to know where they were going. She waited until Arnagh and Enli caught up with her, then led them after the others. In a few more moments, they followed the three dome dwellers through an open doorway and into the light.

They stood on the slope of a hill. Above them, pale gray clouds drifted across the green morning sky. Below, near the foot of the hill, she saw Lusa's blond head. Lusa sat with her arms around the two children; Awan still lay on the plank, unmoving.

"What now?" Jina asked, still holding up Safrah. "Where do we go?"

"Down there." Enli pointed at Lusa and Awan. "And then we wait there with them until Ship sends us the help it promised us."

The two hanging on to Safrah gaped at him. "It's true," Safrah said in a weak voice. "Ship has come back to Home."

"I can't believe it," Mikhail said.

"Come on," Enli said. "We have to get down there and away from this entrance before the others come after us."

"They won't come outside," Jina said. "They're too afraid. Morwen might get as far as this doorway, but even he—"

"Wait." Arnagh was gazing south, toward the lake. Bian looked toward the distant gray expanse and saw dark specks on the water. Boats, she thought, probably the same ones Tarki had seen from the outpost.

"What is it?" Jina asked.

"There are boats on the lake," Arnagh replied. "More of our people are coming here."

"They'll think we were deceiving them," Safrah mumbled in her faint voice. "That we were communicating with

Ship and hiding it from them." She shook off the arms of her companions, although she still seemed a bit unsteady on her legs.

Bian heard a sound behind her. Arnagh spun around and aimed his weapon at the still-open doorway. "Don't shoot," a voice called out from the darkness.

Paola crept outside, her hands out. "You got them really angry," she said. "They're going crazy in there. I was afraid to stay."

"Will they follow you?" Arnagh asked.

"I don't know. Terris was moving a little. He and Morwen are really going to be mad once they recover."

"Are you coming with us?" Bian asked.

"I don't know." Paola wrapped her arms around herself. "Yes. Do I have a choice?"

"Yes. Come on," Arnagh muttered. Jina was already descending the hill, Enli at her side. Mikhail, guiding Safrah with one arm, followed her. Arnagh led Paola down the slope as Bian trailed after them watching Paola, still not entirely trusting her. She focused on Paola's back, not wanting even to glance in Awan's direction, afraid that if she did she would see that death had already taken him.

"Look," Arnagh said then, "up there." He was pointing at the sky. Bian lifted her head.

A strange light shone at the edge of the thick gray clouds to the east. The edges of the cloud turned a bright gold, and then the light grew so bright that Bian had to shade her eyes. Paola dropped to the ground, whimpering, and covered her head with her arms. The sound of a distant hum grew into a low roar that beat against her ears.

The long silvery vessel dropped through the clouds, a much larger ship than the one that had carried her and her friends to the outpost. Bian waited as the shuttle glided in with a roar and landed in the field of green grass below the hill. The roaring sound broke off so suddenly that Bian feared it had deafened her until she heard someone moan.

Paola rocked back and forth, still moaning. Arnagh and Enli moved slowly along a weed-covered trail among the domes as they descended the hill, followed by Safrah and her two friends. Bian reached for Paola's arm and pulled her to her feet. "Come on."

"What is it?" Paola grabbed at Bian, nearly pulling her to the ground.

"Come on." She held on to Paola as they stumbled down the hillside. Lusa was on her feet, the two children clinging to her legs. Bian forced herself to look at Awan. His eyes opened slightly and then closed; his fingers clutched at his shirt. He was still grasping at life.

Ship's vessel awaited them. An opening formed in its side and expelled a ramp.

Enli and Arnagh, aided by Jina and Mikhail, bore Awan through the high grass toward the ramp. Lusa followed them with Paola and the children. Safrah, hobbling unsteadily next to Bian, seemed stronger. Bian had cleansed her wound with water from her waterskin, but the tightness around her lips showed that she was trying to ignore her pain.

Lusa glanced back and then halted, waiting for Bian and Safrah to catch up with her. Paola hurried ahead, heedless of the children, apparently wanting nothing more than to get aboard Ship's vessel as quickly as possible. The children scrambled after her, wailing as they cried out her name.

"Here," Lusa said as Bian and Safrah approached. She

held out the pouch with the comm. "Take it." She pressed it into Bian's hands. "I won't need it now."

The comm seemed to move in her hand. Bian slipped it out of the pouch and saw that it was glowing.

"Ship," she said.

"Get aboard as quickly as possible," Ship said in its alto voice. "I'll tell you what to do for Awan once you're inside the shuttle, but the sooner he is inside my infirmary, the better his chances will be."

Lusa turned away and hurried toward the vessel. The two children followed Paola up the ramp. Arnagh, Enli, and the two other dome dwellers had already disappeared inside with Awan.

Safrah stared up at the craft's opening. "Go," she said to Bian. "I'm staying here."

"But why?" Bian asked.

"I can't just leave the rest of the children behind, not with Terris and Morwen there." Safrah bowed her head. "And there are your people, too, Tarki and the others. What about them? They'll leave their boats and come here looking for us. If they start searching inside the tunnels and domes, the young ones will give them a battle, one they won't be expecting. They'll be at a disadvantage. Some of them will be hurt, and some may die. They have to be warned."

Bian looked toward the craft, then back at Safrah.

"I can't go with you," Safrah said.

"And I won't leave you here by yourself." Bian lifted the comm to her lips. "Ship," she said, "the others are all inside your craft. Safrah and I are staying behind."

Ship did not answer. Bian realized that she had been

expecting Ship to argue with her, but there was no time, not if Awan's life was to be saved.

The ramp withdrew into the vessel, and then the opening abruptly vanished. She stood with Safrah and watched as the shuttle rose.

23

Bian and Safrah followed the pathway that ran along the sides of the old ditch. Safrah's head throbbed, but she forced herself to keep moving. The intermittent bursts and flickers of light that she had seen while stumbling through the tunnel with Jina and Mikhail were gone, but there was a film over her eyes, and the ground under her feet felt as though it might give way at any moment. She had lied when she told Bian that she was feeling better, that Morwen's blow had not injured her that much. By now Bian had to know that she had lied.

Safrah now regretted her hasty decision. Bian would not have been here if she had boarded the shuttle; she would have followed Safrah aboard. They might have been resting inside Ship now, in one of the rooms she had seen in the records. There might have been a chance for her to heal, and time enough to return later to warn Tarki and his people about the dangers they would face at the settlement.

No, she told herself; she could not have counted on that. She might have come back to a battle raging inside the settlement. She wondered how Ship would have judged her and her people then.

"There are over thirty boats out there," Bian said. They were close enough to the lake for Safrah to see that for herself. Most of the boats were still out on the water. Only a few people had come ashore, one of whom she thought might be Tarki. She squinted, but could not see the distant figure well enough to be sure.

Bian slipped an arm around Safrah, who let the smaller girl support her. She needed to stop and rest, just for a little while, even though it would soon be night, and the closer they were to the lake when it grew dark, the safer they would be.

"Let me sit down for a moment," Safrah said. "Just a moment, I promise." Bian eased her to the ground and sat down next to her. "Maybe you could ask Ship if Awan—" She paused. "If he's all right."

"Ship will let us know if—when it has something to tell us," Bian said. "This may sound strange, but I'm afraid of asking Ship questions right now, especially when I know it must be doing everything it can for Awan."

"No, it doesn't sound strange." She was growing more fearful of Ship herself. Had she boarded the shuttle, she would have had to tell Ship that Morwen was responsible for Awan's injuries, that she, Jina, and Mikhail had been forced to flee from the children they had cared for and guided. Ship would find out what poor examples they had been to their young and how badly they had failed, and perhaps wonder if those who called themselves true humankind were worth preserving.

Bian passed Safrah her waterskin and a few pieces of dried fruit. Her dizziness and nausea were fading and she was somehow able to swallow the food and water. She managed to get to her feet without asking Bian to help her stand, then said, "Let's go."

"Are you feeling up to it?"

"I'm better." Her head was still pounding, but not so badly. She allowed Bian to take her arm as they walked along the pathway.

The first moon was rising as Safrah and Bian neared the lake. The yellow light of a fire flickered at lakeside, but only two tents had been raised. It seemed that most of the boatpeople were staying aboard their craft for the night.

Four shadowy shapes crouched around the fire. One of them turned in their direction, quickly stood up, and ran toward them. Safrah recognized Tarki only a few moments before he threw his arms around her.

"You're safe," he said.

"Yes," she said, leaning against him.

"I've been worrying about all of you ever since I found my boat here with no one aboard. When we saw that vessel come down from the sky and then head back up again, we didn't know what to think." He stepped back, but kept holding her arms. "You're hurt." He touched the side of her head gently.

"I'm all right."

He reached for Bian and clasped her hands. "I'm glad to see both of you, but what about the others?"

"They left on that shuttle you saw," Safrah replied. "We

asked Ship to help us, and it sent the shuttle for us. By now they should all be aboard Ship."

Tarki was still, obviously absorbing this news. "You must have plenty to tell us." He slipped one arm around Safrah and reached for Bian with the other. "I told the others that your people weren't concealing Ship's return from us, that you were just as mystified as we were and hadn't been able to contact Ship yourselves. They didn't believe me. Thought maybe I'd let myself get fooled somehow. Then when I saw that vessel take off, I didn't know if I still believed what I told them, either. You must have a tale to tell."

He led them toward the fire. The three boaters sitting at the fire were all from Westbay, although a few of the boatpeople out on the lake had come there from Lakeview. The woman's name was Inessa, her mate was called Uric, and the white-bearded man who offered Safrah and Bian pieces of the roasted wild bird they were eating was Vered.

Bian told them everything that had happened, beginning with her first encounter with Ship's probe, pausing once in a while in case Safrah had anything to add. Safrah, seeing the distrust on the faces of the boatpeople with Tarki, was content to let the other girl tell the story. By the time Bian had finished speaking of the vessel that had carried their companions into the sky, the fire was dying, but there was enough light left for Safrah to see the puzzled looks on the faces of the three strangers.

"And you can actually talk to Ship?" Inessa asked. "Even now?"

"Yes." Bian reached into the pouch hanging from her neck and took out the comm. "All I have to do is press this button, and when it lights up, I know that Ship can hear me."

The woman gazed at the comm, then shook her head.

"Put it away," she murmured. "I'm not so sure I have anything I want to say to Ship."

"Well," Uric muttered. He peered at Safrah from the other side of the fire. "All this time, I was thinking that there must be hundreds of you, maybe thousands, living in your settlement and maybe even building new homes for yourselves in other places to the north. And now this girl tells us that you're no more than a few children. I've got a lot of questions for you."

"Save your questions for tomorrow," Tarki said. "We can all use some sleep." He waved a hand at Safrah and Bian. "They may have saved us all some trouble by coming here to tell us what's happened."

Vered nodded in agreement as he stroked his beard.

Tarki's boat was only a few steps from the fire, tied to one of the poles sticking out of the water that were all that remained of the settlement's docks. He settled them in the cabin, Safrah on a mat and Bian with a blanket.

"Go to sleep," he said in the darkness. "I'll sleep on the deck until it's my turn to keep watch."

"What are they going to do now?" Safrah asked. "The people who came here with you, I mean."

"Time enough to discuss that tomorrow." Tarki left the cabin.

Safrah stretched out on the mat. Those people owed her nothing. Bian could speak to Ship on their behalf, or even show them how to use the comm themselves. Ship might prefer to deal with the river and lake people now that it was only too aware of the flaws of her own. But none of that would change what she was obligated to do now.

She dozed for a while and woke to the sound of Bian's

deep, even breathing. She lay there imagining that she might find herself back in her dome, with Jina asleep nearby, Mikhail and Awan in their room, and everything as it had been. What if Ship had not returned? They would have gone on as they always had, pretending that they could maintain their settlement. She might never have come to understand how completely they had failed.

She got up and crept out of the cabin. Tarki was stretched out on the deck. He sat up as she moved toward the bow.

"I didn't mean to wake you," she whispered to him.

"I'm a light sleeper." He hopped down from the deck, followed her to the bow, and sat down next to her. "I thought you'd be sleeping soundly after all that's happened." He patted her on the shoulder. "That was a good thing you did, you and Bian, coming here to warn us. The other boaters weren't about to go back home until they knew for sure what was going on with you dome dwellers."

"It would have been dangerous for them to go there."

"I know, but their curiosity would have driven them on anyway."

"The young ones would have fought. You might have won out in the end, but it would have been a hard-won battle. They know the tunnels, and you don't. You couldn't have starved them out, not with the food dispenser to give them food, and they could have kept recharging their weapons for the fight."

"It would have cost us," Tarki said, "and maybe more than a few lives. There would have been Ship's judgment to face afterwards. I wonder what it would have thought of its seed after that, after seeing us at each other's throats." He sighed. "And we still don't know what Ship intends for us."

"It's trying to save Awan's life," she said. Perhaps that

meant that Ship would show them some mercy. "What are you going to do?"

Tarki cleared his throat. "I suspect most of the boaters will want to head back to Westbay once they hear what's happened, and there's no reason we shouldn't go with them. If Ship has anything to say to us, surely it can speak to us through that device of Bian's as easily in Westbay as here. What about you, Safrah?"

"Whatever happens, I have to go back to the settlement."

She heard him suck in his breath. "But why? Is it revenge you're looking for? I don't sense that in you."

"Because they're my people. Because they're all that's left of our children."

"They could have killed you, you and your friends."

"They were frightened," she replied. "They didn't mean—"

"You told us they tried to kill your comrade Awan."

"That was mostly Morwen's doing. The rest of them—"

"You might already have lost your friend. And now you want to go back there, when those young ones are probably even more afraid than they were, which makes them even more dangerous."

"I have to try," she said. "Maybe Ship will be able to help them somehow." Maybe Ship could mend the mistakes she had made caring for them.

Tarki said, "You can't go back there by yourself."

"I will if I have to."

"No, you won't." That was Bian's voice. "I won't let you." She came out from behind the curtain hanging in front of the cabin. "I'm going back with you."

"You've got your father Kwam's courage," Tarki said, "and also his recklessness."

"No, I don't." Bian sat down in front of them. "I'm just as afraid as I always was, but now I'm hopeful that Ship can help us." She reached for her pouch and took out the comm. "Ship," she said softly as she pressed her thumb against it, "can you hear me?"

Safrah stared at the jeweled light of the comm. "Bian?" That was Enli's voice. "Where are you?"

"At the lake, with Safrah and Tarki, on his boat. Can't Ship track us with the comm?"

A moment passed before Safrah heard Enli's reply. "Ship probably does know where you are," he said, "but I don't."

"We need to speak to Ship," Bian said.

"It'll hear everything we say," Enli said after another pause, "but I don't know if you should speak to it right now. We're inside a room that Ship calls an infirmary. Awan—" There was a long silence. "He's still alive. He's lying on a bed just a few paces away from me. Jina and Arnagh are doing everything Ship tells them to do, scanning him and feeding medications to him, but—well, we still don't know." There was another pause. "What did you want to ask Ship?"

Bian held out the comm to Safrah. "I'm going back to the settlement," she said. "I'd go there alone if I had to, but Bian says she's coming with me."

"And I'm not about to let you two go there by yourselves," Tarki muttered.

"Tarki just said he's going to come along, too." Safrah took the comm from Bian. "I can't leave the children there," she continued.

"And what about that boy, the one who went after Awan?" Enli asked. "What are you going to do about him?"

"I don't know. I thought Ship—" She sighed. "I was hoping Ship might be able to give us some tools, maybe even replace some of what was lost in the library, but even if it doesn't, we should be able to get by. I can understand why Awan wouldn't ever want to live there again after what's happened to him, and why Jina and Mikhail wouldn't either, for that matter. They'd all be better off with your people."

"You'd stay there?" Enli asked. "By yourself? With those children? With somebody who tried to kill your friend?"

"They won't do anything now. Once they find out Ship has returned, they'll be too afraid to harm anyone else. I can make them believe that Ship would punish them harshly if they do." Perhaps evoking that kind of fear would be enough restraint, and also a suitable punishment. "Maybe people will still come back and trade with us once in a while for whatever we might need."

We can't let the settlement fail, Moise had told her long ago. But it had already failed. No matter what happened to her and the children, she would have to see to it that they were the last generation to grow up inside the domes and tunnels, afraid of everything outside their settlement. Perhaps some of the children, in time, would lose their fear of the outside, and the river people would eventually accept them in their communities.

"I don't know what else to say," Enli said.

"Is Ship listening to us?"

"It hasn't said anything," Enli replied, "but I'm sure it heard every word."

She waited, thinking that Ship might speak now. The comm's gem glowed in the silence. At last she said, "Be sure to speak to us as soon as you know if Awan—when he—"

"Yes," Enli said. "Of course."

She handed the comm back to Bian, who whispered, "Farewell," and then slipped the device back into her pouch.

"If we're heading north tomorrow," Tarki said, "then we'd better use the rest of the night for sleeping. In the morning, maybe I can convince a few other people to come along with us. The more of us there are, the more likely it is that those children you're so worried about will listen to us."

24

Tarki and his three companions carried Bian's tale to the boaters near shore, swimming out to their boats and telling the story as they shared a morning meal. Soon those boatpeople were taking their boats farther out on the lake in order to share the story with others. Tarki easily talked Inessa, Uric, and Vered into accompanying Safrah, largely because the three were intensely curious about the settlement they had never seen.

Nonetheless, by midmorning, most of the boats were heading south. Safrah had hoped for that. Those people would not come to harm for her sake, and they owed her nothing. Even so, she felt disappointed.

Those who were staying filled their waterskins at the

lake. Tarki and Uric hefted two sacks of provisions over their shoulders. Safrah had expected more questions from the boatpeople, but they were silent as she led them north. On the way, she explained what she intended to do, while Tarki gazed at her with a worried expression on his face. When they reached the settlement, she would enter through the tunnel that led to her own dome, since the younger ones did not know about that particular passageway. No one would be expecting her, and if she kept herself hidden, she might be able to find out what was going on before she revealed herself. In any event, her place was with her people.

Tarki had scowled almost the entire time she had been speaking, as if wanting to object.

She had been so certain the night before of what she would have to do, but now doubts troubled her. If more people had been with her, the young ones might have surrendered, but she and her companions were too few in number for her to hope for that. And if the children fought, wouldn't it be better to retreat than to try to overcome them? But if she abandoned them, how would she explain that to Ship?

As they walked, Tarki watched her from out of the corner of his eye, as if picking up on her growing doubts.

When the sun was high, they stopped to rest. "It might be safer if I led you farther east," Safrah said, as Uric handed her some dried fruit, "so there's no chance of anyone seeing us approach."

"Thought your young ones were afraid of the outside," Tarki muttered.

"Someone might be watching from an entrance."

Inessa glanced north at the hills of the settlement. "Simpler and faster if we keep to this path," she said.

She was being too cautious, Safrah told herself. The young ones feared the outside too much to be on watch, and even Morwen's rage might not be enough for him to overcome that fear. But she reminded herself that Paola had fled from the domes and had brought two children out with her. Fear had driven her outside. Anger might do the same to Morwen.

They got up and continued on their way. Occasionally Bian touched the pouch that held the comm, but there was no signal from Ship.

The night sky was cloudless. In the east, the first moon rose, while the unblinking point of light that had to be Ship was dropping in the west. The empty field stretched in front of them, between the two hills of the settlement.

"You'll be safe for the night over there," Safrah told her companions as she gestured at the ruins on the hill to the east.

No one moved. At last Tarki shook his head. "I'm coming with you," he replied.

"So am I," Bian said.

Vered looked toward the eastern hill and then shrugged. "I might as well stick with you, too."

"But I told you—," Safrah began.

"Doesn't matter what you told us," Tarki said. "You said the ones inside don't know about the entrance you want to use, so I don't see why we can't come inside with you and wait for you there." Inessa and Uric nodded in agreement. "You might need us."

Her eyes stung. She wiped at them quickly. Tarki took her hand for a moment and then let go.

She led them past the greenhouse and up the hill. Small patches of light were visible farther up the slope. As they climbed, Safrah saw that light was shining from what was left of the library, through holes in its walls.

"Wait here," Safrah whispered. "I'll find out what's going on." Tarki grunted, but said nothing.

She hurried toward the library and peered through one of the holes. Five small children were in the library, four of them asleep on tabletops or the floor. Tryne, the only one of them who was still awake, sat near the entrance. The little girl's blond head was bowed and her shoulders shook; Safrah realized that she was crying.

She motioned to the others. They came up out of the darkness and stood with her in the light. Tarki gazed into the library for a while, then said in a low voice, "Uric?"

"Yes?"

"You and Inessa stay here and keep an eye on those children. If they wake up and start wandering off, shoot them and tie them up before they come to. If by any chance the charge in your stunner gives out, do what you can to keep them quiet."

"You mustn't," Safrah whispered. "They'll be terrified."

Tarki said, "It'll be five fewer to give us trouble."

She could not argue with him. She turned away from the library and led them up the hill to her dome. The door of the entrance was still partly open. Tarki came to her side and stood there, cupping an ear and sniffing at the entrance.

"Nobody's in there," he said softly.

She crept inside; the others followed her. The darkened rooms no longer felt like home. They came to the common room, where she moved toward the shelves and felt around for a light wand, then flicked it on.

Bian sat down in one corner. Vered looked around the room, his eyes wide. "This is where you live?" he asked.

She nodded.

"All closed in like this?" He rubbed at his beard. "Feels like I'm already dead and in the ground."

"Now what?" Tarki asked.

"Wait for me here," Safrah said. "I'll find out where the rest of them are, and come back for you."

"And then what?"

"I won't know until I see how it is with them."

"I don't like it," Tarki said.

"I won't be gone for long," she said.

"That had better be a promise," Tarki said, "because if you are, I'll come looking for you."

Safrah moved slowly through the tunnel that led to the dining hall, halting once in a while to listen. Her weapon was in her hand. If anyone suddenly appeared around the next bend in the tunnel, she would shoot and save her questions until after the child had revived. She was fairly sure that most of the children would not shoot at her, at least not right away. She was not so sure about what Morwen or Terris might do.

A sound that might have been a cry echoed through the tunnel. She stopped and held her breath. The first words out of her mouth would have to be about Ship. Hearing that Ship had returned might be enough of a shock for all of them to be still for long enough to listen to what she had to tell them.

We can stay here and go on as we have. She could begin with that. Jina and Mikhail might prefer to live among the outsiders, but they would surely come back here to trade, and perhaps Awan would, too, if Ship managed to heal him. Ship might be understanding enough to give them what tools they needed to keep the settlement going, and perhaps it would not judge Safrah too harshly for her failures. You're still children, she would say to them; Ship won't hold you responsible for anything that has happened here.

The entrance to the hall was up ahead. "Stay over there." She recognized Morwen's voice. "You heard me," he went on. Another cry reached her through the tunnel, and then there was the sound of a slap. "Shut up!"

"Steady, Morwen." That was Terris, and his voice sounded strained. Safrah stopped and stood still.

"Running away," Morwen continued, "they're all running away. Said they wouldn't go, but they left anyway. They never really cared what happened to us. Well, now I don't care about them, either."

"Morwen—," Terris began.

"We've got everything we need," Morwen said. "We can take care of ourselves. We don't need them anymore, with all their gab about preserving humanity and keeping our lines going. That's nothing to us—we don't need anybody else."

"Morwen." That sounded like Carrei, and she was crying. "Maybe they'd come back if you promised—"

"Shut up!" Morwen was screaming. Safrah crept closer to the open doorway. "We don't need them. Hear that? We're on our own. Even if Ship came back, there's nothing it can do for us. We can't even talk to it now, but you know what? I wouldn't talk to Ship even if I could, even if it did come back. We don't need it, we don't need it!"

Safrah had never heard such rage and bitterness in his voice, in any voice. She stepped closer to the entrance, her hand tight around her weapon. Perhaps she could bring Morwen down with one shot. She would have to do that, because she was unlikely to get a second chance. Then she would shout to the others that Ship had returned, and maybe that would be enough to keep them from shooting at her. When Morwen revived, he would learn that he had not been abandoned, that Ship had not forgotten them after all.

"Morwen," Terris said, "maybe we shouldn't have gone after Awan. Maybe you should have left the library—"

"We don't need the library," Morwen muttered.

"The radio might still work," Terris said.

"No, it won't. It'll never work again, I made sure of that. I thought I'd taken care of it before when I went there to take it apart, thought it was ruined, didn't think Awan could fix it, but it's dead now. I wrecked it—hear me? I went there and I wrecked it, and they thought they could hide what I did from you, but they couldn't. What do we need a radio for? There's nothing outside this place for us, nothing and nobody."

Morwen had admitted it. Safrah held her breath.

"You?" Terris sounded as though he was deeply wounded and in pain. "You took the radio apart?" There was a long silence. "But why— What if—"

"We don't need it!" Morwen shrieked. "Are you stupid? We don't need it, or anything else. I'll decide what to do."

"We'll never be able to talk to Ship," Terris said. "If it ever comes back, we won't—"

"It's never coming back, don't you understand?"

Safrah peered around the door and caught a glimpse of Morwen as he struck Terris with his weapon. Terris staggered back. Morwen spun around, looked at her, and took aim. She threw herself to one side as a burst flew past her.

She rolled away from the entrance. "Stop!" she cried. "Listen to me!" She heard another burst of fire, and then a second burst. She crawled toward the lighted space outside the open door, then got to her feet. "You have to listen to me!"

The silhouette of a small child, who she recognized as Carrei, appeared in the doorway. Carrei hurled herself at Safrah, grabbing her around the legs. Inside, Morwen lay on the floor as Terris knelt over him. Terris's arm rose and fell, hitting Morwen's chest, then rose and fell again. Safrah pulled Carrei off of her and stumbled into the room.

Morwen's face was misshapen and swollen. There were gashes on his arms and a gaping wound in his chest. Terris, still holding his knife, stood up slowly and staggered back as Safrah walked toward him, then fell at her knees.

Morwen stared up at her. He seemed unconscious, with blood flowing from his mouth. She slipped one arm under him and held him.

"I wasn't going to leave you," she said, knowing that he was already dying and that she could do nothing to help him. "I was going to stay here for as long as you needed me. Ship came back, Morwen. It's the truth, Ship didn't forget its promise. Do you hear me? Ship didn't forget us."

A rasping sound came from his throat. "Safrah," he whispered.

"Ship came back. It didn't forget."

His eyes continued to stare at her, but his body felt heavy in her arms. Other children gathered around her. Some of them were crying, while others stared at Morwen as she lowered his body to the floor.

"He told me he did it," Terris said, "that he ruined the radio, told me we'd never—said he'd—"

"You killed him," Safrah said.

"Shot him with my gun first. But he wouldn't go down, just started swaying back and forth. And then he fell." Tears ran down his face. "He did it, he wrecked Ship's Room. He didn't even care. I was so mad—it was like something else was making me stab him, and it wouldn't stop moving my arm, it just wouldn't stop."

She picked up the weapon lying near Terris's foot while keeping her own gun trained on the boy. A memory of Morwen as a small boy came to her, of a time when she had sat with him and told him a story; remembering the way he had once smiled at her made her want to weep.

"Safrah," Terris said, "what's going to happen now?"

"I don't know," she said.

"You won't go away, will you?"

"No, I won't go away." She sat down, suddenly too weary to move, mourning for the dead boy whom she had failed.

She did not know how long she had been sitting with Morwen's body when Tarki appeared in front of her, Bian at his side. Somehow they had found her. She sat there passively while Tarki questioned Terris in an oddly gentle voice. She noticed then that Vered was standing near the entrance, helping Bian lead the children away.

Tarki was still talking to Terris in a calm and kindly voice, and then he reached for her and pulled her to her feet. She let him lead her out of the hall and through the tunnel. He held on to her with one strong arm while he clutched Terris with the other.

Soon she was back in her dome, where children lay on the floor of the common room, some of them sleeping, others drinking from a waterskin Bian was passing around. Tarki led her through the room she and Jina had shared, where three more children were resting, and into the next room, which was empty.

"I told them I wouldn't leave them," she heard herself say.

"Get some sleep," Tarki said.

"Maybe it's fair, what happened. Awan is gone, and now so is Morwen."

"Go to sleep, Safrah." He waited until she had stretched out on the mat, and then left her.

Safrah was dreaming. People seemed to be drifting past her, whispering to one another before they disappeared into the darkness. Once, she woke to the sound of voices in the next room. "Don't be afraid," someone was saying behind the wall. She tried to listen, but exhaustion overcame her once more.

She awakened to silence. The dome felt empty. She heard the sound of a door sliding open, and then footsteps. She opened her eyes as a lantern was set down at her side. Bian crouched next to the light and Tarki stood behind her.

Bian handed her a waterskin; she drank, and then remembered. "Terris," she said, almost choking on the name. "He—"

Tarki said, "Vered's keeping an eye on him."

"Where are the children?" Safrah asked.

"They're waiting in the tunnel," Bian said.

Safrah sat up, bewildered. "Why . . . what are they doing there?"

"They're afraid to go outside," Bian said. "It might be easier for them if you're there to encourage them. A few of them have been asking for you."

She peered up at Tarki, but could not see his face clearly in the shadows. "But where are they going? Do you think your people will agree to take them?"

"They won't have to, at least not now," Tarki replied. "It's Ship who has agreed to take them."

Safrah managed to stand up. Ship would not be offering them a refuge, but a judgment.

"Listen." That was Bian's voice. Safrah looked down and saw a red gem glowing against the blackness.

"Come to me." That was Ship's voice. Why did it sound so uncertain? She had to be imagining that. "I can help, and I need you."

Safrah leaned toward the light. "I don't understand."

Ship said, "I need you, and the children who are with you."

A hand gripped her arm. Safrah allowed herself to be guided through the entrance to the tunnel. Someone held up a light wand, and she saw the children sitting in a row against the wall.

"It's all right," she heard herself say. "It's all over. You're safe now, I promise you that. I'm going with you. Don't be afraid." She walked past them to the end of the tunnel and looked outside.

Above the dark blue early morning clouds, a spear of flame pierced the deep green sky as the shuttle descended.

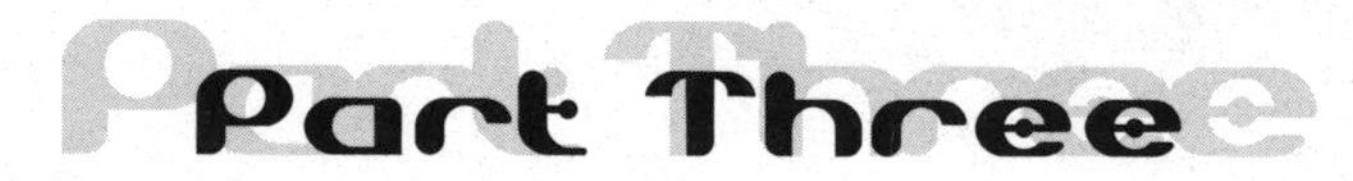

Part Three

25

Safrah woke up one morning and immediately knew where she was. That surprised her. Morning, in this place, was whenever she happened to wake up. For some days now, she had opened her eyes only to lie there in the darkness, feeling uncertain and lost, afraid again.

She was inside Ship. That no longer seemed so strange to her, yet she tensed with apprehension. She wanted to close her eyes and open them again and know that she was back on Home, perhaps at the outpost or the tower, maybe even inside her room at the settlement.

But she would not have wanted to stay there. She did not want to think about the settlement, the ruins on the eastern hill, the burned-out library, the debris-strewn room where Morwen had died.

Ship would judge them for all of that. Ship had said nothing to them yet about their failures, but her fear of its judgment remained.

Paola and the two other children who shared this room with her were still asleep. Light would have filled the room if they were already up. For the past couple of nights, they had slept soundly. Before that, Safrah was often awakened by either Tryne or Carrei screaming in the darkness, terrified by whatever dreams had troubled them. Sometimes she had heard Paola's muffled weeping as well.

Time for them all to wake up, she thought. She had promised Ship that she and her companions would bring the younger ones to the Hollow today.

She sat up slowly as the room grew lighter. She had grown used to that as well, seeing light fill the room when she got up and having the room grow dark after she and the others had stretched out on their mats. The first time she had slept here, there had been beds in the room, with cloth coverings and round padded objects for their heads. Safrah had been unable to sleep on the bed, which seemed to shift under her and mold itself to her whenever she turned over or changed position, and the others had voiced similar complaints. Now the beds were back inside the walls of the room and the cloth coverings had been laid over mats. She preferred the mat and lying against the hardness of the floor.

Paola mumbled a few words under her breath, then sat up. Tryne had covered her head with her arms, while Carrei still lay on one side, knees pulled up to her chest. Paola got to her feet, rubbed at her eyes, then wandered toward the lavatory. They had learned how to use the unfamiliar fixtures in the lavatory, which was also considerably cleaner than the latrines in their settlement, and did not even have to worry about how much water they used for washing themselves. Ship offered them food through slots in the walls or from the dispenser in the large dining hall at the end of the corridor outside this room. It had even given them new clothing: tunics and pants in various colors and foot coverings that didn't pinch their toes, rub against their heels, or give them blisters and calluses.

All the small daily discomforts she had endured most of her life, the occasional itching, the aching muscles, the twinges of pain in her jaw and legs, and the pinched nerve in her neck, were gone. She had hardly even been aware of them until Ship banished them. She and the others had all been scanned, and Ship had then told them that small cylinders would be pressed against their arms briefly. Arnagh and Jina, who spent much of their time in the infirmary when they weren't in the library, had helped by holding the children and soothing them while following Ship's instructions; Arnagh had explained that the substances in the cylinders were medications like the potions and herbs used by the healers in his village. Even though the youngest children had screamed with terror at the sight of the medical tools wielded by Jina and Arnagh, they had admitted, when it was all over, that the slight pressure of the cylinders was painless.

They could have whatever they liked without having to struggle for it or worry about what might happen if the devices that fed them failed or their supplies gave out. Or at least they could do so until Ship decided what to do with them.

Carrei opened her eyes and stretched. Tryne pushed her pillow to one side. "Time to get up," Ship said gently in its alto voice. Safrah was still not used to hearing Ship's voice unexpectedly, to knowing that it was, as far as she could tell, able to watch them all the time.

Tryne scratched her blond head. "Can we eat here?" she asked.

"There will be food in the dining hall," Ship said. "I suggest that all of you eat your breakfast there."

Tryne frowned, while a fearful look passed over Carrei's face. Suggestions from Ship had the force of commands; they would go to the dining hall.

Paola emerged from the lavatory, drying herself off with a towel. "I'd rather eat here," she said.

"It would be better if you went to the hall and joined the others," Ship said. "You'll be going to the Hollow after you eat, and it would be simpler for all of you to keep together until then."

Paola grabbed the green tunic and pants draped over one of the chairs near the wall, then sat down to pull on her shoes. Tryne looked even more unhappy. Carrei got up and went to the lavatory. The two girls would not argue with Ship, however annoyed they felt; Safrah was certain of that. They would be remembering the story Ship had told them after they arrived here, when the youngest and most frightened of the children had finally calmed down enough to be able to listen to the tale.

A battle had been fought inside Ship before the human beings it carried had settled on Home. The young people who were its Earthseed had been divided, and Ship had discovered that some of the Earthpeople who had sent it on its mission had hidden themselves inside one of its rooms, putting themselves in cryonic suspension until they could awaken near the end of their journey and take control of Ship. A battle had ensued, and some had died in the struggle. After peace was restored, Ship had discovered that its builders had deceived it about much of its mission. Ship had believed them to be noble and wise representatives of an advanced civilization, but they had revealed themselves to be discontented, angry people who had hated their fellow Earthpeople and who dreamed of preserving a kind of human culture that the people of Earth's solar system had long since abandoned.

"I might have forgiven them for that," Ship had said after concluding its tale, "but I could not forget their violence, their attack against me that closed off my sensors and left me blind and deaf, what they did to their own offspring. Yet I also could not allow another wrong to be committed against them. In the end, it was your ancestors who decided that they should be put into suspension once more until a new world could be found for them. They sleep aboard me still, because I have not yet found such a world."

Several of the children had shrieked at that. Safrah had found herself thinking of what it must have been like to feel oneself slipping away into unconsciousness, not knowing when, where, or even whether one would wake up again.

She stood up, wondering again what Ship would decide to do with them. Perhaps that would be the simplest solution, to postpone any decision and put them all in suspension, force them into that long sleep so much like death. Her fears gnawed at her once more. Whatever happened, she would not abandon the younger ones, at least not until she knew what their fate was to be and if she would have to share it.

Bian sat in the Hollow, on a hill overlooking a forest. She had been to the Hollow several times since arriving inside Ship, finding its landscape more comforting than the rooms and the lighted corridors connecting them.

The forested landscape stretched on below the hill, but the distant horizon seemed higher than it should have been, and there was no sky above. Instead, she saw the tiny green tops of other trees, the thin silvery threads of rivers, and tendrils of clouds drifting far overhead.

A world turned inside out, she thought. The Hollow, Ship had explained, was an enclosed sphere, a world inside Ship that was surrounded by rock, shielding, corridors, and shells of rooms. The Hollow was a part of Earth that Ship carried, where plants and animals that had once thrived on Earth still lived. This place was much greener than the yellow and pale green plains of Home, the air more humid and filled with the odors of soil and strange wildflowers and the sharp but pleasant smell of the forest, but even with those differences, the Hollow felt more like Home than any other part of Ship.

Bian sat only a few paces from the nearest entrance, as Ship had warned her to do. She did not know the Hollow, and Ship had told her that there were dangers here, animals like those her ancestors had brought to Home, and places where she might get lost or injure herself. Even with sensors inside the Hollow, there was a limit to what Ship could do if she got lost in the forest, fell from a ledge, or was carried down a river by a strong current, especially since her companions, the only ones Ship would be able to summon to help her, were as unfamiliar with the Hollow as she was.

At least she and Arnagh and Enli and Lusa were able to come to the Hollow and stay here for a while, even for what would have been the length of a day back on Home. Safrah, Jina, and Mikhail had come there occasionally, too, although they spent much of their time looking out for the younger ones who were still too afraid to enter the Hollow.

Below her, Arnagh and Awan descended the hill. The two had been up and down the slope twice since she had been sitting here, Awan with a walking stick to support himself. He still tired easily and complained of headaches, but he was growing stronger. At the bottom of the hill, not far from a grove of trees, Enli sat with Lusa; her blond head rested on his shoulder.

"What are you thinking about, Bian?" Ship said in a soft tenor voice.

She looked around, searching for hidden sensors. Even after a number of conversations with Ship, hearing it suddenly speak to her still startled her.

"That I'm happy Awan's getting better," she said at last. "Arnagh has been a good caretaker to him."

"Yes, he has," Ship murmured. "He shows both an aptitude for and an interest in medicine."

"But I'm also worried about Lusa," Bian said. "She's not happy here."

"Then why hasn't she asked me to return her to her home?"

"You mean she can leave?"

"Yes."

Bian frowned. "You might have let her know that," she replied.

"Have I ever said that any of you were not free to go?" Ship asked.

"You haven't exactly made it clear that we didn't have to stay."

"That is because I am still uncertain of my future course," Ship said, "and because it might be best if the youngest children had more time here and some experience with the environment of the Hollow before going back to your world, since they've known only the enclosed spaces of their settlement. And perhaps because I have seen no signs that the rest of you are longing to go back."

"Maybe that's because we're still as uncertain as you," Bian said, "and I know Safrah's still afraid of you. I can pick up that fear whenever I'm around her, even when she's pretending that she's all right. I think she fears you even more than the youngest children do."

"I did not intend to instill fear in any of you," Ship murmured in its baritone.

"I know you didn't." Bian tried to sound comforting, even though Ship hardly needed any comfort from her. Her first conversation with Ship in the Hollow had disturbed her, having to listen to its disembodied voice with nothing else to guide her in her responses, but lately she had found other clues to its inner states. When Ship lowered its voice, she sensed uncertainty behind the more authoritative and deeper tone; when it spoke in its alto, it sounded both curious and calm; and its tenor made it sound dispassionate. It seemed to have some understanding of emotions, but perhaps that was only because it could draw on all the knowledge it carried of humankind, rather than because it had any feelings of its own.

"What I think," Bian went on, "is that you ought to tell everyone outright that they're free to go as soon as possible."

"Yes."

"In fact, I don't know why you didn't do that right after you brought us here."

"Perhaps because I had reason to think that if I did tell you that you could go, all of you would decide to abandon me immediately."

Maybe she was imagining it, but she thought she heard loneliness and longing behind those words.

"You said before that Lusa was unhappy here," Ship continued.

"But she also doesn't want to leave Enli."

"Yes," Ship said. "Of course."

Ship could watch them all the time, even here, yet the kinds of questions it often asked Bian revealed that, whatever it had found out about them, it could not see that deeply into their thoughts and feelings. She answered its questions as thoroughly as she could without betraying anything her companions might prefer to keep to themselves. Ship, she had discovered, considered all the people of Home, those who lived along the river and those who had dwelled in the ruins of the settlement, its Earthseed, which had eased her deeper worries about how it might regard her people. Whether they carried pieces of Home inside themselves or had diverged genetically from their ancestors did not seem to matter to Ship.

"Those who built me," Ship had told her during one of their earliest conversations, "programmed me to believe that the destiny of their species lay in seeding other worlds. I believed that humankind had overcome its more violent instincts and was prepared for such a mission. But they fought against one another when they were inside me, and I discovered that my creators had deceived me, that they had retained the older, instinctive, unthinking ways of their kind, while most of their species back in their home system had long since transcended them."

Ship had paused for a moment before continuing. "I had thought that those who made me were representative of Earth's civilization, but in fact they were only a discontented offshoot who hated what their kind had become and wanted to return to an earlier stage. They had programmed me to believe that their mission was one that all their people supported, when in fact most of humankind had abandoned Earth to live in habitats throughout their planetary system, artificial worlds they had made for themselves. Most of them were content to remain in their own sunspace while exploring the rest of the universe through probes. Those who made me were those who had turned against what the rest of their species had become. It was after I found that out that I began to have doubts about my mission. Now that I'm here and can see what has grown from my seed and been shaped by this world, I have come to question my purpose again."

Such words had frightened Bian the first time she had heard them, and she had not understood everything Ship was trying to tell her, but since then, she had spent more time in the library near the room where she slept. The library held records, in words and sounds and images, of those who had lived inside Ship. Bian had read the journals some had kept and viewed the records of their lives, including their battles. Ship had explained that the written records might be inaccurate, since those who had written them were recording what they believed and felt as well as events that had actually happened, while many of the visual records were reconstructions based on what Ship remembered or had been told, but even so, they had opened much of the life of her ancestors to her.

The growth of her own curiosity had surprised her: The more she found out, the more she wanted to know. She longed to find out even more about the civilization that had existed in Earth's sunspace and how those people had tamed the more destructive impulses that might have destroyed them. Eventually, she thought, she would work her way back from her immediate ancestors' times to earlier events, perhaps even to the beginnings of human history.

But she would have such an opportunity only if Ship remained in orbit around Home, or at least gave them the means to build a new library on their world if it decided to leave this system again.

"What do you want to do, Bian?" Ship asked. "Stay here, or return to your people?"

For a moment, she almost believed that Ship had sensed her thoughts. She would have to return to Home eventually, if for no other reason than to assure the people of Seaside that they did not have to fear Ship's judgment. They would have other fears, though, even after receiving that reassurance—the fear of change, of the disruption Ship and the technology it could offer them would bring to their lives, of the way they might judge and measure themselves after they learned more about their ancestors and the civilization that had sent them to this world.

"I miss Home," she said carefully, "and my mother must be worrying about me. But—" She paused. "I think I would want to come back to you after a visit, if there were others living here with me."

"You'd have to work if you stayed here," Ship said. "There would be lessons for you to study, and much that you would have to master."

"Does that mean you'll stay in orbit around Home?" she asked, and waited, but Ship was silent.

Enli and Lusa climbed toward her. Bian saw the other girl's unhappiness in her slumped shoulders and empty pale eyes. "You want to go back," Bian said as the two sat down near her. "You can admit it, Lusa."

Lusa sighed. "Yes, I do."

"Ship will let you go if you want to leave."

The other girl seemed confused. "What do you mean?"

"I am willing to send any of you back to Home," Ship said. "I would have done so at any time if you had asked me."

"It's just that Ship was worried that we'd all decide to leave," Bian added, "and then it would be alone again."

Lusa's eyes widened in surprise. "I didn't realize—"

"And I don't want to go," Enli said, "at least not right now."

"You want to stay and listen to all the music in Ship's records and make more of your own music and do other utterly useless things," Lusa said, but her voice was soft and gentle, and she managed a smile. She reached for Enli's hand. "I don't mind, really I don't. It'll be easier for me to go back by myself, to get past all of this. And maybe by the time I see you again, I'll be—" She let go of him. "I miss Overlook. I've been missing it and my family ever since I left them. When can I leave?"

"You may prepare to leave now," Ship said. "I will find out if others wish to go with you."

Lusa stood up. "Farewell, Enli." He seemed about to rise, but she held up a hand, then hurried away.

Lusa has told me that she wants to return to Home now," Ship was saying. The children sitting near Safrah, still finishing their breakfast, looked around uneasily at the sound of Ship's voice. "If anyone else wishes to go with her, speak now, and I will direct you to the ship in the port bay."

Vinn gobbled down the rest of his fruit. "I don't want to go," he muttered.

"Me either," Carrei said.

"You don't have to go," Safrah said, "not now, anyway." The children seemed relieved. Even with Ship breaking in on them to speak from time to time, and a dreaded excursion into the Hollow lying just ahead, of course they would not want to leave, at least not until they were assured that they could go back to a place that would allow them to be as idle and careless as they had always been.

"Hai," a familiar voice said behind her. Safrah looked up into Tarki's broad face. He wore black pants and a short-sleeved blue shirt that showed off his muscular arms. "I'm not all that anxious to leave myself," he said as he sat down next to her, at the head of the table. "In fact, I wouldn't mind staying here for some time." He looked up at the bright ceiling above them. "Mind if I stay?"

"Not at all," Ship replied.

"There's too much I still have to find out here." Tarki turned back to Safrah. "For instance, how Ship can talk to us here while it's probably carrying on another conversation with somebody else and looking out for other concerns at the same time."

"There's no mystery to that," Ship said. "I am capable of responding to a number of stimuli simultaneously. There are records in the library that will explain my workings to you in detail."

"Hope I can stay long enough to look at them, then," Tarki said. He might have remained on Home with Inessa, Uric, and Vered, who had all stayed behind because somebody needed to let others know what had happened, and also because none of them dared set foot inside the shuttle. Tarki had, however, insisted on coming along and had barely left Safrah's side since then. Safrah had only a dim memory of their journey aboard the shuttle; the children, strapped in their seats, had been too terrified to do more than whimper. She did recall looking up at a screen to see a lighted space filled with other shuttlecraft appear in the blackness and then expand until it filled the screen, a sight that indicated they were finally inside Ship.

Farkhan jabbed Vinn with his elbow. Tarki glowered at the two boys and they looked away and bowed their heads. "Thought you might need some help herding this bunch to the Hollow," he said.

Safrah nodded. "Thanks."

"You've hardly been there yourself, have you?"

"Only a couple of times," she replied.

Jina came toward them, trailed by another group of children. "Ready?" she asked, with a smile on her face and nervousness in her eyes.

Safrah stood up. "I guess so." Mikhail was already leading four other young ones to the door.

Most of the children still sat near the top of the slope, just inside the entrance. Several of them sat with knees drawn up and arms wound tight around their legs; others looked up or around themselves with both fear and wonder in their faces. Terris, crouched down with his hands over his eyes, seemed even more frightened than the rest.

Enli had taken out his flute only a few moments before the children entered the Hollow; he tucked it back under his belt. "How soon do you think they'll be ready to go back to Home?" Enli asked.

Bian shrugged. "That depends on how quickly they can adapt to the Hollow." Their ancestors had lived here long ago, mastering the skills they would need to survive on

Home, and the children of the dome dwellers would require the same skills if they were ever to return to their settlement or live in any of Home's villages. Her people would probably be willing to take in the youngest of the children, if they could overcome their fear, their lassitude, and their occasional outbursts of anger and impatience. She did not know if any of the villages would welcome Terris once they found out what he had done.

"They may not be able to adapt that quickly," Ship said in its tenor voice.

"What happens if they can't?" Enli asked.

"Perhaps they will have to live out their lives in the Hollow," Ship replied, "or in my rooms and corridors. They might prefer to go back to their settlement, but I am not at all sure that they could maintain it by themselves. Rebuilding it might have to be the work of another generation."

Bian lifted her head. "Are you saying—?" She paused. "Do you mean that you're going to stay near Home?"

"I have much to consider, Bian, and perhaps more time among my children here will help me decide what to do. That, of course, will depend on whether your people want me to stay."

"You could stay whether they want you to or not."

"I would have to consider leaving if my presence would distress them."

Tarki and Safrah descended the hill. His arm was looped around hers, as if to reassure her that she was safe here. Tarki grinned at them as they passed, and Safrah managed a hesitant smile before they continued down the slope. Her cousin's growing feelings for Safrah had become so obvious that Bian wondered when Tarki was going to speak to her of them.

"I don't want you to go, Ship," Enli murmured, "and if you ever did decide to leave, I think I'd want to go with you."

"You would have much to learn before undertaking such a journey," Ship replied, "more than the music that so entrances you."

"I'd be willing to learn," Enli said, "and there are others like me, people who would want to come here and learn whatever you could teach them."

"There will be time enough for me to find out if that is so," Ship said.

Safrah sat down next to Tarki, then glanced up the hillside. The children were still cowering near the entrance. She doubted any of them would work up the courage to walk down to her, but at least no one had yet fled to the safety of the corridors. To her surprise, she felt calmed by the Hollow and by the sight of the forested land below, even by the landscape overhead. She had expected to feel more disoriented, as she had during her brief earlier visits; perhaps she was at ease only because Tarki was with her.

Arnagh and Awan emerged from the trees at the bottom of the hill. For just a moment, she felt revulsion, and then the feeling passed. The two lovers would soon make a pledge, probably one that would bind them for life. Awan could never have been a mate to her; she knew that now. She no longer had to torment herself with the conviction that some defect in her had been the barrier between them. She had worked hard not to betray her feelings and to treat both Awan and Arnagh as the friends they were to her, even though she suspected that Arnagh could glimpse some of her inner discomfort. Perhaps eventually her feelings would catch up with her reason.

Tarki was looking up the hill. "They're still there," he said. He turned back to her. "Maybe those young ones will do better than I thought. They'll adapt to this place, and maybe having to take care of themselves here will bring them out of their lazy ways. Maybe they'll grow as curious about everything they can learn here as I already am."

"I worry about Terris," she said. Sometimes she thought it would have been better if he had died with Morwen, then despised herself for thinking that.

"He's been punished, if that's what you're thinking. He's punishing and tormenting himself. My biggest fear about him is not that he'll hurt somebody else, but that he'll disappear and then turn up dead by his own hand."

"Ship wouldn't let that happen," she said.

Tarki said, "Ship isn't all powerful." He paused. "I'll be staying here for a while, as long as you're here and Ship doesn't decide to send us all back. All these years, I've been looking for something and not knowing what it was, and now . . ." He sighed. "About the only thing I really miss is my boat. I wouldn't mind piloting it along some of the waterways here."

He reached for her hand. She let him hold it. "Safrah," he continued, "I'll say it again. As long as you're here, I'll stay."

"That's kind of you," she said, "but I can look after the children myself, at least until they're able to function on their own. Mikhail and Jina wouldn't just leave it all to—"

"Why don't you listen to what I'm actually saying for a change?" He grabbed her by the shoulders, forcing her to look into his face. "I want to stay with you for a good long time, whether it's here or on Home or anywhere else Ship might carry us. I'm telling you that maybe it's time I had a partner, a mate."

Tears stung her eyes. She did not know what to say.

"You could think it over, at least," Tarki said. "You don't have to start weeping over the prospect."

"Oh, Tarki." She leaned against him, letting him hold her.

"You don't know what answer to give me now," he said, "and that's fine."

A breeze carried the odors of leaves and flowers to her. She suddenly felt like a stranger to herself, to everything around her, disoriented by the green of the Hollow, the absence of sky, at thinking of herself inside this vessel that was falling around her world. What lay ahead was uncertain enough to make her fearful; she and her people might still fail, might call down some judgment of Ship's upon themselves because of that failure. Ship might abandon Home to sow its Earthseed elsewhere.

But for now, she was content, with Tarki at her side.

26

"I'm trying to talk her into saying something to you," Bian's voice said, "but she keeps shaking her head at me."

Ship called up an image of Bian's face. The girl had apparently forgotten that Ship could pick up images through the communicator that she held. Since she seemed more at ease believing that Ship was only listening to her voice, it decided not to remind her that it could also see her as she spoke.

"If she doesn't wish to speak to me," Ship replied, "then she needn't."

Bian's face disappeared and was replaced by an image of sand and an expanse of gray ocean. She was sitting with her great-grandmother Nuy on the beach to the south of her village. She had arrived there a few days ago with Arnagh and

Awan, aboard one of Ship's shuttles, hoping that others of her people would agree to return to Ship with her. So far, she had been unsuccessful in convincing anybody else to make the trip. As soon as the people of Seaside had understood that Ship had not returned to Home either to judge or to punish them, but only to observe them and offer whatever tools they needed or were willing to accept, they seemed content to stay where they were. Arnagh had been equally unsuccessful at persuasion, and had not communicated with Ship for nearly two of Home's days now. Awan was apparently still preoccupied with meeting Arnagh's family and friends.

"Nuy," Bian was saying, "Ship says that you don't have to speak to it."

"I heard what Ship said," an unfamiliar voice muttered. The voice was low and hoarse, but not unpleasant.

Bian said, "But it would be good if you did."

"Ship doesn't need to hear from me," Bian's great-grandmother replied. "The only question I would have to ask is why it's willing to offer us gifts for nothing. Surely it'll expect something in trade from us later on."

Nuy had guessed that Ship did, in fact, hope for something from them. Ship meant to scan as many of these people as possible, since its scans of those it had already brought inside itself had revealed some interesting features. They had diverged from their ancestors, and carried genes that differed from those in Ship's records. They had acquired parasites as well, alien bacteria that lived inside them that might have aided in heightening and sharpening their senses, although that remained a hypothesis. Even the young people from the original settlement on Home carried some unfamiliar genes, although not nearly so many as did those whose forebears had left the domes.

Scanning all the people at Home and noting individual variations would tell Ship more about how these human organisms had adapted to this world. That was the trade it sought for whatever help it offered, but Ship would be patient; it could wait. Those who had sent Ship on its voyage had sought to preserve what they thought of as true humankind, but had they remained unchanged themselves? They had been the children of a species that had mastered biotechnology; however much they had resembled earlier human beings physically, they had themselves been the product of genetic engineering. Ship had pieced together enough from its somewhat incomplete records to know that, and their descendants had been altered even more by the world they called Home.

"You are correct," Ship said, "in that I do seek an exchange with you." There was a sound like that of a sharp intake of breath. "I wish to find out as much about your people as I can. What I learn will guide me in carrying out my mission."

"Thought your mission was to seed this world with human life," the old woman said, "and then seed other worlds." Ship saw her face now, a wrinkled brown one framed by white hair and dominated by alert dark eyes. "You've accomplished your task here."

"Nuy," Bian's voice said, "Ship will think its help isn't wanted."

The old woman sighed again. "It isn't that." Nuy's eyes narrowed. "I worry that in time we might grow too dependent on what you can give us."

"That is a possibility," Ship said, "but I will do what I can to limit my gifts to tools you'll be able to re-create."

"Why would you give us things we could make for ourselves? And if you offer us devices that we can't make now, we'll have to learn how to make them, and that will change us. People capable of making screens or objects like this comm won't be able to live as we do."

"There are other ways to live," Bian said.

"Yes," Nuy added, "ways that will divide some people from others who would rather that our lives remain as they are." She peered more closely into the communicator. "Perhaps we seem simple to you, and backward, but the way we live has its compensations. What you offer may only bring conflict."

"That is a possibility," Ship said, although it intended to do whatever it could to avert such an outcome.

"When I first looked up and saw that new light," Nuy said, "I was hoping you hadn't returned. But now . . ." She was silent for a few moments. "Bian wants to go back and live inside you and swallow as much of the knowledge that you carry as she can. She tells me that my grandson Tarki is the same way, that almost all he thinks about now is mastering such lore." A shadow fell across her face and then Nuy's face vanished.

An image of Tarki appeared. He was sitting on the floor of the library, his back against one of the chairs, a screen on his lap. Safrah sat at a table near him, bent over another screen.

"Bian tells me that he's happy, though," Nuy's voice continued. "He wasn't happy here; it's why he left Seaside years ago."

"He seems content now," Ship said.

"Maybe it's good that you returned, that you kept your old promise. Maybe I'm only worrying because I won't live long enough to see the changes that will come to Home, the good and the bad."

The old woman had lived a very long life by the standards of her ancestors, yet another reason Ship wanted to scan more of her people. The genetic changes in them might be responsible for that increased life span. Still, however long their lives might be now, Ship was only too aware of how brief they were compared to its own. Something inside Ship rebelled at seeing the existence of any intelligence cut short.

I do not want to lose my companions. There was also that longing inside Ship. Perhaps it could find ways to prolong their lives.

"May I leave this comm with Nuy?" Bian asked. "I won't need it after I'm back."

"Of course," Ship replied. Perhaps when more of the people there had spoken to Ship, more might be willing to board one of its shuttles. "Will Nuy be willing to talk to me if you do?"

"Yes," Nuy said in a low voice. "I have many questions for you, all still jumbled up inside me, but eventually I'll sort them all out. We'll have much to talk about."

"I'm closing the channel now," Bian said.

Ship opened another channel and saw that most of the children had joined Jina and Mikhail in the Hollow. The two had planned a short expedition for them through the woods. The children, however timid they still were, had promised to hike with them as far as the next clearing. Only the boy called Terris and the girl named Paola remained behind; they were in one of the rooms near the library, playing a game on their screens. A few vials lay near them. Terris had taken to stealing medications from the infirmary. Ship, rather than confronting the boy, had instead allowed him to steal only those medications that might ease his inner torment without harming him. Terris and Paola drifted through Ship now, wandering the corridors, eating, sleeping, playing games, and swallowing their stolen medications. That could not go on indefinitely, Ship knew, but in time, maybe the pain they both carried inside themselves would fade. Terris no longer spoke of wanting to be put in suspension, of wanting to lose himself for good, and Ship occasionally saw a smile on Paola's face. Perhaps those were signs that they were beginning to heal.

In the Hollow, on the hill just below the entrance, Enli sat with Weneth, the girl who had returned with him after his recent sojourn on Home. She was like him, entranced by the music they had discovered in Ship's records, apparently content to spend much of her time listening to those sounds and creating her own. They, too, would have to turn their attention to mastering other skills, but for now Ship would listen to the girl sing and the boy play his flute and take pleasure in the patterns of the sounds they made.

Ship would remain in orbit around Home at least until the next generation of Home's children reached adulthood. What it would do after that remained uncertain, but Ship was at peace with uncertainty for now. Whatever its creators had intended, Ship was beginning to realize that another mission might lie ahead, one that offered new possibilities instead of perpetuating the mistakes of the past. Its creators had been too bound by their resentments, their more violent instincts, and their limits. They had deceived Ship and hidden much of their true history, but Ship had recovered enough of the records they had concealed to know that in the solar system they had abandoned, there were minds like its own, living among humankind's descendants.

By leaving this planet, by abandoning its children, Ship

had deprived them of the means to transcend the more problematic aspects of their heritage. To abandon them again would only consign them to repeating their ancestors' mistakes.

Ship would learn what it could from the people of Home, and teach them what it could, and perhaps in the future they would use the tools they had mastered to remake themselves. A vision came to Ship of a voyage that might lie ahead, a journey it would make with the descendants of the people of Home. They would return to the cradle of humanity, that distant star system that had given birth to all of their kind.

And then at last I will be with others like myself.